THE

CISTERN

AN ALCREST MYSTERY

THE CISTERN
Copyright © 2014 by Lorne Oliver

ISBN 978-0-9738132-5-8

Dad

We don't talk much, but I love you.

Thanks for telling me all your stories.

Dad-in-Law

We miss you.

Acknowledgments

Dear voices in my head;
You can shut up now! Many years ago I wrote a story called *The Core*. It was about the core of the writer's mind. In mine all the characters I ever wrote met for a night of poker. The mysterious writer guy, that would be me, sat in the corner observing it all. During that story a couple of characters complained about not being complete and out there. One set of characters was Jake Hart and Chrys Flower. They've gone through a couple of formations, changing from a couple to brother and sister. The only problem is that they won't shut up.

Dear Brandi;
Back in 2012 you got a little side job of going into abandoned foreclosed houses to take pictures…clean them out…and collect the cash. The first house we went to, and still refer to as *The Creepy House*, is the very one in this book, you know, minus what Spencer and Chrys find. So yet again I owe a lot to my lovely wife and I'm sure she will remind me. Love you.

Thank you to some great people. Thank you, Donna for your hard work and advice. I've never been so grateful to see the marks of a red pen. Miki and Jessica, two of my greatest supports, thanks for lending me your names and sorry I had to kill you. Cara, you did a great job again.

An enormous thanks goes out to Elizabeth Frances. In January, 2013 I went looking for the face of Chrys. I looked at the faces of several Aboriginal women, but was always drawn back to Elizabeth. I asked if I could use her image and she said yes. The fact that the two women are very similar is just bonus. Elizabeth is an actor staring in movies such as *Drunktown's Finest* and *Ghost Forest*. Her image gave the character life.

Jordann and Wylie, you are my everything. In many ways you are Chrys and Spencer.

Dear Reader;
A billion times, thank you. I saved my thank you to you because I've been trying to think of how to express all that I feel for you. I've had this writing dream since I was 10 and it is becoming a reality. I hope you love the characters and the story as much as I do. Thank you a billion times more.

CISTERN

"sistern"

A tank for storing water, especially one supplying taps
or as part of a flushing toilet

An underground reservoir for rainwater.

Prologue

Twenty years ago

He wondered what the cat wanted more - to be let out of the wood box or to have the cinderblock lifted from its tail.

Meeerrrooowwww

He stared at it, with what his mother called his big baby eyes. The cat screeched and thrashed about wildly without getting anywhere. Its feet dug into the bottom of the box wanting to pull its tail out from under the concrete block. One of its nails had pulled out and was stuck in the plywood bottom.

The boy's tongue flicked out and licked the saliva collecting on his lips. His head tilted to the side as he pondered how long it would take before Whisker's tail popped off.

He smiled. It was like that rhyme before you flicked the dandelion head off the stem with your thumb. "Momma had a baby and her head popped off."

Meeooooowwrrreeeooowww

Things were tingling inside the boy. He didn't know why or how it all started, but he didn't want to let it stop. He wanted to see how far it would go. If the boy saw Whiskers pull its tail off would he moan in ecstasy like those men in the movies his father watched after everyone went to bed? Would he be shocked?

This was different than the cat he put in the barrel of rain water. He watched Tabby try and swim to the edge. Then he pushed the cat back to the center with a stick. It splashed around a long time, but then just gave up and it was over.

Whiskers was different. His face got warm.

Meeeoooowwwwwrrrrrr

He knew that if the grey cat could pull its tail out...

"Momma had a baby..."

...it wouldn't be over. Any bone, or whatever was in a cat's tail, was crushed. He could still hear the sounds from when he tipped the heavy cinderblock over.

Meeooooowwwrrrrrrooowwwrrr

"Hush kitty," he said in a calming tone. "Everything's okay." He reached out a hand.

The cat riled up. Its paw swiped.

The boy pulled his hand back. There was pain on his fingers. He looked down as crimson bubbled to the surface and squeezed through the thin holes left by razor-sharp feline blades. He put his fingertips in his mouth and sucked.

Stupid cat.

He searched the yard. There were more cinderblocks. He could take one, hold it above the box, count to three...

"What are you doing?"

Mmmmmrrrrreeeeeoooooowwwwwww

2

He spun around. The girl from down the road stood at the corner of his house. It was only the two of them and the howling cat.

The boy's eyes narrowed. He tasted blood on his tongue. Cats and dogs were one thing. He took a step toward the girl. This was going to be something altogether different. Part of him grew.

"...and her head popped off."

Chapter One

Maeve's face scrunched up as her teeth tore at the flesh of the other woman's arm. She chewed quickly and forced herself to swallow, the gulping noise echoing in her ears. She tried not to think about what it tasted like. It sure as hell wasn't chicken. How long had it been since she ate real food? Two days? Three? Four? She couldn't tell. *So hungry.*

Her stomach lurched. Her body wanted to reject what she was putting into it. She closed her eyes and tried to remember what daisies smelled like, what sun on her skin felt like. She imagined the ocean's water lapping against her belly. It wasn't that long ago she had been on the east coast on one of Prince Edward Island's beaches. She could almost feel the breeze coming in with each wave. The last time she was there some people invited her to join their cookout. She remembered the smell of the steaks cooking.

Her chest suddenly burned. She felt the fire shoot up into her throat. On instinct she turned. The brick wall scratched hard against her forehead. Pain and heat cracked through her skull. Her body fell forward onto hands and knees. Water splashed up her limbs. Her bare breasts dipped into the water covering the floor. As her mouth opened the two bites of flesh came shooting out with searing stomach acids in one reaching heave. It splashed into the water. *The water that I drink*, she thought. Her body pitched as she tried to vomit more. With each thrust pain scorched her throat. She thought something was scratching to get out of her chest. It was suddenly hard to breathe. Tears filled her eyes.

The sweet daisies were gone. The soft breeze wasn't there. The only thing remaining from her dream was water. It filled the floor of the square room high enough to cover her legs when sitting. It tasted foul. It was the worst thing she had ever put to her lips, but she had to drink something. It was stale, as though it had been in this room for a long time and she knew there were *things* in it. It left a metallic taste in her mouth. Every time she drank it came back up, then when she couldn't stand it anymore she had to drink again.

All she could smell was rot. The body of the other girl gave off a stench that seemed to soak into Maeve's skin. Only when she drifted to sleep did the smell go away, then it exploded in her senses the moment she woke. Just thinking of it again made her body toss forward with more dry heaves burning her chest and throat. No matter how much she tried to remember the smell of flowers (it was barely a memory) she couldn't stop. Even light was quickly being forgotten. How long had she been in there?

Was anyone looking?

Elisa.

She pushed back with her feet and hands until her body was in a corner. Cold damp cinderblock pressed against both shoulders. It was there in the corner that she felt okay to sag against the two walls and fall asleep.

When she first got there, when the other woman was still alive, she explored the room in the dark. Her hands walked the walls as she counted steps in the water. Seven steps in each direction. She knew the ceiling was a good jump above her head. The only entrance was a trap door that was now above the rotting corpse. That was how Maeve came to the prison. She was dropped through the hole, barely awake, barely aware of what was happening. Her ankle snapped when she landed and the cold water splashed over her body. Then the door slammed shut and she was in darkness. The only other thing she found when she limped around the walls was a one-inch plastic pipe sticking through the far wall almost near the top. It drizzled water once.

The sound had echoed through the square room; she lurched across on one knee pushing with her good foot to drink the water coming down. The other woman had screamed. She wanted to drink too. She needed the water. Maeve was able to move and she needed it. She would have brought some to the other woman if she had some way of carrying it. *How long ago had it been?*

Should I feel bad, she wondered. The woman was already dying. She coughed blood and had welts all over her body. All she did was cry and whimper. Until it was over.

Maeve closed her eyes and rested her head against the wall. She tried to focus on something other than the darkness she saw with eyes open. Her body tried to pull in a new breath. The smells stuttered through her nose and down to her lungs. Her eyes opened. She saw eyes in the darkness. They were blue with yellow in the whites like stars. She remembered those from when she was taken.

Those eyes would never leave her mind. *Was it real or a remembered movie? Did a man take her? A monster?*

Where was he?

Usually when he came, he had a large flashlight that he shone in her eyes. She couldn't see his face. All she saw was the pipe soaring down on her. Her screams echoed through the square room. She didn't know for how long it continued, at some point it all stopped. Her world went dark.

The second last time he came the trapdoor opened and fresh water poured down. Maeve stood in the corner paralyzed with fear. She didn't want to get hit again, until the moment she heard the water pouring down into the water covering the floor. She pushed herself away from the wall and stumbled across the room. Her ankle had gone beyond pain. Her body fell over the other woman as she hungrily drank the falling water. She let it fill her mouth and throat until natural instinct made her pull away. She took a breath and opened her mouth again. The water stopped. The trap door shut. She knelt there for a long time staring up at the door wishing for it to open again. He didn't come back that day or that night.

She couldn't think about what he had done to her or what he had done to the other. She needed him. She needed him to come back. Maybe that was the point.

She needed him.

When was he last there? She didn't want to remember it, but that thought consumed her. Light had cascaded in blinding Maeve for a minute as her eyes tried to adjust. Before she could see Maeve heard the water move as he lifted the other woman to see if she was dead.

The dying woman moaned and said, "Please." All she could say was, "please." Please save her? Please bring her death?

Maeve didn't want to open her eyes, but she had to. She had to see what was going on, what was going to happen. She wanted to know if he was coming for her. She wanted to see if he had the pipe. She watched him drop the other woman and slowly walk through the water toward her. All she could see was a different black moving within the darkness. Light from the door opening let her see the curve of his shoulders and head. His hand reached out. Maeve let out a scream that echoed around the cube. She tried to scramble away, but he was too fast. He grabbed her shoulder and pushed her. She fell against the wall, her palms scraped against the blocks. She turned. He hit her. He threw her around the room until she fell into the water and couldn't get up again. Then he stopped.

"Please," the other woman moaned from under the trapdoor opening.

Maeve raised her face from the water. Her body had to fight to keep above the surface. She watched him walk slowly through the dark liquid.

"Please."

He stopped below the opening. Maeve thought he looked down toward the begging woman there.

"Please."

A black boot slowly rose out of the water. He put it down just as slowly. The woman's face disappeared beneath the surface. For a few minutes (Maeve wasn't sure of the time) the black form just stood there staring down. Then he suddenly reached up for the ledge around the trap door opening and pulled himself up and out like a Ninja in one of those late night movies.

The door closed with a slam enveloping Maeve in darkness and still silence.

Tears began to fall down Maeve's cheeks. She felt the heat rise inside her chest again. *How could she need him?* He was a monster. He drowned that poor woman as if she was nothing, worthless. She had to do something. She had to save herself. She couldn't just give up and let him hold her head under water with a boot.

Like Enid. The other woman's name was Enid.

Maeve tried to reach the trapdoor by jumping when she first got in. She almost touched it though the fiery pain from her ankle danced up her leg like lightning. If she could jump up and grab him when he looked in maybe – maybe she could startle him. Maybe she could pull him down. If she was lucky he would hit the concrete floor beneath the water with his head and break his neck. Or if he didn't maybe he would be so angry he would end it all.

Save herself or welcome death? Either way, she wanted to be the one to choose.

Chapter Two

Chrysanthemum was hit with sensory overload as she crossed the threshold of The Alcrest Gastropub. Since she was a child she loved the smells of onions, garlic, and charbroil that always filled her nostrils when she walked through the door, back when it was just The Alcrest Pub to now. Her ears overflowed with the sounds of singing, guitar playing, and voices talking a dozen conversations and challenging the music. Across the room a man in a flat-brimmed cowboy hat began to add the wailing of a harmonica to the sound. Saturday nights were always so full of loud energy. As the patrons consumed more spirits, the next singer would have to get louder or surrender in defeat. The best part about the restaurant was that the kitchen was right in the dining room, adding to the sights and smells. Chrys watched the three men and one woman move between the barrier of a bar ledge and the heat of a large stove. A ball of flame exploded from a pan. Her foster brother commanded his troops in their white coats as they played with fire.

Damn, I love this place, she thought. She didn't always feel that way after a long night of serving customers, but that quickly faded.

"Spence," she called out with a little whine to her voice. A high barrier ran most of the length of the room with the kitchen and bar on one side and the customers on the other. Her weight hitched onto one leg as she leaned over the pass where plated food was handed to the servers and rubbed her hands under the hanging heat lamps. She tapped her thumb against the hot tile on top of the barrier so that her ring clicked. *Click, click, click.*

Over his shoulder Spencer said, "Burger, well-done with fries and a fish and chips."

"Burger-well, heard."

"Spence."

"Two side fries and fish, heard. Can you pass the fish?"

Spencer reached into the small lowboy fridge beneath the counter and passed the skinny fry cook a clear plastic container with equal-sized fish fillets inside before looking up at Chrys. His family had taken her in as a foster kid when she was three, he nine. "What?"

"Are you busy tomorrow?" She knew this was a loaded question. Her brother (after twenty-two years being in the same family there was no "foster" about it) was usually all business. You shouldn't let the tattoos peeking out from under the rolled up sleeves of his chef jacket and the backwards baseball cap fool you.

"I'm busy, now." Emphasis on the *now*. He took two plates from the right side oven. They didn't turn that one on. It was full of plates that got warm from the residual heat coming from the 400 degree oven on the left. On the plates he loaded mashed potato and the day's vegetable then left them there for the grill cook to add the perfectly-cooked steaks.

"I see that, but are you busy tomorrow?" Emphasis on the *tomorrow*.

12

He spun around for a moment to grab the pan of mushroom sauce sitting on the back flame. He turned back and added the sauce to the steaks. As he slid the plates up under the heat lamps he said, "Come to think of it, shouldn't *you* be busy *now*?"

Chrys checked behind her to see the front-of-house manager, Jessie, walk by. Jessie gave Spencer a smile, he returned with a twitch of his lips and a nod in her direction. Chrys didn't get why the two of them acted so indifferent to each other. They weren't hiding anything.

"I'm serious." She stated.

"So am I."

One of the servers checked the order ticked with the plates and then took them away.

"Where have you been anyway?" Spencer asked as he quickly wiped the butcher block counter (marked from years of knives gone wild and burn marks) on his side with a damp cloth.

The smell of garlic butter hit the air as the big man behind him put a hamburger bun on the grill. He was more than twice the size of the chef, but somehow the two of them could dance around each other in the small space. They had less than three feet between the butcher block and the stove. Gordie worked the grill while Spencer cooked anything having to be cooked in a pan beside him and did most of the plating.

Click, click.

Chrys lowered her eyes for a moment. "I was at my new job."

"Order in, Chef," One of the servers slipped an order slip in front of Chrys. The two women gave each other a faint smile. Chrys usually liked everyone, but something about Hanni, pronounced Honey, rubbed her the wrong

13

way. Maybe it was the three-inch spike heel boots she insisted on wearing. Maybe it was the way she flirted with everyone with a banana hanging between his legs, especially her brother. She sniffed and twitched her nose before walking away.

Spencer called over his shoulder, "Adding on mussels and fries, Alcrest salad." All cooks concerned announced that they heard the order. To the cold side cook, and the only female on the evening team, Spencer said, "Give us five minutes." He turned on a burner and nothing happened. He flipped a rag from his apron string and snapped it against the burner, hoping the air from the rag would pop the flameless burner awake. Nothing. "Damn, piece of ... Gordo, lighter."

After lighting the burner, almost frying off the hairs of his arm, he placed a sauté pan on the heat. He looked across the pass with no real expression on his face. Sweat glistened on his cheeks. "What about this job?"

"Oh fuck off, Spence. I'll go up and change in a minute. Are you busy tomorrow or not?"

Sunday was the only day he took off, and even then he spent most of it sitting at a corner table doing paperwork and fighting the itch to get in the kitchen.

Click, click, click.

Spencer sighed, "No, I'm not busy tomorrow. Why?"

Chrys's full, *Angelina Jolie* lips formed into a bright smile. "I'll tell you in the morning."

"Why don't you tell me now?" In one smooth action he took a container of mussels from the small fridge below, turned and poured some into the hot pan. To that he added diced onion and a spoonful of minced garlic from the cold inserts hanging through the countertop into the top back of the fridge. A little splash of Shiraz and he covered it with a

14

metal pie plate. As he turned back to the heat lamps a server was taking the burger and fish plates the others put together and Chrys was gone.

Gordie leaned in close to his boss. "I ever tell you your sister's hot?"

"Shut up," Spencer flicked the side towel in his hand at his grill cook. If he had time to register his feelings he would have sensed dread envelop his entire body.

"Order in."

Spencer took the order chit. "New order."

Chapter Three

The life of a chef was one hidden behind closed doors.
Most customers finished their food, paid their bills, and
went home not giving a second thought to what happened in
the kitchen before, during, or especially after their
wonderful meal. Even if the kitchen is out in the open. At
The Alcrest the end of the night meant the kitchen crew
cleaned down every piece of equipment and surface they
touched, wrapped what they could in plastic film - trying
not to discard anything - and put it all away in the walk-in
cooler in the back room. Then the cooks would go off to
whichever nightlife they preferred. Liz got a taxi home to
her mother's place where she and her daughter stayed,
Gordie usually went home for some *Xbox* and a little
marijuana, and Ranger did whatever the kid - he was
nineteen, but the chef still thought of him as a kid - did.
Spencer was chef and owner, so he stayed at work. Since
his father died four years ago he barely ever left. He had to
check and organize the walk-in, make a prep list for the
following day, get things ready for the Sunday brunch chef
in the morning, then check on how things were going out
front. Only after the last customer was gone, the money
counted, the front cleaned, and the last server gone did

Spencer climb the back stairs to the apartment he shared with Chrys and go to sleep. She had gone to bed an hour before. At three in the morning his head hit the pillow. He lay there a long while wondering what he missed.

Did Ranger turn the fryer off? Are the doors locked? Did everyone enjoy themselves? Is any of the staff thinking of quitting? Is there enough in the bank to pay all the bills this month?

At eight-thirty in the morning, with a freshly baked blueberry muffin warning his knee and a travel mug of coffee in its cup holder, he steered his truck around a pothole and continued thinking about what he missed. His aquamarine eyes, the lids still heavy, hid behind sunglasses even though the sun was not above the trees yet.

"I'm sorry for waking you up so early." It was the sixth time Chrys had said it.

He shrugged his shoulders. "Are you going to tell me why we're driving all the way out to Hillsborough?"

The only thing she had said so far, besides apologizing, was to tell him to drive north into the rural area. They could have gone west, a more visual ride and taken the Lindsen Ferry over the Hillsborough River, but the north route was more direct via highway and gravel road. Along the sides of the highway fields were broken by tired fences and walls of forest. It was beautiful country either way. Most of the leaves had already changed from green to the amazing colours of a painter's pallett. Bright yellow and red flickered from branches. Chrys suggested they should stop on the way home. Her digital camera sat between them along with the flashlight she had noisily dug through his closet for before he was officially awake. She liked taking pictures.

"Foreclosed houses," she admitted.

18

Spencer sleepily responded with a, "What?"

"Banks foreclose on houses, right? Then after a while if the owners can't pay they get the places cleaned and sell them."

His head bobbed. "So you're the middle man."

"Woman, yes. I'm supposed to take pictures of the places then later clean up whatever's there. They pay me for travel, cleaning, everything. You should see all the stuff that was left in this house. There's a nice dining table and chairs, a China set, tons of tools and shit in the garage."

"Isn't this like," Spencer started, "I don't know. Would you want someone going through your stuff?"

She plucked the muffin from his knee. "Come on. It's like Storage Wars or those picker shows you like. These people haven't been in this house for a year. They're not coming back. They've probably forgotten about all of their shit."

"So you've been there already?"

She hummed an answer with a mouthful of muffin. "Yesterday. Hoyt drove me out there to take pictures and change the locks, but we didn't have a flashlight so we couldn't go in the basement."

"So that's where you were instead of at your real job. And how much was Hoyt charging you for working on a Saturday?" Hoyt Heath owned a locksmith shop across the road. He had gone to school with Spencer's Dad.

"Don't start, Spence. The company's paying him."

"The company? Sounds sketchy." He flashed a smile and his dimples showed.

"The bank, you dick." She pulled the other half of the top from the muffin.

"So you're profiting on peoples' bad luck?"

"Hey, the bank lady told me the bank was going to work with them, but they didn't want to. The bank made phone calls and sent out letters. As far as they know the family just disappeared. It looks it too."

"What do you mean?" Spencer looked over at Chrys.

She was already silent looking out the side window lost in her own thoughts. Spencer's parents had fostered their fair share of children over the years, but the parents of most of those kids worked their issues out and got their kids back or a family member took them or a couple of the kids aged out of the government system. For Chrysanthemum Wanderingspirit, now Alcrest, there was no one. One day her mother was just gone and there was nobody else to take her but the Alcrests.

She pretty well matched the photograph of her mother she had wedged into the edge of a mirror in her bedroom. Dark chestnut hair fell down past her shoulders and against her light caramel skin. Her aboriginal ancestors were more than kind to her. The only difference from the picture was that she had full lips, the bottom especially, and her mother's were thin. Something from the father she didn't know perhaps. She had a thin and athletic body that included what she referred to as humble breasts.

"Jessie didn't stay last night," she said after fifteen minutes of nothing but the radio.

Spencer took a swallow of coffee. "No, she didn't."

"She is your girlfriend, isn't she?"

"She's not my girlfriend." Jessie and Spencer had moments where they were a happy couple and moments where they didn't speak to each other. He thought it worked.

"Your fuck buddy then. Is that better?" She looked down at her cell phone. "Oh look who's texting. She wants

20

me to work Tuesday night." She texted back that she would.

"I don't know what we are. We're just off and on."

"Well she's always in a better mood when you're on. Turn left here. It's the first driveway on the right."

They passed a collection of buildings in a small bundle on the left side – a collection of storage sheds for whatever farmer had his crops in the fields around them. The boards were black from years of weather against untreated wood. The tracks showed somebody went in there. Back in the day Spencer and his friends would have driven around looking for such buildings to explore. You never knew what you could find in abandoned buildings, or buildings that looked abandoned.

Spencer almost passed the driveway where it lay hidden on the grassy side of the road. As he eased the truck into the driveway and down a gentle slope, a feeling of dread fell over him.

Giant evergreens made a square around the house and yard blocking most of the wind coming across the fields. There were ghosts hanging from those trees. They dangled from strings tied around the grey paper to create a head. The grass over the entire yard had grown untouched until it was too heavy to stand up and fell over on itself. On one side the grass was only broken by a small kids' swimming pool deflated and discarded. There was filthy water inside it from rain with piles of dead and rotting leaves turning the water dark. The house itself had an attached two-car garage, the roof shingles had seen better days, and over in front of a glass door was a deck with plants growing up from underneath poking through the floorboards. A vine had climbed halfway up one of the posts around the outside of the deck. It looked as though it had once been screened in, but that was long ago. A storm door stood open beside the garage with the door behind it closed. How long would it take for nature to take over the house?

"This is it?" Nervous energy ran through Spencer's body as he looked around. On the side of the house what looked like discarded furniture and garbage had become a living mound with grass and plants growing over it. He bet snakes and mice and other nasties found a home in there during different times of the year.

Chrys said, "This is it," and slipped from the truck with the camera hanging from around her neck and flashlight in hand.

Even though the wind couldn't get through the trees the chill still made him button up his coat as he got out. A large trampoline stood in one corner of the yard. Dead leaves painted the bouncing surface. Branches from the nearest trees had expanded outward blocking some of the air above it. Those trees creaked and scraped against each other as if in some evil chanting. Witches standing over a bouncing cauldron.

"Where did you say the family went?"

"No idea. All I was told was that they stopped answering phone calls and then the mail started being returned a year ago. Nice house though, eh?" Chrys didn't worry about the cold. When she came yesterday fear fell over her the moment she saw the outside door open. Today she had to show that she was strong. She couldn't wimp out in front of her brother.

"I guess. Seems spooky though, like something bad happened." Spencer sent a hand through his hair spiking up the short blond locks. "Returning to the scene of the crime."

"Spence, don't start freaking me out. Hoyt tried scaring me yesterday. He kept stopping his work saying, did you hear that? And when I said we could go downstairs with our cell phones as flashlights he started telling me he smelled dead bodies."

"How would he know what dead bodies smell like?" Spencer looked to the road as a red pickup sped past spraying a jet stream of dust behind it. *Was someone watching them? Was the house owner going to come back?* It was a ridiculous thought. *If they hadn't been back in a year why would they come now?*

Chrys inserted a key and pushed the door open. "He said he's been called to unlock houses where dead people were inside and the basement had that sort of smell. I didn't smell anything but mold."

When they opened the door yesterday she almost had to be pushed inside. The lights were on as though it had been dark outside when the owner went to work and they just forgot to hit the switch on the way out. Chrys had done that many times herself. They probably got in their car ready to go to work, saw that they left the lights on, and for a split second thought about running back to turn them off, but they were late. No, they were gone.

Right inside the front door was a small landing before three steps up to the main floor. A closed door on the right led into the garage. The window was black from the darkness behind. In Spencer's mind he expected to see a face suddenly appear. On the landing he stood on and the one Chrys stepped up to were shoes simply discarded along the walls. At least a half dozen pairs in different sizes from child's to adult, newer ones to beat-up shoes that had been through the ringer. A yellow rain coat and umbrella hung from hooks on the wall. A wood box underneath those was wide open. There were more shoes inside there.

"They left their shoes?"

Chrys opened another door on the landing. "They left everything."

This one led into the kitchen of the house. Every surface was covered: the horseshoe of kitchen countertop was blanketed in papers, there was a knife block with only one knife in it, glasses and plates were scattered around, there was a small wood box with seashells crudely glued to it, a large green glass bowl kept a collection of those plastic clips that held bread bags closed, there were Tupperware containers, empty pop bottles, candles, and kitchen utensils. It was an assortment of what a stranger would call crap. It seemed as if someone took a couple of junk drawers and dumped them on top of the counter.

Spencer looked at the child's drawings that had been stuck to the refrigerator with colorful flower magnets. Beside them was a school calendar from last year.

"It's hot in here."

"I turned the heat up yesterday. Look at this," Chrys opened a corner cupboard. In just that little space there was a popcorn maker, waffle maker, flat grill, and a crockpot. "There's more stuff in every cupboard."

On the other side of the counter was a dining table big enough for four. Again it was as though things had just been dumped and piled on top. There was unopened mail and store flyers amongst it all. A cardboard box was full of electronic parts, some wires hung out over the edge. Another glass bowl had a collection of tea-light candles inside with colorful stones and loose change at the bottom. A stack of photographs had been spilled across some papers and disappeared under some others. Spencer moved a few around with his fingers. Just everyday photos; the dog that must have belonged to the dog house he noticed by the deck, kids at play on the trampoline, a girl in a pretty dress, a guy in his twenties leaning back on a couch with a cigarette dangling from thin lips. *Who leaves photographs?* Under the pictures he found a school report card. Daniel Linque, grade three, St. John's School. Spencer suddenly remembered all of his report cards collected and secured with a bulldog clip in the same box as his baby book in his mother's closet.

"They left their kids' report cards."

"It's weird, right?" Chrys had a strange smile over her face. She always enjoyed a mystery. "And look at this," she walked into the open living room pointing at the inner wall. The room itself was empty but for papers and clothes strewn over the floor. Candle holders were fastened to the far wall. On the wall Chrys pointed at, neither of them could tell if there was red painted over white or the other way around. Most of the wall was white like all of the others, but on this one the paint had been scraped off showing bright red behind in jagged shards.

"It looks like the blood wall in that movie. Remember the scary one where the blood flowed down the wall?" Chrys loved scary movies.

"It's not blood."

"I know it's not blood, jackass. I'm just saying it looks it." There was definite excitement in her voice. She was having fun. "And they said I'll probably be able to keep anything I want or anything I can sell, so like this dining table and chairs. I could probably get a few for it." She crossed back to it and gave it a shake. It creaked, but stood firm. A few papers floated to the vinyl floor.

"There are only three chairs," Spencer stated. The eerie feeling he got from the house was still there, but it was being massaged away by his sister's excitement.

Chrys pulled two chairs away from the table. One had a small cardboard box on the seat. She said, "They're in good shape though. And the table looks good."

Spencer smiled showing deep dimples on both cheeks. "You can only see the legs. What if the top is all scratched up?"

"Oh come on, I know you're a leg man. I've seen you check out what's under the skirts that come into the restaurant." Chrys took all of her hair behind her neck in one hand. "Oh or at the gym. I saw your head snap all the way around once at ..."

"Or Hanni's legs," Spencer interrupted.

Psst. "She doesn't have any legs and less of an ass. All she has are tight clothes and heels. It's all smoke and mirrors."

"Gordie likes your legs."

"Shut up." She let her hair drop.

"No I'm serious." He opened the box on the chair. "You should give him a shot."

Chrys started sorting through the papers on the table. "You know he's not my type."

"What is your type? In the past few months you dated that business guy and then Corey from the gym. Oh and don't forget, Dawn. Or was she a phase?" In the box were two stacks of compact discs, all the same album. "You ever hear of Maeve Campbell?"

The front cover of the CD showed a woman with long blond hair leaning against a red wall. The thin strap of a white dress was all that was over her otherwise bare shoulder. It said, *Maeve Campbell Songs for Elisa.*

"Nope."

"She's pretty."

"Let me," Chrys craned her neck. "You can only see half her face."

Spencer flipped the disc case around. The back was a picture of the same woman lying on grass. The view was looking over her breasts mounds. A straw cowboy hat was pulled low and black sunglasses hid her eyes.

Chrys said, "Her boobs are small."

"So are yours." He slipped the CD in his jacket pocket.

"Shut the fuck up. Jessie's are even smaller than mine. And what are you doing looking at my boobs anyway?" She gave him a quick kick to the shin. Mr. Alcrest always told her if she had to fight a man to kick him hard in the shin and run like hell. This one was more like a sisterly kick.

Spencer hopped on the other foot and rubbed his leg. "All Gordie does is talk about your tits. That hurt." His eyes looked down at a grey skateboard turned upside down under the table like a tortoise on its shell. He took his jacket off and slipped it over the back of the chair.

Chrys clapped her hands together. "Come see the bedrooms."

The bedrooms were all variations on a theme. The first one must have been for a preteen or teenaged girl. Flowered drapes still hung from a bent curtain rod. There was another pile of photographs. These too were of kids and family stuff. There was some of winter fun and a collection of older people all with the same light hair. A cardboard box with a bunch of books sat in the middle of the room. It held novels about girls and horses, two of the Twilight novels, a Harry Potter, a bunch of Goosebumps and other books. In the corner was a stuffed blue rabbit.

Over the floor were random papers and scraps of garbage. Justin Bieber stared from pages torn out of magazines and thumbtacked to the wall. The second bedroom was a little girls'. There were a half dozen stuffed animals on the floor, crayon drawings on the walls, and hand-drawn pictures tacked beside them. The strangest thing was that the bedroom door barely hung onto the wall and only by the bottom hinge. The top one was still on the door but long screws hung from the other half of the hinge with bits of wood in the threads. The wood on the frame was splintered. Room three, the last bedroom down the hallway must have been Daniel's room. On his walls were pictures of Star Wars characters and sports cars. There was a small makeshift table with green soldiers scattered over it. In the closet, bags of clothes and papers were piled halfway up. An old computer monitor sat underneath. Each room told a story of who the occupant was, but nothing of where they had gone.

"What the hell happened to these people?"

"No clue." Chrys's dark oval eyes went up to the tiny attic door just outside the third bedroom.

Spencer followed her gaze. Because of her love for scary movies he refused to look up in attics. "And it's been over a year?"

"A guy came to do this a few months ago, but he told the bank he refused to finish this house."

"Why?"

"Mice droppings or something."

Spencer looked up at a mobile of the solar system attached to the ceiling in the boys' room. Outside the bedroom window he had a good view of the back yard that was pretty much the same as the front with overgrown grass that had been left to grow out of control. On the back deck was a giant pile. There was a mattress sticking out of it, but the majority was clothes. He wondered if the people opened their windows and just chucked it all. *Why do such a thing? If you didn't want to take it, why not donate it? Or had this pile been made long before the foreclosure? What were these people like before that happened?*

"There are empty hair dye tubes in the bathroom." Chrys pointed to the twisted packet on top the shower door. "The really good stuff is in the garage. There's a dresser and a couple of mountain bikes, a lot of fishing gear, and a shit load of tools. Did you want to see that or do you want to go to the basement?"

Spencer passed the broken door as he walked through the little girls' room. He wasn't sure why, but he put each foot down with care on every step. He looked around some more then glanced out the window. Trees, already bare, stood back of the house with gnarly claws reaching out.

Everything about the place gave him an eerie feeling. It was probably all in his imagination, too many suspense novels read while unwinding from the restaurant. He understood his sister's enthusiasm about the prospects of the house, but there were too many questions bouncing around in his head. Where did the family go? It was probably something boring and mundane. The bank was taking the house and the land, so the owners applied for jobs elsewhere. An opportunity came and they had to leave quickly. A brand new start. But then why throw all that stuff out on the deck? He saw a large shed far behind the house being taken over by nature. What was going to be in there? He wasn't sure he wanted to look in anything anymore. He knew there were going to be more questions than answers.

He said, "Basement, I guess."

Chapter Four

Maeve Campbell's head snapped up. The back of her cranium bounced off one cinder block wall then another. For one brief confused moment she didn't know where she was. Then the smell hit her and her body shivered with violence. *Was the smell worse? Was the water colder? Was that woman's body still out there in the dark?*

She had been dreaming. She actually fell asleep sitting in the corner. And she dreamed. There were daisies again, only this time they were woven in and out of her long blond hair. Her mother always said Maeve belonged in the sixties, a flower child reborn. She stood on a beach and her bare feet dug into the sand as the ocean's waves came over them. A strand of green seaweed wrapped around her calf. She wore a shear red dress that flowed with the wind and danced on the surface of the water. You could see the outline of her body when the light was right. Her guitar hung from one hand beside her.

The rotting smell was back. There were no flowers in her hair, no seaweed around her leg. She saw nothing in the darkness.

What made her waken? There was no water dripping from the pipe. She struggled to hear if there were any sounds, but the hits to her head made it ring from inside her skull. Perhaps she just woke because it was time. She longed to be back in her dream.

What was that? There was a sound. She knew the top of this room had a wood ceiling and above that was another. *Was it all the way up there? Was it all in her head? Was it Enid?* Maybe she had come back to life and wanted revenge for being eaten.

There was the sound again. Footsteps? It was so faint she could barely hear it over the ringing. Her heart pounded. It was him. Maybe he was back to kill her. Maybe he was back to finally do the things she feared the most. She knew some of what he had done to the other woman. Her body ached from the games he had played already. She felt so week.

She pushed away from the corner. Maeve didn't want this to go on.

More sounds came from above, something along the floor. Something scraped like it was dragged. Another woman?

He's found another. If he had another girl to play with then this might be Maeve's last chance. She was going to be held under the water.

She rolled forward onto her hands and knees and began crawling through the water. She couldn't see, but knew where the trap door was. She had to get under it, behind it almost so that she would still be in the shadows when the door opened. Her hand fell on the leg of the dead woman. Enid. Her hand flinched away. She gently put her hand back on the body and followed down the leg to her toes. At the far wall she let her hands crawl upward until she was standing. Her weak legs wobbled beneath her. Her ankle was in violent pain. Unless she was lucky, she wasn't going to win. Maeve knew her only chance was to grab him when he looked in with his flashlight. All of the possibilities played through her mind. Either way she was going to fight. She was going to claw and scratch and kick and bite until either she killed him or he ended it. She widened her stance, arms out to keep balance.

Where was he?

She felt an almost excitement growing inside her. She had tried to be nice to everyone her entire life, but she was going to kill the next person that came through that trap door.

Chapter Five

"So why didn't you guys come down here yesterday?" Spencer stopped halfway down the basement stairs

"Couldn't find a light switch and we didn't have a flashlight," Chrys pushed the on/off button on the flashlight and flashed it in her brother's face. He reached for it and she pulled back. "Ladies first." She slipped past him and headed down the stairs without a thought of fear.

Someday that's going to get her killed, Spencer thought as he headed down after her. He found the flashlight application on his phone just as Chrys found a light switch at the base of the stairs.

A dull light erupted above them. The smell of mold and dampness filled their nostrils. It was a finished basement so at some point in time someone had money and cared. The room they were in was a big open area that looked like it was a family room. A computer desk sat against one wall covered in more papers, a couple of speakers, some video games, and discarded wires but no computer. The base of a futon, no cushion in sight, had a pile of clothes and toys on top. A dresser stood at a strange angle in the middle of the room and there was an entertainment stand made of particle board opposite the computer desk. It looked like they had taken the furniture they cared about and left everything that could be replaced. Across the room one wall was lined with red brick thinning to a chimney-sized end ascending upward as though there had once been a real fireplace there.

As Spencer watched Chrys go through a door his eyes caught movement. A fan stood in the corner oscillating back and forth on a tall skinny pole. The lone soldier fighting off the mildew, and losing. In his mind he imagined some scene in a movie where a pack of the undead or mutated inbred creatures would come stumbling around the corner. His damn sister and her scary movies.

"What's over there?"

"Bedroom. Maybe the master. Nothing in it though, just some boxes."

Another open door showed a bathroom with a toilet, sink, and shower. The shower was full of broken-down cardboard boxes.

Spencer walked into the last open room, his phone's bright light leading the way. This was the furnace room. He pulled on a chord and a single light bulb burst into brightness. Along the wall was a homemade shelf with junk overflowing on each board. There was an old aquarium, boxes with books sticking out, papers were everywhere. It was amazing how many papers people collected.

"That a guitar case?" Chrys asked as she snapped a picture.

Spencer poked the hanging black fabric case. "Empty. Check out the mold over there."

All along the wooden inner wall (the shower was on the other side) rounds of black mold spread. Chrys wondered how much of it was in the air. She took a picture.

A folded baby playpen leaned against the corner blocked in by a high chair. Children's toys were piled in front of them. Their children were too old for them, so these were probably things the family couldn't bring themselves to throw out or perhaps they were hoping to sell or donate someday. A cast-iron framed coffee table stood on its end and leaned against the outer wall. One leg hung down at an unnatural angle. A plastic tub held Christmas wrapping paper and bows.

Spencer walked around the furnace and hot water tank, both looked relatively new. Behind them was a wall of cinderblocks that was just taller than his almost six-foot frame, but didn't reach the ceiling. It didn't extend to the side wall of the basement either and left a thin path between them. He looked around expecting to see just the one wall, a barrier for the furnace maybe. Another wall extended from the corner of the smaller one and stopped just before the far wall. This didn't make sense. He pushed up onto his toes. There was a top. It was a room. A room made of thick cinderblock walls and mortar with a plywood top.

"Ah, Chrys."

The hairs on her arms felt electrified at just the way her brother said her name. He was already moving forward.

Spencer felt drawn to walk around these inside walls. There had to be a door or something. There had to be a reason for them to be there. He said, "This is a concrete room. The walls don't go up."

"What?"

"They don't go all the way to the ceiling."

"What? Why?"

The light from Spencer's cellphone didn't reach around the corner as he moved toward it. Shadows were cast and danced. Why was there a room like this inside the house?

Every horror movie popped through his head. Pennywise the Clown liked basements. Zombies often got locked in them. Freddie Kruger. Jason. In his head he saw all of them turning the corner from the far side or maybe crawling along the top of it waiting for the next time he looked up.

"What are you doing?" Chrys pointed the flashlight on her brother.

He jumped. The phone almost fell from his hand.

"You shouldn't go over there, Spence. We should just go." All of her courage had instantly left. The only feeling she had at that moment was that they should get out of there. "I've taken pictures. We should just go." Her brother was in the grey shadows and she stood under the light bulb. She realized her body was trembling. She looked back toward the family room at the stairs. All she heard was the fan blowing and turning. She should have locked the front door. Somebody could be coming down those stairs right now and they wouldn't know it. They would be trapped.

"There's a ladder." Spencer stood at the far corner. The short wall made a ninety degree turn. It was indeed a square room right underneath the kitchen.

"Spence, come back." Chrys watched him disappear around the corner. She looked out to the family room again. Her head spun to look at the tiny window high on the wall and covered on the outside by the tall grass. *Could someone be watching?* She knew her thoughts and fears were irrational.

"I'm just going to see what's on top."

"Forget it. I have enough pictures." She wanted to get out of there.

The closer he got to the ladder, made of rough-cut two by fours, the more Spencer smelled something foul. It wasn't that bad from where he stood. Was this a compost thing? Something in his head said he had to continue. He grabbed the top of the ladder and pulled himself up with his phone leading the way. The dark shadows covered everything behind him. The phone sent light over the top. All that was up there was a small skimming net with a metal handle. There was also a square block nailed to a larger square on the top just a foot in front of him.

He took another step up. Spencer said, "There's a trap door up here."

"Shit. If I give you the camera can you get pictures?" Chrys forgot about her fears and followed the path her brother had taken.

Spencer grabbed hold of the block and jerked upward on the trap door. The whole square jumped out of the hole. The foul stench was instantly stronger. The smell encircled him like a cloud rising from the cube. It was a mixture of rotting meat and garbage. If it was a compost then it shouldn't still smell after a year of sitting there. *Did people really have composts in their houses? If they did, did they make them with cinderblock walls? How would they get the stuff out?* He couldn't see right down through the open hole. At the angle he was looking all he saw was his light shining off something. He had to get a better look.

"I think there's water in there."

"What?" Chrys checked behind her. There was nothing there. Her stomach churned. The hairs on her arms still stood up. Her breaths came quickly. She turned the corner and pointed the light. There was the ladder her brother had talked about. She brought the light up until she saw Spencer's hiking boots. "Why don't you come down?"

"In a second." He pulled himself forward. He had to know how much water was inside this concrete box. *This tomb*, he thought. He put his cellphone flashlight in his palm and reached inside. There was something in the water.

His eyes went wide. Spencer saw the hands appear out of the black. Fingers encircled his wrist. The phone fell from his grasp. His weight slipped forward. There was nothing in front of his eyes but darkness.

"Spencer? Fuck, Spencer."

Chapter Six

Spencer tried to reach for the edge of the hole. His phone dropped. The light spiraled down before fading beneath water. His hand grabbed for the wood. A sliver of wood speared into his fingertip. He was suddenly falling through air into the darkness. Who grabbed him? What was he falling into?

"Spence!"

His arm reached out to brace his fall. There was water, then a concrete bottom. The snap echoed to his ears as if it was inside him. Pain shot through every nerve from his wrist to his brain. A scream surged from his throat. His face hit something solid that, at the same time, was not. Chest, stomach, legs hit the shallow water. His knees surged through to hit the bottom. It filled his mouth drowning his yell.

Spencer pushed his head up above the surface. His body suddenly lurched in a coughing fit. He had to get the water out. *What am I tasting?* Between coughs that pulled at his insides he tried to spit. It was rot. It was that Tupperware container you found in the back of the fridge after God knows how long. You know you shouldn't open it, but can't help the curiosity. He gagged. It was like nothing he had ever put into his system, and as a chef that was a wide range. His throat clenched tight. His chest burned.

There was another scream. It wasn't Spencer. It wasn't his sister. *Who?*

Something slammed against his back. Spencer pitched forward, his head went under the water again. His eyes closed. His hands reached down to try and push himself up. This time his scream reverberated through the water. Claws pulled at his hair.

He had to get up. He had to fight back, save himself. Save Chrys.

The wind had been knocked out of him from the fall and it was a struggle just to get his mouth above the water and catch a breath amidst the coughing. His heart raced. He tried pushing up, but what was on him pushed down. Spencer felt a knee in his back. Hands forced his head into the water.

It was trying to kill him.

He thrashed side to side. He had to get this thing off him. Its grip slipped. One knee got underneath him. He gasped for air. Violent spasms took control of his body coughing out the foul water.

Fingernails suddenly tore at his skin. His arm went up and the creature set its sights on it.

Light shone down. Spencer's eyes opened. The creature had bright blue eyes. It was a woman's face. Her mouth opened wide. Her teeth were stained, but still looked sharp.

"Get the fuck off of him bitch," Chrys screamed. "Spencer."

The woman pushed away. She half crawled as fast as she could into the far dark corner. The water splashed in her wake.

"Spence, you okay?" Chrys leaned over the opening spotlighting the flashlight's beam on her brother. Her face scrunched up from the smell.

Spencer tried to push himself up. The water was high enough that it almost covered him where he lay. With his right arm he pushed himself to a sitting position. The coughing wouldn't stop. He hocked up some phlegm and spat into the water. It didn't help much. The taste of the water seemed to coat his tongue.

The smell definitely came from in there. It was a mix of rot and something metallic. Between coughs he said, "I think I ... broke my wrist." His eyes found where his phone's flashlight was still lit at the bottom. After plunging two phones in the kitchen sink, another in the toilet, he had decided it was time for a waterproof phone. For extra protection it had a case that he could supposedly drive over. It had been under water and was still working. The driving over thing he didn't really want to try.

"Who the fuck was that?"

He brought the light up and shone it into the corner.

The woman covered her eyes with dirty hands. Her hair was grimy and in a mess, but he could tell it was blond. She had her knees pulled tight to her body. He was pretty sure she was completely bare. Her skin was covered in grime. The part that really got his attention was all the bruising. Even in the low light he could see that parts of her body were mottled with colourful marks, her legs and arms especially. From around her hands he saw her face was puffed out and her skin seemed an odd colour. In some places it was normal flesh tone, but in others it ranged from purple to a worrisome green. One of the fingers covering her face was bent at an unnatural angle.

43

"Spence," Chrys' voice was full with enough strain and panic that he had to look up at her right into the flashlight. "What the hell's that beside you? Oh fucking shit on a duck."

He looked down at the lump in the water. His eyes had watered from the pain. What he saw was something looking back at him. A face, it was a face.

"That's a fucking body."

"Jesus." He pushed away from the lump in the water. Pain shot up his arm. He turned his head as he spewed into the very water he had ingested. "Chrys, you have to find something to get me out of here."

"My phone's out in the truck. Give me yours." Chrys lay on the wood top and reached down as far as she could. Her eyes darted into the dark corner where the other woman had gone.

"What about getting me out of here?"

"I have to call the cops, don't I?"

Spencer didn't know if his sister was fearless or stupid. The debate went to both sides depending on what crazy stunt she was doing. He shone the light on the creature in the corner. She watched him through her fingers. He felt scratches to his arm and face starting to sting. Did she kill this other person? "Give me the flashlight then."

"What am I supposed to use then?"

"You have lights out there. I've got nothing. You're not leaving me in the dark, Chrys." Even he was surprised how close to panic his voice sounded.

"Don't be such a chicken shit."

"Don't be such a foul mouth. Just give me the flashlight."

Spencer pushed himself to his feet. His legs felt wobbly and his entire body ached. Behind the pain of his left wrist he felt another pain in his knee. It must have struck the bottom when he fell. His eyes watched for the body in the water. With the toe of his boot he nudged it away. The face tilted and fell beneath the water with a splash. He turned his light on the other girl. She hadn't moved. He felt his heart beating rapidly through his chest. Reaching up, he passed the phone to his sister.

In the two seconds it took Chrys to lift the phone up and hand down the flashlight Spencer was cast into darkness. His head spun. *How could anyone survive in there?* He sensed to the black all around him. *How long had she been there? Who put her in?*

Chrys reached down with the flashlight. "Here." As the light fell on Spencer's handsome face she held her breath at how it had changed. His oval face was painted with the blood of someone else. Small scratches around his eyes looked ready to burst. The worst part was that she saw terror in every feature.

Spencer took the flashlight and pointed it at the woman. She had not moved. Her back was hard against the wall, hands still covering her face. The woman was huddled as tightly as she could make her body. She was making a noise. It sounded like singing, but he couldn't make out the words.

"Shit. I'm not getting any service down here. I have to go outside." Chrys hesitated at the look her brother gave her. As if channeling his thoughts she added, "I'll be careful."

Spencer watched his sister disappear from the open hole above him. His ears strained to hear her climb down the ladder and run back around the square room, but even with the lid open he barely heard a thing. *What was it like for this woman? What if someone shut the door?* At least he had a flashlight. The woman had nothing.

His legs threatened to let go. He stood over the dead body; he didn't want to sit there. Spencer backed to the closest wall and rested his back against it before sliding down until he was practically sitting on his heels with his butt in the water. The flashlight lay on his knees, the beam pointing at the woman against the far wall.

He moved it away from her face, but only slightly, so that he could still see her in the edge of the beam. "I'm Spencer," his voice trembled. It didn't have the usual confidence he portrayed. "What's your name?"

She stopped her singing.

Spencer adjusted himself and let his butt drop right to the floor. Pain shot from his wrist. He closed his eyes and tried to breathe. Opening them again, he focused on the girl. *Had she moved? Was there something else in the dark room?* He turned the light around the room, then quickly put it back near the woman.

"My sister went to call for help. She's not really my sister. I mean, she is, but she isn't. She was my foster sister and then she changed her last name." He didn't have a clue why he was talking. It just seemed to put him at ease. As long as he was hearing his own voice things were still okay.

With his right hand he carefully placed his left arm across his legs. The cool water actually seemed to soothe it. "This is sure going to be a pain at work." He winced. "I'm a chef. I bet they'll have to put it in a cast. And I'm left-handed, so this is really going to suck."

Spencer looked back at the woman. She had let her hands drop to her chin. In the dim light he could barely recognize her as a human being. Her face was bruised and

46

spotted with welts that cast shadows over her features making her appear almost demonic. One eye looked like it was almost swollen shut. The pain she was probably in made his wrist seem like nothing.

"You should come for dinner. I mean after you get all fixed up. We'll get you out of here, get you to a hospital, and then I'll make you a special dinner. If I can cook with one hand. Do you like seafood?" She didn't move. "I hope you like seafood because I'm planning to add a new halibut dish to the menu. It's going to have a sweet corn zabaglione with it. I have this supplier who has bushels of fresh corn on the cob for me. It's going to be so good." His enthusiasm was getting the better of him and making him feel better.

He heard the woman say something. It was rough like her throat was dry and raw, but she did make a sound. Spencer stared across at her as she stared back. After a moment she opened her mouth again.

"Where," she tried to clear her throat. "Where is she?"

"Who, Chrys? She's outside calling the cops and ambulance and everyone. If anyone can make some noise, it's Chrys." His eyes turned up to the open hole and the faint light from the lone bulb by the furnace. "So what's your name?"

Again she went silent.

Spencer moved the light so it was brighter but by the look on her face, she didn't seem to notice. It, bruised as it was, was a mask of terror. She was afraid of what might come through the square opening. She was terrified about what had come through there before. *How long had she been stuck in here, her only companion a slowly-rotting corpse? Or was the dead woman still alive when she was put in there and she had to watch her die?* A fate that she must have been certain she too would have had.

Spencer suddenly realized how quiet it was. He could almost hear the pumping of blood through his temples. Outside the furnace kicked off. The woman was breathing heavily. He held his own breath. Chrys should have come back. What if the person who put this woman in here, who beat her to the point of being unrecognizable, who killed the other woman, was out there waiting? He could have been driving that red truck that went by. *He could have Chrys*, Spencer thought.

There was a noise. Someone was up on the main floor.

The woman fell forward onto her hands and knees and crawled toward Spencer. "You have to kill him. If he comes in here you have to kill him." He had never heard such a serious person.

"I, I can't," he looked up. There was someone on the stairs.

The woman pushed back. She wanted to stay in the shadows. Her good eye was on the opening. "You have to kill him. You have to." Her voice dropped to a soft tone that seemed to dissipate in the square. "Please, please." Her voice dropped to a whisper, "Please."

If this was the *him* she was afraid of, Spencer knew he would have to make quick decisions. His sister was out there. He had to make sure she was safe. Carefully, he got up on his feet again. The pain completely way through his body. There were footsteps. Someone was out there. Someone was coming.

"Spence," it was Chrys. She leaned over the opening. Her eyes were comforting. She said, "Help's on the way."

Chapter Seven

"It's a cistern."

Spencer winced as the volunteer fireman tightened the sling behind his head. His left arm was fastened between two orange boards wrapped in towels to keep the bone stable. The only thing they had for the pain was ibuprofen and it wasn't helping.

The area around *The Creepy House*, as Chrys had begun to refer to it, now looked like a staging point for battle. White police cruisers and trucks with the yellow and red stripes of the Royal Canadian Mounted Police were parked on the lawn. A yellow box fire truck sat behind Spencer's truck. It was manned by the area's volunteer fire team. Their personal vehicles were parked along the sides of the road. They were farmers, students, retirees, teachers, one was actually a nurse; their beepers went off and they left their lives to respond. A helicopter from the city's hospital sat in the field across the road. Its rotor blades circled slowly above it churning the long grass.

"There you go. That should hold you until you get to the hospital." He pushed his sunglasses back up his nose with the back of a latex gloved hand. "What was I saying?" Dr. Ken (he introduced himself as "*Kenneth, but everyone knows me as Dr. Ken"*, when Spencer was brought out to him) was a veterinarian in the city.

To get Spencer out of the cinderblock cube they lowered a ladder through the trap door opening. One of the volunteers had to go in to help him up. As they came close to the naked woman she began to scream and flail her limbs, trying to hit anyone who dared go near. By the time Spencer was leaving the opening they had a female RCMP officer down there attempting to get close to the wild woman. You couldn't blame her though. Spencer could only imagine what she had gone through, but he really didn't want to know.

Spencer stared at the front door of the house. He didn't want to know, in depth, what happened to her, but he did want to see what she looked like in the light. He absently said, "A *sistern?*"

"Right, cistern. Basically it's a holding tank usually used for rain water. Nowadays they're plastic and buried underground but lots of these older farm houses still have them inside. People use the water for laundry, animals, washing dishes, watering gardens. In big cities high-rises have them on their roofs. The tank at the back of a toilet is a cistern." He ran his forearm over his black hair trying to get at an itch without having to take the blue latex gloves off. Spencer saw splashes of silver glisten in the light.

Chrys walked out of the house with her arms wrapped tight around her body. A female RCMP officer, Dawn, walked with her, her hand resting on the other woman's back. She was the one RCMP officer the two Alcrests knew.

"Are we done?" Spencer asked Dr. Ken. The last thing he wanted was a history lesson on water tanks.

"Sure, sure. Do you need a ride to the hospital? They'll have to cast that arm."

And it was his good hand. His knife hand. Spencer let out a sigh. "No thanks. I've got my truck."

Dr. Ken started putting things back into his large tackle box of medical supplies. "I don't know if you should be driving. That arm's going to be in some pain."

"Goodie, I get to drive." Chrys bounced on the balls of her feet. She flashed the volunteer fireman a bright smile, but it didn't go through to her eyes.

She obviously didn't see the ring on the finger of this man who was old enough to have kids their age, Spencer thought. "I don't think so. Hey, um …"

"Kenneth. Dr. Ken. Whichever."

"Dr. Ken, can I hold onto this?" Spencer wiggled the maroon blanket draped over his shoulders. Since going into *The Creepy House* the temperature outside had dropped a few degrees. All of his clothes were still wet and were intensifying the cold.

The veterinarian flashed a perfect set of teeth. "Oh sure. I'll come by your restaurant some time and get it."

"You can check out Bullet too. I think he needs to go on a diet or exercise program or something."

"That's the bulldog you told me about? You can always bring him by the clinic if you want." God forbid a doctor, of humans or animals, ever made a house call. "Here's my card. Just drop by and I can take a look." *Dr. Ken Stewart, Middleton Vet Clinic*. He went back to putting things away.

"I got your coat." Chrys held up Spencer's black cashmere coat.

"Thanks, but I'll keep this blanket on. I don't know what was in that water, but it smells nasty." It was attached to him, in his hair, on his clothes. He had to sit in the cistern for over an hour waiting for the police to come and determine how to get him out. The stench had probably seeped into his skin. The taste was still in his mouth and up his nose. "Do you have any water, Doc?"

Chrys scrunched up her face as she took a sniff. "You fucking reek."

Spencer took the bottle of water Dr. Ken handed to him, cracked the top by sticking it between his knees, awkwardly turned the cap with his bad hand, and filled his mouth. He swirled it around, sloshed it through his teeth, then spit it into the grass. He bent over at the waist and poured some into his hair.

"What are you doing?" Dawn's voice raised to a squeal. "What?"

"You might have evidence in your hair. We need your clothes also." Her voice went flat. "Evidence."

Spencer smirked. "Evidence of what? That I should look before putting my head in a hole?"

"Good advice for anyone," Chrys responded with a twinkle in her eye showing some of her normal self. She bumped her hip against the other woman's.

Dawn smiled at the tan-skinned woman. It disappeared the moment she turned back to the brother. "Your face bounced off a dead body. You might have some particulates on you, so we need to take your clothes. You'll get them back." Her last sentence had that teenage-girl attitude behind it that would have been followed with a, *duh*, and the cocking of a hip. All she did was cross her arms, the cop sign of attitude.

"And what am I supposed to wear?"

Dawn shook her head and rolled her eyes. "I have some gym sweats in my car. You can borrow those."

"I have to wear your clothes?"

"Oh Spence, quit being a fucking dick." Chrys gave him a little push.

"Screw you, Chrys. And how am I supposed to get my shirt off?"

"I have scissors," Dr. Ken stated.

Spencer looked at him as if to say, "You're supposed to be on my side."

Kenneth held his hands to the side after passing the scissors to Chrys. "I wouldn't complain if I had two pretty young ladies telling me to take my clothes off."

"Dude, she's my sister and this one's ..."

"Don't worry, Spencer, I'm in no rush to see what you've got. And did you seriously just use the word, *dude*?" Dawn glared at him.

Chrys snorted and started snipping the left side of his shirt with the medical scissors.

Dawn spun on her heel and marched off to one of the RCMP cars. Spencer watched her thinking how her uniform fit her well. She and Chrys had dated, but she never got along with him. They had a moment once, both swore never to talk about it, not to even think about it. She came back moments later with a large brown paper bag and a pair of navy sweat pants.

She watched Chrys peal the shirt off of the chef and was a little surprised at the muscle tone, the cold made his nipples instantly hard. A second later she realized she was staring. "Put your clothes in here. Here are some pants. I don't think my sports bra'll fit you, so you'll have to go shirtless."

"Great."

They all looked to the house as a flight paramedic backed out lifting the stretcher wheels over the threshold and gently lowering them to the ground. The woman from the cistern was strapped to the gurney; her face was smeared with blood and dirt, eyes closed. An oxygen mask covered her mouth and nose. A police officer walked alongside her holding an IV bag in the air as the ambulance attendants rolled her up the driveway. Nobody spoke or moved until the helicopter was in the air and heading to the city.

"Any idea who she is?" Spencer watched the flying machine get further and further away.

"We think she might be this woman who disappeared from the train a few weeks ago, Maeve Campbell."

Spencer remembered the CD in his coat pocket. His hand had to adjust to catch the blanket over his shoulders. He thought of telling Dawn about the CD, but she would want it for evidence and he didn't want to let it go.

"What about the other woman?" Chrys asked.

Dawn said, "We don't know yet. Hey, *dude*, you have to take your pants off."

As Spencer tried pushing his pants down the blanket slipped from his shoulders and fell to the ground. Chrys grabbed for his pants. He stepped back almost losing his balance on the blanket. "I can do it myself."

"I've seen you naked before, dear brother."

"Not lately. Not on purpose."

"It was too on purpose."

"What?" Spencer and Dawn said at the same time.

Chrys put her hands on her hips. "Sonja Aldren dared me to take a picture of your," she wiggled a finger in the direction of his crotch, "your better half, one time when she slept over."

"Seriously?" Spencer walked around to the far side of his truck. He opened the door so it would at least block him

54

being seen from one direction. "Are you telling me there's a picture of my thing out there?"

"Oh for fuck sakes. Are you going to run for god damn office or something? Hurry up. And you're the one who sleeps naked, so get over it." Chrys yelled across the truck before going back to quiet whispers with her former girlfriend. It felt good to have her there.

Spencer walked around the truck and handed the police officer the full paper bag. He wore the maroon blanket over one shoulder, the navy blue pants with RCMP across his ass, and hiking boots. He tried not to notice the police officers and volunteer firemen looking in his direction, probably snickering at him. The pants were too tight and, though they were unisex, in his mind they were women's pants.

Dawn pointed down. "Boots too."

~ * ~

"You getting back with Dawn?" Spencer asked after he and Chrys were seated in the emergency room waiting area at the hospital. He meant to ask her during the drive back to town but got pre-occupied with directing his sister's driving. If it wasn't her lead foot that bothered him it was her eagle-eye precision at aiming the truck for every pothole.

Chrys leaned forward in her chair, elbows on her knees. "Why do you ask?"

"You two were awfully flirty."

She sat back in her chair and let her head slowly roll toward him until her chin sat on her shoulder. She gazed at him with sleepy eyes. "I'm flirty with a lot of people."

"When there's a tortured and dead woman right nearby?" He wasn't too worried about being overheard. As soon as people got a whiff of him they decided to sit somewhere else.

"That's how I deal with shit, you know that."

"Spencer Alcrest?" A nurse stood between the waiting room and a set of doors leading to the trauma rooms. She had on blue scrub pants and a scrub top with characters from the *Muppets* on it.

Spencer slowly got up. To his sister he asked, "Are you coming?"

"I'm going to find some food."

Spencer followed the nurse through the two doors that opened at the push of a button. He couldn't help himself. His eyes went down. Sure enough, the scrub pants were wedged between her butt cheeks. Those things always seemed to do that.

At the far end of the hallway was an RCMP officer in the dark blue pants, yellow stripe down the leg, and a pale blue shirt with dark Kevlar vest over top. He sat in a chair outside one of the rooms.

Spencer looked in the room as he walked past. The woman from the cistern was in there asleep on a bed. They probably had her drugged in order to keep her calm.

"Are you Spencer?" A woman walked from the hospital room with a white coat covering plain clothes. The woman's dark red hair was in a loose perm. The roots were a lot darker than the rest of the hair. Her eyes were bright.

He nodded. "How is she?"

"She asked for you." The doctor folded her arms around a medical chart and held it to her chest. "We've sedated her so she's sleeping now and will for awhile. I can't even imagine what she's gone through but all things considered she's doing well. We'll be moving her to a floor soon so you can try to see her tomorrow." She gave him a faint smile and walked down the hallway, her heels clicking on the floor.

"This way, Mr. Alcrest." The nurse raised her voice more than she had before.

~ * ~

It took Chrys ten minutes and switching her sitting position thirteen times before she decided it was time to get up. For eight of those minutes she watched a late afternoon talk-show on the television up in the corner. She didn't recognize the host, who had as his guests a mother/daughter porn team. They appeared in movies together often having sex with the same guy at the same time, but never touching each other. *Creepy*. The mother had this deer-in-the-headlights look as though her daughter somehow talked her into it and the daughter wore an angry scowl as if she knew her mother was better-looking with a sexier body and she was pissed off about it.

A few years ago Chrys played with the idea of having naked pictures taken to try and get herself in the magazines. She tried to convince a boy who had a crush on her to go into a store and buy whatever nudie magazines they had so she could get addresses. She modelled when she was younger, she had a very pretty face, and the moment she hit sixteen she knew she had the body men liked to look at. Her breasts were humble, but all of her other curves were sharp. The thought of pimply-faced boys having her hidden under their mattress for whenever the creature stirred wasn't really that appealing, however, and she cared about what Mrs. Alcrest would have thought. She cared more about that than what her real mother thought, wherever she was. Plus she knew it was a short climb from pictures to dancing to movies. Chrys knew two girls who put topless pictures on *Twitter* all the time. That wasn't her style.

Maybe she was turning into a stick-in-the-mud like her brother. She laughed to herself. It would take a long while before she ever got that bad.

It took only a few seconds to realize she didn't like the snacks available in the ER vending machines. The healthiest thing was *Sun Chips*. She wasn't a health nut, she was just in the mood for something else. She often got cravings that had to be satisfied.

Chrys wore her favorite pair of Steve Madden ankle boots - blue jeans faded on the fronts of the legs - a blue blouse - and her dance studio's jacket. The chunky block heel of her boots barely made a sound as she quickly descended a flight of stairs to the basement and started along the hallway toward the cafeteria. On most people the heel would click against the tile floor, but years of dancing meant she walked mostly on the balls of her feet when she was moving quickly. It was that clicking noise she bought some of her other heels for. When the heels make that *clicky clacky* noise there was something about it that just gave her a bit of a confidence boost.

She didn't notice that there was a clicking this time.

An orderly pushed a cart heading in the opposite direction. The moment she said, "Hi," he looked up at her. Bright white teeth appeared in a dark face.

Okay, Chrys had to admit she loved the way most people looked at her.

"Hey, how are you?" The contents of the cart clinked together as the orderly came to a sudden halt.

Five minutes of flirting, Chrys's number on Marc's phone along with a spur-of-the-moment picture, and she was off again heading for the cafeteria.

The clicking was no longer there.

After a tour around the food court Chrys settled on a fruit cup with a good amount of red grapes and a bottle of water. She hadn't eaten anything since Spencer's muffin in the morning. It had taken all day out at *The Creepy House*. After Dawn had Spence's clothes they had to wait for a forensics person to go through his hair - which was not top priority. Then they sat for a long time in the waiting room upstairs watching others go in to be taken care of – a broken wrist also not top priority. Hospital ER's were a model of efficiency. Not! Supper time was two hours ago, so there weren't too many people sitting at the tables. She took a quick drink from the bottle before paying her money and heading back down the hallways.

Click, click

With the fruit cup between index finger and thumb, bottle of water carefully hanging between little and ring finger (all in the same hand) she took her cellular phone from her bra. She either carried it there or in the waistband of tight-fitting pants. More than a dozen texts from more than a dozen people since the last time she checked it in the waiting room.

Where are you, flower girl?
What are you doing tonight?
Was that you guys on the news?
I can't make class tomorrow.
There's a sale this week at Ardenes. 50% off!
Practice Tuesday at 6.

Most of them she skimmed over. The class one was from one of her dance students. The practice was for roller derby. She'd have to try and switch shifts at the Alcrest. Jessie was going to be pissed.

"What were you doing at the house?"

The deep voice made her jump. Her feet stopped. A hand was suddenly pushing against the back of her neck, so she had to keep moving forward. Chrys realized the clicking was down at her feet, but it wasn't from her boots.

"What the fuck ..."

"What were you doing at the house?" The voice cut her off. His hand was still on her neck.

Chrys stared at the glowing-red Exit sign above the door to the stairs. Further down the hall was the elevator. Her heart raced inside her chest. She could probably make a break for it, but she really wanted to know what the hell was going on. She started, "Who the ..."

Her hair was pulled back sending her eyes to the ceiling. Pain shot through her scalp. The water bottle hit the floor and skidded toward the stairwell door. Fruit scattered across the tile. Her phone fell from her fingers followed closely by the distinctive sound of the screen shattering on impact. She let a faint sound escape her throat then tried to pull it back in. She couldn't breathe, she couldn't think.

"I was hired to check it out," Chrys said louder than she needed to.

"Who hired you?" He pulled her hair again.

She wasn't going to let herself scream. He could pull her hair right out and she wouldn't yell. Her neck was open and vulnerable. As she stared up at the florescent lights her vision went fussy from tears.

Bing.

The elevator.

Chrys shot her foot backward. The second time it connected with something solid. The grip on her hair

slackened. She leaned forward. Her foot kept kicking
back.

"Get your hands off me you cock-sucking feneuter," she
screeched out.

"What are you doing? Let her go."

She was shoved forward. Her feet stumbled and tripped.
Her knees hit the tile and pain shot through her legs.

The orderly was suddenly there. His strong hands
caught her body before she went any farther down. One
hand brushed across her breast.

Chrys spun around, but whoever had been there was
gone. The door to the stairs clicked shut.

"Who was that guy?" Marc helped her to her feet.

"I, I don't know." The fear in her own voice was
surprising. Chrys's chest tingled with excitement and terror.

"Are you okay? Do you want me to call security or the
police or something?"

"I … I'm okay. I want, I want …" The only thing Chrys
knew about the situation was that she didn't want to tell her
brother what happened. The last thing she needed was him
saying, "I told you so." He already had a broken wrist from
The Creepy House. She didn't need him to be stressing
about this too.

Chapter Eight

It was black. Everything was black.
There were eyes. Eyes came out of the darkness.
A hand.
A tongue. A mouth. Teeth.

Spencer lurched. Pain shot from his wrist up his arm into his brain, it gave him an instant headache. His eyes filled with flashes of red as though he had been staring at a light bulb. The television was on; an episode of *Storage Wars* was playing. A petite face stared down at him from the armrest of the couch. Pointy ears were erect off the top sides of its head. A pink tongue flicked out almost going in its own nose. Spencer would never admit it to his sister, but he loved her chocolate Chihuahua.

Bullet, Spencer's British bulldog, wasn't that fond of Breeze, the Chihuahua, however.

Bullet's chin sat on the couch cushion beside his owner's side. His soulful eyes flicked between Spencer and the tiny dog on the arm as though asking why she got to be up there and he didn't. He always looked sad from his wrinkles hanging down and, because of a wrinkle above each eye, the white and tan dog either looked like he was in deep thought or surprised all the time. He let out a half snort, half groan.

Breeze gave a sharp bark in reply, *"Ha ha I can climb up here and you can't!"* The bulldog made a sound like an old man clearing his throat.

"Alright, I get it."

"What's going on?"

He jumped. It was a woman's voice. What woman? *Maeve?* His heart raced.

No, Chrys. Chrysanthemum.

As Spencer sat up pain soared through his arm again making his head ache even more. It swirled around his entire brain. *When was the last time he took ibuprofen?* He couldn't remember. All he knew was that he still smelled like the foul water. When they got home his sister washed his hair in the bathroom sink. He was told he couldn't shower until the next day so that his cast could set.

He was laid out on the couch, Chrys was on the lime green *Lay-Z-Boy* that had been his father's. She had the foot-rest up but her body was practically curled all the way onto the seat with her fluffy *Scooby-Doo* blanket tucked around her. The only light in the room was from the television. Her hair fell over her face. Her feet stuck out from the blanket and absently fought with each other.

Spencer said, "The dogs want out."

"Okay, I'm getting up," said Chrys as she began kicking her legs to get out from under the blanket.

"I …" he cringed, "…can take them for a walk."

"Spence, you don't have to be all tough." Chrys sat up and flicked her head back sending her long hair arching over her. "I've seen you crying over fucking mosquito bites."

Breeze bounced from the armrest to the cushion to the floor and scurried over to her owner's feet where she started yapping and bounding up and down.

Chrys scratched her behind the ear. "You're hurt, so I'll take the dogs for a walk. Did you sleep?"

"Yeah, a little."

"Where's Bullet's harness?" Because a bulldog's neck is larger than its head, a traditional collar wasn't enough.

"In the hall closet." He sat up cradling his arm and rapidly did the math in his head; the last time he had an *Advil* was during the *Criminal Minds* episode, which came on at midnight. It was now five-thirty a.m. He awkwardly popped the pill bottle top with his unfamiliar hand and tipped two out on the table. He swallowed them with a mouthful of flat *Dr. Pepper*. It was strange trying to learn how to do things with the wrong hand. Everything was backward. He knew most things were made for right-handed people, but to him it was just wrong. He asked, "How did you sleep?"

Chrys shrugged her shoulders. "Fine."

"You were having nightmares."

"Was I?" She pouted making her full bottom lip even larger. "I don't remember."

She did remember, but she couldn't tell him. If she told him she would have to tell him about what happened. The nightmare was about being alone and having someone grab her. Only in the dream she felt a cold knife blade against her throat and another in her side. The tip pushed into her belly. She wasn't sure how there were two knives, but it *was* a dream. Then she was thrown in the cistern and left alone with nothing to eat but a rotting corpse. *What would it be like with no colour, no light – nothing? What did Maeve Campbell have to live through? Was the man who grabbed her the one who put Maeve in there? What did the other woman go through? Who was she?*

Spencer stared at his sister. When they got home last night she turned on every light in the house and checked every room. He saw her casually flick the curtains to make sure there was nothing hiding in them and then she stared down at the front street. Every time he had suggested she go to bed she said she was fine.

"What are you thinking about?"

Startled Chrys asked, "What?"

"You have this serious expression on your face." Spencer tried to get his shoe on with his wrong hand. It didn't want to work.

"I do not." Chrys went back to wrestling with Bullet trying to put on his harness. She got one leg in and then as she put his second foot in he stepped out with the first. Breeze circled around the pair begging them to hurry.

"Yes you do. Your mouth stays slightly open and you stare off into space when you're thinking about something."

"The hell I do. Where are you going?"

"With you and the dogs." He just shoved the second foot into his running shoe and wiggled it around until it was set. The tongue got squished down. *Screw it.*

"Spence, you don't have to."

"I want to." He guessed the day's events at *The Creepy House* spooked her. His over-active imagination ate its way into her own and brought on the fear. When he closed his eyes he saw Maeve coming out of the darkness, so he could relate.

She sighed. "There's no point in arguing."

There were two ways to get in and out of the second floor apartment. One door opened to stairs that went down to the back room of The Alcrest. Across the apartment another door lead out to a small deck and wood stairs going down to the back parking lot.

Breeze had to be carried down to the ground. Bullet was too heavy to lift. He practically fell over the edge of each step and stopped on the next one. By the time he got to the bottom he was already panting. Spencer's truck was the only thing parked out back. The bulldog had to stop and sniff the tire before leaving his mark and waddling after the two females. He resembled a linebacker with too much muscle in the chest. He was like the bulldog that fought with *Sylvester the Cat* in the *Looney Tunes* shows.

When they got to the front of the restaurant Spencer glanced at the building. Everything was in place. The building was red brick, faded from all the years it had been there. Next to the front door was a slab of polished black granite attached to the wall with Alcrest carved into it. Above was a lion's head carved in white and protruding from the wall. When he was a kid he could never tell if the lion was snarling, smiling, or was about to sneeze. His father didn't know what their family crest was, so he settled on a lion.

Chrys looked up and down the street. She felt a chill that was something other than the cold morning air. It was as though there were eyes on her somewhere. Or was it in her head? There wasn't really anyone around. This was mainly a business area with not too many living in it. That was a good thing. Or was it a bad one? Nobody would hear her screaming. She looked at the two cars, three half-ton trucks, and a mini-van parked on the curbs as though there was something more to see. A blue light flashed in almost all of the windshields signalling alarm systems.

There was a man standing by the corner. He seemed to be searching the sidewalk for something. Cigarette butts, maybe.

"You okay?" Spencer caught up to his foster sister. They headed toward the corner away from the solo man. The flower shop there had a patch of grass out front that the dogs liked.

Bullet waddled along between them while Breeze dashed back and forth from one side of the sidewalk to the other like a sweeping metal detector.

"I'm fine. Why?" She looked behind them.

No businesses were open this early, theirs would be the first. The only people who lived on this part of the street were in apartments above some of the stores. Most shops had a little night light inside so passing security or police could see that things were copasetic. Spencer liked that there was a butcher shop a few doors down and the Asian market across the way. On the other side of the street, next to the locksmith, was a comic book and games store (board and card games, not video) once a month they held a board game night at The Alcrest. Beside that was the tattoo shop he had used. At the far end was the credit union he used. It was a pleasant street. During the day it was crazy busy with people driving up and down or walking along window shopping, but this early there wasn't much going on.

It was an area called Fairmont within the City of Middleton, close enough to the downtown that they got people going back and forth for work but not so close that they were over-run. Luckily for the Alcrest their street was a shortcut to avoid a long set of traffic lights.

"You keep looking behind us."

"Do I?" She looked over her shoulder.

Spencer looked back behind them too. The man at the corner was staring in their direction. He said, "Yes. Shouldn't I be the jumpy one after being in that concrete box? What are you so creeped out about?"

"I'm not creeped out about anything." She scrunched up her face and focused her eyes on Breeze. "Not as bad as that woman should be."

"Maeve?"

"Yeah, she's going to be fucked up for a long time."

Spencer had to tug the bulldog a little to get him to move. As he pulled, his eyes gazed at the man walking behind them. While still looking back he said, "Well maybe she'll be strong enough to get past it."

After the words left his mouth he didn't believe it was possible. He didn't know what she had been through or what she would have had to endure if the two of them hadn't come along. *How would anyone recover from that?* He still remembered being ten years old and picking up his black and white puppy after it had been hit by a car. If he closed his eyes he could still feel Winston's hot guts spill over the back of his hand and the sound of his own scream as it startled him. He could recall the burning in the corner of his eyes after wiping the tears away with a dirty palm while he buried the dog in the back yard by himself, so *how was this woman who had probably been tortured and raped going to move on?* He saw the bite marks on the dead woman. He knew what she did to survive. *Was there a way to get past that?*

"I wouldn't." She stopped for a second almost forgetting everything she was going to say. Chrys's mind was back in her own past to secrets her foster brother didn't know. "Dawn told me there were bite marks on that dead woman as though Maeve was eating from her. How do you

69

get past that?" She was walking, but she wasn't looking where she was going. For a moment she thought she saw a red light behind a windshield almost as though someone took a drag on a cigarette and the ember burned bright.

"I don't know," Spencer answered.

Bullet stopped and turned around. He made a noise that wasn't quite a growl.

Spencer held his breath as he stopped and looked at the lone man. *Who was this guy? Why was he out and about so early?*

Was there someone in that car, Chrys thought. Her neck craned to try and see. It was a truck. She took a few steps before she realized her brother had stopped.

Chrys turned and caught her own breath. Her heart started to race.

The man who had been at the corner when they first stepped out was almost on them. He walked as though his feet didn't want to function properly. He stumbled from one side to the other in and out of the streetlamp lights. His tanned skin was tight and wrinkled at the same time, leathery almost. His grimy clothes hung off his limbs. His eyes almost seemed to be red under his baseball cap.

Breeze started to bark.

"Ju ave a smoke?" His words slurred together. His eyes, which had burned red a second before, seemed to fade into the sad eyes of a clown.

Both of them shook their heads and the man kept walking. It took a couple minutes standing there feeling like fools before they turned around and headed for home.

~ * ~

"What the bloody ell'appened to you?" Sandra Husk was in the dish pit room when Spencer came down the stairs and through the door at the bottom. The smell of fresh baked muffins had already wafted up to the apartment.

"I fell." Spencer smiled. He had called her last night to tell her the crew may need her help today and she might have to stay late, so she already knew the basics.

He went through an open doorway to his office, past his clean chef coat that was always hanging on a hook by the door, and sat behind the desk. His office was about as organized as his side of the apartment. The messiest part was a bin on one side of the desk with a stack of papers sitting at all angles. By the door was a stand-up freezer that held mostly meat and some ice cream. Just about everything in the restaurant was prepped fresh so only a small freezer was needed. A filing cabinet with the printer on top was in the corner, bulletin board with schedules on it by his coat. He opened his laptop computer.

He looked at the cover of Maeve Campbell's CD as he slid the disc into the computer. The woman on the cover had waves of thick blond hair falling over her shoulders. Her eyes, barely seen from under the hair, seductively looked back at him over one shoulder. She wore a white summer dress with a thin spaghetti strap over her shoulder. It made her look like the girl next door. The sound of a single guitar came through the speakers. It was joined by a throaty soft voice that you expected to hear in a 90's coffee shop. The first song was titled, "Wind." He sat for a moment listening to the words about her walking along a dirt road with wind blowing against her face and sending her hair out behind her like a superhero's cape. It was the kind of music he listened to back when he was younger and dreaming of the women who sang them.

The only messages on the answering machine were reporters wanting to talk to him. He didn't bother writing down their names. His emails were the same. He responded to one from his mother, hunting and pecking with the wrong hand. Even before he clicked "Send," Spencer decided that was enough typing. He went through his morning routine of checking the night's sales against the money that was in the safe under his desk. Jessie did it so he knew it was going to be right.

By the time Sandra brought in a fresh-from-the-oven banana nut muffin and a cup of tea he was putting everything away.

"So how's your arm?" Her English accent only came out once in a while in some of the words she used.

Spencer wiggled the digits sticking out of the cast. His thumb remained immobilized. "My fingers still work."

"I said a prayer for you last night." Sandra had been at The Alcrest since before Spencer's father had died and he took over. Compared to the other employees she was ancient. She as more than double her bosses age. She had a full head of grey, almost white, hair that was short in a puffed-up style. She was the morning baker and brunch lady. "Shouldn't you be upstairs in bed?"

He shrugged. "Can't sleep. I'm fine anyway."

"It's not nice to lie to an old lady, Spencer. Your eyes are puffy and you broke your wrist. Did you *get* any sleep?"

"Do you and my Mom check notes? She asked the same thing."

The oven timer she wore attached to her apron started buzzing. "Oh, me rock cakes." She turned to walk out saying, "Get rest Spencer or I'll tell your mum," over her shoulder as she left.

He checked Sunday's schedule against the time cards. Liz had been twenty minutes late for her shift. He would have to have another one of his talks with her. She was always showing up late. One of the servers left early. He wondered if it was just getting slow and she was sent home or if she just left.

On one wall of the dish pit were shelves with some canned goods, buckets of spices, and other dry ingredients. The walk-in cooler was at the back corner. It was smaller than others he had used. One side held everything for salads – the greens, prepped vegetables and fruits, and house-made dressings. The back shelf had raw meat, bottles of different condiments, and bins of vegetables. Along the third wall were rolling racks with different objects held on large sheet pans – wrapped desserts, house-made pasta, and thawing meat that had been taken out of the freezer before closing the night before. On the middle rack were sheet pans with insert containers used in the kitchen all covered with plastic wrap. He lifted a couple corners of plastic and got his nose right in there to take a sniff. The chicken didn't have a clean smell. It probably just needed a new container. One of the dressings on the other side still had a ladle in it. That was a no-no. It was something for him to address with the kitchen crew about when they got to work.

Spencer left the back, passed the staff washroom, the public washrooms and proceeded into the restaurant. One server was already there. On the left was the kitchen, on the right beside the hostess stand was a glass case for the baked goodies to be displayed.

In daylight things looked a lot calmer. Sandra was the only one in the kitchen; she was moving rock cakes from the cooling rack to a wicker basket that would go in the display beside the new muffins and the day old ones left over from Sunday brunch. Also behind the case were the coffee and cappuccino machines. The smell of roasted beans brewing fought with that of the baked goodies.

When Spencer's parents started the restaurant (more as a pub then) they thought it rustic and cheaper to get their coffee mugs from yard sales. The tradition continued, so during the summer Spencer or Chrys would still go around to yard sales and buy up more cheap mugs. They had a couple boxes from the recent summer down in the basement. Customers liked it too. Some had specific mugs they asked for. The tables and chairs were dark wood. They made an L shape around the kitchen and bar. In the far corner was a small stage with a fire Exit door behind it. When there was nobody performing they could pull a screen down and project something on such as television shows or sporting events. Around the corner was a separate room, cut off from the main part of the restaurant by a wall of empty wooden window frames suspended from the ceiling and another completely closed-off room that accomodated about sixteen at one long table. *The Frame Room* was still open to the sights and sounds of the main room, but it felt more intimate. It had a bookshelf with novels and games on it, plus comfier chairs. This was where the comic store did their board game nights. It was really more like a lounge really than an expansion of the restaurant.

On the walls of every room were paintings or photographs by local artists. Some frames contained poems or quotes by local and famous authors. In each room was a hanging tapestry with the meaning of the Alcrest name;

A-fter

L-abour

C-omes

R

E

S

T

The others replaced the word "Labour" with Life, Love, and Living.

Nobody was certain where the breakdowns had come from. They had just been with the family for many years. The name, the meanings, and the restaurant were home.

Spencer checked the small fridges beneath the butcher block countertop to see what was in them. They were completely empty. One needed to be scrubbed. In his morning routine he checked the whole kitchen then stepped to the bar and made sure everything was where it needed to be. He had to carefully stand up and crouch down trying not to move his hand the wrong way.

"Good morning Chef," Megan looked up briefly from the table she was wiping. Today her black hair had a couple streaks of bright purple. There as a bright orange flower behind one ear. Her eyes changed when she saw his arm and the marks on his face, but she didn't say anything. The morning shift was not one people were fighting each other to work, so he was lucky to have her. All of the servers wanted the evening shifts because there were better tips. Megan had afternoon college courses that she attended around her shifts.

"How are you?" he asked.

She looked up at him again and gave him a smile. She had a piercing through the side of her nose and a ring through the center of her bottom lip. "I'm good."

They both turned at the sound of the bell above the door ringing. Two men in police uniforms stopped for a second just inside the door. When they saw the man behind the bar one said, "You Spencer Alcrest?"

Chapter Nine

Chrys walked through the doors to the bank and let her eyes fall on everything. It was all clean and modern. People in line for the tellers stared back at her. It took a second to find what she needed.

After their walk and her brother had gone downstairs she sat in the living room, Bullet snoring at her side and Breeze curled up on her out-stretched legs. She flipped through TV channels stopping to learn the trick to making the perfect brownie and the eerie secrets of the Jersey Devil. For a few minutes she stopped on the shopping channel. There was a special on shoes, and she wondered how much was left on her credit card. None of it was going to help her fall back asleep. The man in the bowels of the hospital saw to that. When she closed her eyes she felt his hand on her. She could still smell the cigarette odor from his breath.

Cigarettes? The ember in the truck.

He had to be the same person who put the women in the cistern, but why was he asking about the family? Where were they?

Today she was in black jeans and a red scoop-neck blouse with her dance jacket over top. The only make-up she had used was to darken her oval eyes and brighten her lips. Her Aboriginal features looked exotic, Asian – but not quite. As she stepped up to the information desk she flashed a bright smile.

"Excuse me, can I see Robin Cranston?"

The woman across the desk adjusted her glasses, clicked something on the computer, and fixed her with a big *welcome* smile on her face. "Do you have an appointment?"

"No I don't. Is that a problem? I just need to see her for a quick second."

The woman tilted her head slightly and said said, "You really should have an appointment." "She's in a meeting right now and has more all day." The tone of her voice was saying, *go away little girl.* She clicked something with the mouse. "It looks like Ms. Cranston will have time Wednesday afternoon."

"That's, um… Do you think she'd have five minutes between meetings? I can wait for a while." Chrys had learned a long time ago that being nice and sweet could get you a lot, and being a bitch could get you the rest.

The woman looked at the computer screen again and shook her head. Her red hair, the kind of red that came from a bottle, didn't even move. She said, "I really don't think so."

Chrys looked over her shoulder at the people in the teller line. At that moment there were five, three of whom were looking in her direction. Two were men. A man talking to a teller looked over his shoulder toward her. One of them could have been him. The hairs on her arms stood up. Normally she liked being the focus of people's attention. She suddenly felt exposed like standing on a stage naked.

Don't ask how she knew what that felt like.

Of course they could have just been looking in her direction for the sake of looking at something. They may not have even been looking at her.

Chrys leaned on the counter between her and the woman. "Look," she started, "yesterday I came face to face with a dead body at one of the houses Robin sent me to. I want to see her. It'll take five minutes and I'm not leaving until I do." She fought the strong urge to use profanity.

The woman stared straight at her for a long moment then said, "Please have a seat in the lounge area."

The leather chair creaked as she sat down. Magazines that looked like they had never been touched were fanned out perfectly on a shiny coffee table. She never really understood why banks always had fancy waiting areas. Nobody ever seemed to wait in them for long. Forty minutes later Chrys was still there.

She started to get up a couple of times, but was halted by, "It'll just be a few more minutes," and a sly smirk that said, *you should have made an appointment*.

Chrys got lost in her phone. She was lucky the guy at the phone repair place had crush on her. A little flirting got her phone screen replaced while she waited. However, she didn't like when he said, "See you soon," as she was walking out.

By the time she heard her name called she had downloaded three free books for her *Kindle* app, checked her email, checked her *Facebook*, played a dozen levels in *Angry Birds*, tweeted about waiting at the bank, texted a dozen times about absolutely nothing. The only text she got that she needed to deal with was Jessie telling her there was a staff meeting after lunch. She started reading the latest *Beverly Preston* novel when there was nothing left to do.

"How are you doing today, Chrys?" Robin Cranston flashed bright white teeth. Her hand reached out.

Chrys said, "I'm good."

Robin led the way through a line of offices. She wore a maroon skirt with a matching blouse. Her hair was long, straight, and blond with black underneath the bottom as if she wore a shorter blond wig over longer black hair. She turned into an office and motioned Chrys to take a seat. Nobody shut the door.

Chrys positioned her chair so that she was more at an angle with the window looking out on the corridor.

"I heard you had quite a day out at the house yesterday."

Understatement of the year. She tried not to show her annoyance. "It was something I won't soon forget."

"No, I guess not. How's your brother doing?"

"He has a broken wrist, but he's okay."

"That's good." Robin's hands moved around her desk straightening things. "The police were here first thing this morning asking questions about the house. I can't believe what you found in there. I told them exactly what I told you; the house was foreclosed on last year and we haven't been able to get in touch with Dan and Kate Linque."

"So you don't know where they went?"

"None of their contact numbers work at all. I remember something about them heading east, but I don't remember where it came from." She tapped a blue tipped fingernail on her watch as if to mention that time was ticking. "Was there something you wanted to talk about, Chrys? Everything at the house is suspended, of course, pending the police investigation. Even after that I don't know how we'll be able to sell it. I do have some other houses if you still want the work."

Chrys shrugged her shoulders and scrunched up her face. "I don't know about that." She paused trying to find the right words. She wasn't sure if she still wanted to go through all of that. What would she find in the next house? "Do you know what happened to the family? You said the bank was going to work with them, right? Why would they just leave like that?"

"I really have no idea. At first it seemed like they were going to work with us, but then they stopped answering my calls, stopped checking in …"

"A lot of their stuff is still there. It was like they left in a hurry or something. People don't really leave like that, do they?"

Robin craned her neck to see through the window into the hall. There was no one there, but she stood and quietly closed the door to the office anyway. All the sounds from other offices stopped. She sat down again and moved her hands, re-straightening things she had already straightened. "Chrys, you really should forget about it." She was staring down at the papers on her desk. "You did a good thing finding these women. Now let me give you some other houses to clear out."

Chrys had never felt more awkward and uncomfortable. "Come on, Robin. What's going on?"

Robin looked across at the young woman. Her eyes were watery. She checked the hallway again. "Have you ever heard of Liam O'Donnell?"

Chrys shook her head.

"Well look him up and then you'll know why you should let it all go. He had someone come ask questions about the Linques shortly after we lost contact. I never heard from either again, so I just assumed …" she had to swallow and take a breath, "Well I just assumed. I waited to see if they would come back and they didn't." "I didn't tell the police because ..." Robin got up from her chair and opened the door. She looked up and down the hall, "I just didn't."

In Chrys's eyes the woman looked like she was shaking. She wanted to press on, but knew she wasn't going to get any more from her. "Didn't you say someone else had gone to clean the, ah," *creepy*, "house before?"

Robin Cranston looked at her watch again. Her hand tapped the door. "I really have to start my next meeting."

"But who was it? Why didn't he check out the house?"

Robin stepped around the desk. She shuffled Chrys out into the hallway. "I told you before, didn't I? He said he saw rats or mice or something. I guess he was lucky he didn't go further."

"What's his name?"

"Kevin Bird. He has a garbage hauling business. He used to do a lot of our houses."

"Used to?"

"Excuse me." Robin plastered a smile on her face before heading back to the open area. She didn't speak another word to Chrys as she crossed to greet the couple for her next meeting.

~ * ~

As Chrys stormed through the front door of The Alcrest she locked her brown eyes on the closest staff member and went right for him. "Where's Spence?"

Ranger turned so fast his legs almost tied together. Not a good thing in front of the deep-fryer. He grabbed the bill of his ball cap and pulled it lower almost covering his bushy eyebrows. His mouth opened. He shut it without saying a word. He turned to the fryer and inspected what was going on. All that in ten seconds.

"Chef? He is, um …" he had issues with talking to women. He was nineteen and constantly nervous. Chrys wondered how he could stand working out in the open like he did. "Chef's not here." Almost every day his job was to cut the potatoes for fries then blanch them to the half-cooked stage. During service they could then be fried again in a short amount of time and would come out crispy. His hands twisted up his apron.

"Where is he?" Under normal circumstances Chrys might play with the guy and try to make him so nervous he'd break a sweat, but she wasn't in the mood. She stretched up to see her brother's table that was kitty corner from the door – even though he had an office he preferred doing his paperwork in the restaurant. He wasn't there.

"The cops took him."

"What?"

"He said, the cops took him." Gordie said as he came from the back hallway. He carried a thick wood cutting board with a grey bus-bin on top. In that were mostly roma tomatoes, plus a couple of English cucumbers and some red onions. As he squeezed past Ranger he said, "Sandra said they came and took him a few hours ago. Something about the girl from the house would only talk to him." He pulled out a larger metal bowl from beneath the steam table. It took a second for him to choose a yellow-handled serrated knife. A dozen or so sat, blade down, in a slit in the butcher block. "Hey," Gordie wiggled the knife toward Chrys, "you were there right? What was it like? Was it all gross and shit?"

"What?" Chrys put her hands on her hips.

"Hi, Chrys."

"Hey, Sue." Chrys quickly eyed the other server as she passed.

Gordie let his eyes linger on Sue until she turned and gave him a smile. Everyone seemed to let their eyes linger on Sue. He turned to Chrys. "The bodies; were they all gross and rotting like in the movies? Were there maggots?"

"There was only one body and I didn't get a close look." *And I didn't want to*, she thought but didn't say.

"That's not what the radio said. On my way in I heard them say multiple bodies were found." Gordie cut the tops off some tomatoes then started slicing them, gave them a quarter turn, slice, turn, and another slice to make diced tomatoes for bruschetta. Unlike the younger cook he did not wear the full apron. He folded his in half and tied it around his waist under his belly. It had smears on both hips where his hands rubbed. He had his Alcrest ball cap twisted at an angle.

Ranger lifted his head, but not enough for Chrys to see his eyes. There were some people wearing suits sitting at one table, a couple of men played chess by the stage, a regular customer (Mr. Oh as everyone called him) was at his usual table right next to the windows, some guys were playing the latest table top game in the frame room. It was the regular after-lunch crowd. The kitchen crew was prepping for dinner as the servers prepared their side. Everything was normal and as it should be at The Alcrest.

But they didn't always talk about dead bodies.

"What else did the radio say? Did they mention us?" Chrys held her breath. She didn't want the world to know it was them who went in the house, found the woman and the body. She didn't know why. At least one person knew already.

"No, they just said they were found."

"Good," she said and looked around. She felt like everyone was looking at her differently.

"They have your picture though."

Chrys jumped as Jessie stepped up beside her. The front-of-house-manager was a little shorter and thinner. Her hair (what the hair dye wheel called *sun-kissed brown* hair) was cut short in a boys' cut, a little longer on the top. It really emphasised her strong jaw line and cheek bones. Spencer called her eyes "smokey" and said once that when she didn't smile her eyes and face seemed to take on a darker tone as if she was withholding dark secrets.

"You and Spence were in the background of a picture taken from the road that was in the paper. No names though." Her voice had a touch of huskiness. "Is he okay? Sandra said he had a cast on his arm." She was dressed in black slacks and a black shirt with the top two buttons open and sleeves rolled to her elbows.

"I don't have time for this." Chrys stepped around the front of the pass and rested her arms on it. The heat lamps were off but the tile was still warm. "Do any of you know a Kevin Bird? He picks up people's garbage or some shit."

"Staff meeting in five minutes." Jessie said with a sigh as she walked away.

"I guess he has like a trailer or something." Chrys continued as if she didn't hear her boss. The two of them never really got along. She didn't know if it was because their personalities clashed or because the other one was sleeping with her brother. She watched Jessie walk around to the space between the line and bar where she washed her hands quickly.

Gordie rubbed his bearded chin in the crook of his elbow. "Nope. Ask Mr. O. He knows everyone."

"Chrys! Good someone impartial. Excuse me. Behind, behind," Liz passed through the line carrying a sheet pan covered with a lot of different containers. Her strawberry hair was pulled up under a black knit cap with a few of her bangs swirling over her forehead. All her edges were round and the apron did little to hide the paunch left from having a baby eight months earlier. After putting the pan on her table she came back and poked a finger at Gordie's belly. "Would you tell this guy that bakers are better than cooks?"

"Bullshit," Gordie exclaimed. "How do you figure? If it weren't for cooks, this place wouldn't run. We don't need baking."

Chrys rolled her eyes. This was the same argument they had every couple of weeks.

"A baker can cook regular food too. Cooks can't bake."

"I can bake." Gordie's voice went up to a squeal.

"Guys," Jessie raised her voice. "Staff meeting in the private room."

Nearly everyone was in the small room sitting around the long table. Hanni was at the end with her feet crossed on the table. The ankles of her spiked knee-high boots connected perfectly and her skirt rode up too far, but she didn't seem to notice or care. Wylie had some of his law books spread in front of him - he had been there a while. Jen, Dee, and Mario sat across from the wannabe lawyer. Megan stood by the brick fireplace (it was fake) checking her phone. Sue brushed passed Chrys lightly touching her ass. The two gave each other knowing smiles. There were a couple of servers who were not there, they had classes during the day, and Sandra had gone home.

"Chrys, check these." Dee thrust out one leg. She wore a black shoe with a three-inch heel, black and grey fur around the ankle, and chains strung around the front. "Pam sent them from China. Aren't they cute?"

"Adorable." She noticed Hanni crane her neck and sneer.

"This won't take long," Jessie said as the cooks shuffled in and she came last. "Megan, you know everything I'm going to say, so can you watch the front? I'll just be about five minutes."

Chrys sat at the far end of the table. It was too close to Hanni for her comfort, but she needed to be farther away from the boss lady. As Jessie started talking about what had happened to Chrys and her brother the day before, she leaned close enough to the table where she (but no one else) could see her phone underneath. She went online and typed in "Kevin Bird." She clicked on a link that took her to a cheaply made website for Kevin Bird's Yard Clean-Up. She bookmarked the page then typed in "Liam O'Donnell."

"… Spencer's injuries, Chrys?"

"What?"

Jessie looked up to the ceiling and took a deep breath. "How is Spencer?"

Chrys looked down at her phone and clicked on one of the Google links. She heard herself whisper, "You're sleeping with him, you tell us," but didn't mean to say it out loud. She looked up, saw the dark shadowed eyes staring at her, and realized she did say the words. *Oops.*

Jessie folded her arms over her chest. Her cheeks were going red. She bit down on her bottom lip. Everyone else in the room was quiet. Their eyes moved between the two women.

"He fractured his wrist," Chrys blurted out. "He has to wear a cast for a few weeks."

Jessie bit her lip for a little more. "So we will be out of a chef for a few weeks. I'm sure Spencer'll -"

The link Chrys chose was a newspaper clipping. There were phrases such as, suspected in, rumored to be, and under investigation. Among those were words like drug trade, prostitution, and murder. Her stomach twisted into knots.

"… Chrys,"

She had to blink a few times before realizing she was out in the dining room. The meeting was over. The staff had scattered. She slowly walked toward the back. "What?" She turned back to see whoever had said anything.

Liz gave a little wave. "I just said, bye Chrys."

~ * ~

"Are you Kevin Bird?" Chrys strode around the front of a truck with a long trailer behind it. After the meeting she had gone upstairs to the apartment and took both dogs for a walk. On the way back that she realized her brother's truck was still in the parking lot. He didn't need it at the moment, so she thought she might as well borrow it. A phone call to Kevin Bird told her where he was.

Her stride had her cocky confidence, though she didn't feel that sure of herself. What was she doing investigating this? That's what she was doing – *investigating*. She read Nancy Drew when she was young, but she never had any desire to solve mysteries. Spencer was the one addicted to Sherlock Holmes.

He looked up with deep brown oval eyes, his gloved hands never stopping their work. He had that intimidating gaze of a Canadian First Nations man; they all had it from the business man to the punk on the corner, even the guy hauling garbage. His face suddenly lightened with the addition of a smile. "Hey, yeah. How's it going? You're the one who called?" The man pulled some branches from a pile and walked to his trailer where he threw them behind an old beat-up chair and a few black garbage bags. In the corner of the trailer was also a bin with a variety of handles sticking out.

"Can I ask you some questions?" She reached out and grabbed a branch. "Ouch."

"Careful there, they bite back." He had strong etched facial characteristics; prominent cheek bones and nose inside red caramel skin. Jet black hair was short and hidden beneath a baseball cap. "What do you want to ask?"

Chrys sucked on her finger. "You clear out houses for the banks?"

"Sometimes." He continued grabbing branches and moving them to the trailer. She couldn't tell if he was trying to avoid her or not.

"Did you hear about the house out in Hillsborough?" She watched him closely trying to see if he flinched.

"The one where those women were found? Why you asking, eh?" He wouldn't raise his eyes.

"You were supposed to clear it out, right?"

He put some more branches on the trailer before wiping the sweat off his forehead. "I didn't."

"But you were supposed to." She moved beside the trailer so he didn't have a choice but to look at her. "You went to the house, didn't you? What happened?"

He paused for a moment and stared at her. "I saw signs of rats. I barely even went in the place."

"I didn't see any signs of rats." She sounded desperate. She needed someone else to join her in her knowledge. She needed to know if and why she should be afraid.

He let out a breath and turned back to the pile of branches. "There were rats," he mumbled.

"You don't look like a man afraid of rats." Chrys stepped around and got in front of him. "You sure someone didn't say something to you? Don't you feel badly that these women were held there? Maybe you could have done something. They could have been there while you were getting scared off by rat poop."

His muscles went taut. Chrys couldn't tell if it was anger or frustration. Maybe it was fear.

"I hate rats," was all he said.

"I didn't see any signs of rats. There was mouse crap, but no rats." She put her hands on her hips and watched him move from the brush pile to the trailer and back.

"Do you know what rat scat looks like?" He didn't look up. The anger and tension were rising in his voice. He threw the branches down in the trailer like a frustrated toddler.

"Well no, but …"

"Then you can't really say anything about it, can you?" He stared at her for a moment before returning back to work.

Chrys watched him for a long time. Something in her said not to believe him, though she wanted to. What the hell was she doing?

Kevin Bird grabbed two handfuls of branches and threw them into the trailer. He looked up and down the street as if he was looking for something. His shoulders slouched. His whole being seemed to change. "Take my advice, and take the advice of whoever found you, stay away from that house and leave it alone."

Whoever found her? *He knew.*

"Did he threaten you too?" She started moving around to always stay in front of him. "Did he ask about the family? You have to tell me."

"Look," He put the final branch in the trailer. His eyes followed a car going by until he saw the driver. "No matter how many times I get asked, I don't know. Nobody asked me anything. Nobody threatened me. There was rat shit and I'm allergic or scared of it. Whatever will make you go away is what was there." He gazed at her for a long moment before getting in his truck.

He was lying. She knew he was. As he drove away Chrys stood at the side of the street until the trailer's red lights turned the corner. What did she get herself into?

Her body was raked with a sudden chill. There had been a red truck parked in front of the restaurant when she left. She looked both ways down the street. She was alone and in the open. Anyone could see her.

Chapter Ten

As Spencer stepped from the elevator on the sixth floor
of the hospital he felt like he could finally breathe. He
never did anything *that* bad or *that* illegal in his life, but
still felt a strong fear when police were near. He was one of
those people who drove for a couple of blocks with his eyes
on the rear-view mirror after passing a police car going in
the other direction. He always expected them to pull a
quick U-turn and flip their lights on. He usually wasn't
speeding, his lights were all functioning properly, and his
seatbelt was on, so there was never a reason for the cops to
come after him; he just expected it. Getting picked up by
them nearly gave him a panic attack. Walking through the
large University Hospital with a police escort he didn't
know how to feel. It was worse than being escorted to the
principal's office by Mrs. Zetick for throwing mud on the
playground.

Their shoes clicked and echoed on the floor. People
moved in and out of the hallway disappearing into one
room or another after taking a quick look at the trio. At the
end of the hallway a man in the blue RCMP uniform stood
outside a door beside a man and woman in casual clothes.

They all stopped talking the moment the chef and other officers got near.

"Spencer, glad you could come." Sgt. Heather Finnegan of the Major Crimes Unit gave him a faint nod. Her pant suit was the same charcoal grey as the one she wore when she spoke to him at *The Creepy House* but with a beige blouse underneath instead of white. Her hair was almost completely white with darker roots as if it was trying to keep some of her youth. He noticed the day before that she had perfect posture and always seemed to keep her chin up. It was probably one way of dealing with a male-dominated career.

He couldn't keep his eyes on her, nervously looking around the hallway instead. The arm inside the cast suddenly itched. "I, ah, wasn't sure I had a choice."

The woman in the suit gave him a grim smile. She was plain-looking. Outside of this moment under these circumstances he would have never noticed her. He wondered if she had children and what she looked like to them. "I don't know what kind of impression you made with Ms. Campbell, but she's refusing to talk to us without talking to you first."

"I didn't do anything," Spencer scrunched up his face.

"When the sedation wore off, she started asking for you. Where's Spencer? I want to talk to Spencer. We need to talk to her, but more importantly we need her to talk to us." She took out a notebook and flipped through to a new page. Her hair was short enough that it didn't touch her shoulders. "We need to see if she knows who the other woman was or if she saw her attackers or what she even remembers about any of it. The doctors say she might be too traumatized to remember much at the moment."

Spencer looked at all the faces around him. The other plain-closed officer was much younger. He had dark skin and a body that filled his suit with muscle.

"I want you to convince Ms. Campbell that she needs to talk to us and tell us whatever she knows." Finnegan folded her hands in front of her. "The sooner we can get started in this investigation the better chance we have of catching who did this." On her signal Mr. Muscles opened the door and motioned for the chef to enter the room.

There were two beds in the room, one empty. In the other was a woman, but he didn't recognize who she was. This wasn't the same woman on the CD cover in his office and it wasn't the one in the dark corner of the cistern. Her upper lip was thick in an unnatural way with a slit in the corner and one eye was nearly swollen shut. The top lid was thick and the bottom of the eye was a rainbow of dark colours. The cheek underneath looked like she had a big wad of gum in there. A square bandage seemed out of place. Her blond hair was stringy behind her head. It looked as though it had been washed. In fact all of her had been washed. She didn't look as good as she did on the CD cover, but she looked better than at *The Creepy House*. She tried smiling when she saw Spencer, but it came out looking like a deformed monster snarling.

"Hi," he said as he took a quick glance around the room. There were no flowers or cards. He suddenly felt like he should have brought something. "I'm Spencer. I don't know if you remember. I, ah, have been listening to your CD."

She let out a moan as she tried to sit up. "What do you think?" It sounded funny from swollen lips.

"I like it. It's very Jewel-esk." He didn't know where to look. He didn't want to focus on the bruises and cuts of her

95

face, but that was all that seemed to be there. As he shifted from one foot to the other he started scratching above his cast.

"How did you get my CD?"

"It was at the house. There was a box of them in the dining room." His voice faded off until there was nothing. He watched a cloud fall over her. Her eyes stared off. Maybe she was remembering what happened. He wanted to ask her what actually did happen, though he was sure he didn't want to know. Maybe she was realizing how things were never going to go back to normal, not inside her mind anyway.

After a time of silence she asked, "How are you?" She pointed at his face then let her hand drop. "Did I do that to you?"

The scratches around his eyes had become dark crimson marks that he hardly noticed except when he looked in a mirror or chased an itch and sent pain running through his skull. "It looks worse than it is," he said. He moved his casted arm in its sling and wiggled his fingers. He didn't let on that it hurt. "I'm fine, really. I'll heal anyway. How are you doing?"

He bit his lip and focused on her face. The one eye that was open was a bright blue that seemed brighter because her skin was extremely pale around the bruising. The white of her eye was tinted red. There was bruising on her neck in the shape of a hand. Both forearms also had welts and discolourations. Spencer tried to picture the woman on the CD cover. He could barely see it through the purple and unhealthy green tones.

Maeve's shoulders shrugged and her face twitched. He was sure there would be some sort of smile if she was able. "They have me on some good drugs so I can't feel most of it. Some fractured ribs, broken fingers," her right hand rose showing the bandages and metal splints, "cuts, fractured cheekbone. The doctors say I'm lucky." A tear fell from her swollen eye and streaked over the bruising. "Lucky," she repeated so softly it could barely be heard. Her left hand ran along the side railing of the bed. It too was bandaged and was in an odd shape, like something was missing.

Spencer fought the urge to move to her side and wipe the tear away. His hand got as far as touching the safety bar along her bed then stopped. Her eyes stared at it as if it was a live animal watching her. He was too afraid to touch her. Even the thought of it seemed wrong. She was wounded and vulnerable. How was any man going to be able to touch her? "You're alive, that's something."

Spencer wanted to ask what her captor had done to her, how far had it all gone, but he knew he wouldn't want to relive it if their roles were reversed. That's what the police outside the room wanted her to do. They had to ask her questions. They were going to make her talk about the abuse over and over when all she probably wanted to do was try to forget. She wasn't going to be able to do that and she knew it.

If this had happened to Chrys he would have wanted the blood of the man who did it with no worries about what would happen to him. He wondered if she had a father or big brother.

"I should bring you some food next time I come." He had to change the subject. He didn't want to be the one to make her cry and have that be their moment together. He didn't want that to be what she remembered when she thought of him. *What did he want her to think?* "Do you like seafood? I make a pretty good chowder."

Her hand reached out and touched his. He held his breath. The first thought in his head was to pull away. He didn't. Her bandaged fingers awkwardly held his.

"You don't have to come back," she said. "I just wanted to talk to you before …" she stopped there. Even thinking about the questioning seemed to be enough.

He had to say something. "I know I don't have to. I want to." Spencer flashed his dimples. This time he didn't find it awkward to look at her face. All he really felt was anger from what had happened to her. "Besides, I have to keep coming to see you until I convince you to write a song about me."

Maeve moaned as she shifted position. "If I knew where my guitar was I probably would. It wasn't with my CD's was it?"

"No it wasn't. What did your guitar look like?"

She dropped her eyes. "It was just your average acoustic. It had a blue pic guard and pictures all over it. I drew designs and pictures and wrote song ideas and poems on it with a black marker." She turned a little and mumbled, "Something else gone forever," so softly that Spencer thought he wasn't supposed to hear it. What did this mad man do to her? Her hands rubbed together. As if hearing Spencer's thoughts she said, "He cut off my little finger."

"What?"

"Pruning shears. And then he burned the, the stump. The doctors said it probably saved me from bleeding out or becoming infected." She stared off into space for a long time.

"So, tell me about yourself." It felt weird to say that.

Maeve spoke about where she came from and what she did. She told him about traveling around singing her songs.

Then she told him why she was on that train. After that she became very quiet.

"The police are waiting." Spencer moved his hand away from hers. The curtain dropped over her.

It looked like she tried biting her lip; there was a tooth missing. "I'd like to hear about your tattoo sometime." She reached out to touch his forearm and he flinched away.

"Sure. I have another under here," he tapped the cast. "You never said whether you like seafood or not."

She let her head fall on the pillow. Her eyes looked out the window for a moment. For the first time Spencer saw the beauty behind the bruises. She said, "I'm a vegan actually."

"But didn't you …" He stopped himself before finishing the thought. Remembering gnawing on a dead woman was probably not something she wanted to do. "We're sworn enemies. The chef and the vegan."

"It sounds like a *Brothers Grimm* title."

He shook his head. "The originals never ended well."

"Does any story?"

For a few moments they looked at each other. Twenty-four hours before the woman was attacking the man trying to scratch his eye out. The evidence was still on his face. She wanted to survive then. She wanted to fight back and would have killed to get out of that place. In the sanitized room, laying among clean sheets with the dirt and blood washed away she looked ready to submit. The fight was gone. Spencer hoped the spirit was still in there. If the spirit was gone, whoever put her in the cistern had won.

~ * ~

Spencer didn't have time to thank the police officers for dropping him off at the restaurant before they drove away. The street was busy as all the businesses were getting close to the end of their day. Cars filled the street moving in and out of the traffic like a metallic ballet. The Alcrest was going to erupt in the next hour or two, hopefully.

He had that sudden feeling of someone's eyes on him. It wasn't against all possibility. He had an arm in a cast, scratches on his face, and was just let out of the back seat of a police car. Everyone that witnessed that probably wondered what he had done? Spencer dropped his eyes and headed for the safety of home.

As he passed the lion's head out front he gave it a light pat.

"Where have you been?" Chrys bellowed before the door closed behind Spencer.

"What? I was at the hospital."

Chrys left the stool at the far end of the bar and marched the distance of the restaurant. "You couldn't text or anything to tell me you were okay?"

Spencer looked at the cooks behind the line, all gave blank stares. He asked, "Why would you be worried? Everyone here knew where I went." He looked past the bar as Jessie came around from the frame room. His head popped up with a nod.

"I told her."

"Shut up, Gordo. That's beside the point. We went through this traumatic event yesterday and then … why shouldn't I be worried about you, Fuck-nut?"

"That was yesterday." He was the one who had fallen into the room and was attacked and had his wrist broken and face scratched. Chrys wrenched her ankle a little when she ran to use the phone. *What did she have to be*

100

traumatized about? Spencer checked the reservations book at the front counter/hostess stand. There was the ten-top (table of 10) still expected plus two tables of two he already knew about. A four-top was added. Reservations were normally, on a busy night, just a quarter of the evening business. That could mean they were going to have up to seventy-two guests tonight. He looked at his sister who was staring at him and moved when he moved. "There's nothing more to worry about, is there?"

Chrys opened her mouth as if she was going to tell him something. It closed with a little snap.

"Hey Chef, look at you." A man who had to duck under the threshold between hallway and dining room carried a tray of separated silverware. He was dressed in the server uniform black pants and a black shirt. Today he had a *Tasmanian Devil* tie and Spencer knew without looking that his socks were probably even crazier.

"How's it going, Wylie?"

"Good," Wylie was one of only two male servers at the gastropub. He was a good guy to have around in case court issues ever came up. "This what happens when you piss off a Chihuahua?" he asked pointing at the scratches on Spencer's face.

"Shut up," Spencer said. He tried ignoring his sister whose expression was getting more and more frustrated. "Are you taking the ten-top?"

His eyes intercepted Jessie as she walked toward them. Although he thought she was attractive with an interesting look he always had trouble keeping his eyes on hers when they were around other people. It was as though through her eyes were his secrets. Her sleeves were rolled to the elbow so he dropped his gaze to the words tattooed on the inside of her forearm; "A Candle Within Chaos."

101

Wylie nodded, his perfect head of sandy hair bounced. "Hanni and I are. She'll flirt with the men, I'll flirt with the ladies, and we'll both be happy with big tips."

"Or a fight."

"Either way it'll be entertaining." Wylie and Hanni always worked together on big tables. They were both in their early twenties, good-looking, charming, and very good at their jobs. It made for happy customers and good gratuities. Wylie walked to the bar, which was also the staging area for servers.

Jessie squeezed Spencer's upper arm. He did not flinch. As soon as she mouthed, "Are you okay?" He nodded and said he was fine. He patted her hand then turned and headed down the hallway.

"Spence," Chrys whined as she followed him. "I'm not done."

He walked through the open doorway into the dish pit area where a scrawny man was scrubbing a pot in the first sink. He was in his early thirties, had a thin moustache, and wore blue jeans, an Alcrest T-shirt and a *Toronto Blue Jays* baseball cap. Spencer gave him a tap on the shoulder, then they knocked fists together.

"How's Brian today?"

"Good, good, Chef, good." Brian was mentally slow. The doctors said he was never going to seem emotionally older than sixteen and younger than that mentally. He started at The Alcrest through high school as work experience. Fifteen years later he remained in the same position. After Spencer took over he got Brian prepping some vegetables, but others were afraid he was going to cut off finger or peel away a layer of skin. "Oh, what happened to you?"

"Nothing."

"Spence." Chrys grabbed his shoulder and tugged him toward the office.

"Watch the arm." Spencer protested.

"Screw your arm." As soon as they were both in the office she slammed the door. "You can't just take off like that. Not when all this is happening."

"All what?" He sat down at his desk.

"The fucking kidnapper is still out there, you know."

"And he's coming after me now?" Spencer's eyebrows raised. "I don't think I'm his type."

Chrys looked at him like he had just made the worst joke ever. She let out a strong sigh. "What happened at the hospital?"

"I talked to Maeve a bit. She wanted to talk to me before the cops."

"Did she say how she got in the cistern?"

He shook his head. "She was taking the train across country to officially meet the daughter she gave up for adoption twelve years ago and she doesn't remember getting off. She's not sure how she got dropped in the cistern."

"How long was she in there?"

"She's not sure. She was supposed to meet her daughter thirteen days ago, so over two weeks, assuming she was in it the whole time."

"Did she see whoever did this to her?" She stared at the papers stuck to the cork board.

"No, but most of this I got from the cops, not her. They might not have wanted to tell me everything. I don't think Sgt. Finnegan likes me too much."

"That's the old lady cop, right? What's with you and female cops?"

"Spence?" Gordie pushed through the door. He looked at the woman then his boss. "Can I talk to you for a sec?"

"The door was shut, Gordie," Chrys screeched.

Gordie already had smears on his chef jacket and more on his apron. "This is restaurant business, alright. You're not even working today. Open door policy, remember that?"

"Stop it." Spencer raised his voice. He ran his hand back through spiked hair.

Not only was it a family restaurant, but the employees fought like they were related. Gordie stroked his beard like he was ringing it out. Chrys played with her hair and looked up at the ceiling tiles. Both felt what they needed to talk about was the beginning and end of everything.

"What is it Gordie?" Spencer finally asked.

He took a deep breath. "All I wanted to tell you was that Liz was late again today."

"Really," Chrys started up, "That's what was so cock fucking important?"

"Hey, she was almost an hour late. That really screws up our prep."

Chrys rolled her big eyes. She said, "Go jack a chicken, *Tattler.*"

"Enough already." Spencer stared at his sister. To his sous chef he said, "I'll talk to her about it later." He got a nod from the big man and waited until he was gone with the door closed again before turning back to his sister. "What's going on with you?"

She shook her head. "Nothing."

"Come on, you're acting strange."

"You would too if someone …" She bit her tongue. She looked away quickly. Her lips pressed tightly together.

"If someone what?"

Chrys's eyes closed and she sucked her bottom lip between her teeth. "Nothing. I'm just having a bad day. Can you give me a ride to the dance studio at five?"

Spencer gave her a nod. "I'm just going to call around to some pawn shops, but sure."

Something in him wanted to find that guitar. It could have been back at the house in the garage, in the pile out back on the deck, or maybe it never made it to the house at all. It could have been in the lost and found at the train station for all he knew. He'd check there if the pawn shops gave him nothing. Maybe the guitar case he saw in the basement had nothing to do with Maeve Campbell. The CDs were there though.

~ * ~

The sounds of a busy restaurant barely came through the floor of the apartment. It was a constant murmur that almost made everything vibrate. Cooking odors and the scent of the grill came through, however, making Spencer's stomach rumble. It was very rare that he was upstairs during a dinner shift. He had driven Chrys to her class, the pawn stores he called were closed, and when he got back he was ushered upstairs by Jessie. "*Rest,*" she told him after she pushed him through the door to the stairs and rapidly kissed his cheek. *How could he rest?*

He took the dogs for a walk and counted the cars in the back lot and along the street out front. He intentionally walked them past the windows so he could have a look inside, knowing damn well the windows were tinted. There were a lot of cars though.

Back upstairs he intended to make himself a tuna salad sandwich (ended up just draining the can and eating the tuna straight from there with some salt, pepper and soya sauce on top,) flipped through television shows, looked at recipes on his tablet, and tried to get the dogs to play. Bullet just looked at the ball rolling by as if it was an alien creature. The animal looked up at him and cocked his head to the side. A wrinkled eyebrow curved up almost saying, "Seriously?"

"What's wrong, buddy? You don't want to play?" He scratched the bulldog behind the ear. "You want to listen to some music? You want me to go downstairs and get Maeve's CD? I can do that for you." Perfect excuse for going down to see what was happening in the restaurant. *The dog sent him down for a CD*, sure.

The night dishwasher was too busy when Spencer walked through the door to notice he was there. Bryan was gone and the kid working the evening shift had headphones blasting music into one ear. He banged pans together in the sink as he scraped them clean. The machine beside him hummed.

"Chef, what are you doing here?" Hanni placed two handfuls of wide rimmed bowls on the dish pit tray. The silverware was tossed into a waiting bus pan with soapy water. She sniffed and rubbed the end of her small nose. In general terms her body was shapeless with tiny breasts and few curves, but long legs, high *high* spiked boots, and long silky blond hair made up for everything.

Caught. "I just came down for a CD."

"We could use you out there." Sweat made her forehead glisten. A bead ran down her chest through the barely-held-together shirt. She liked gel brass and shirts that were one or two size too small. "The kitchen's falling behind. Customers are getting pissed." There was desperation in her voice. She never seemed to have faith in the kitchen crew, always wanting her food in an unrealistic time.

It was enough for Spencer. "Come here." He stepped into his office and grabbed his chef coat from its hanger. "Help me get this sling off."

"Chef, you can't …"

"Yes, I can."

"Jessie'll kill me."

"Just help me." He writhed around like a magician trying to get out of a strait jacket. Pain seemed to envelop his wrist and shot right up his arm for the first time in a couple hours. As Hanni's hands took hold of the sling and she leaned in to lift it over his head he got a good whiff of her perfume. She helped him get the casted arm into the white jacket, fastened the buttons for him, and rolled his sleeves to the elbows. Her nose twitched as she made a sniff noise again. Her nose twitch was sort of cute.

Hanni's high heeled boots clicked on the floor as Spencer followed her down the hallway. Before they got to the end sound thundered. Every table seemed to be filled with customers. A couple of tables scattered around the room could be quiet, more than half the restaurant may have been a dull rumble, but the moment you filled the place with people eating and drinking the light fixtures trembled. Everyone had to speak over everyone else in order to be heard. Hanni was sucked into the crowd and was soon nothing more than a blond head moving along. The hostess looked at Spencer with a bewildered expression. A middle-aged couple standing in front of her looked at him with hope. Jessie, luckily, couldn't get around them without being rude. It was Monday night. They were never busy on Monday nights.

As his father always said, if he could predict when the restaurant was going to be busy he would have made his money and got the hell out of the industry.

In the kitchen everyone seemed to be moving, but nothing was happening. On a slow Monday night Gordie could do the grill and pans section with no problem. Ranger was there to help with plating. At the moment they both looked stunned as though they were waiting for something to happen. Pale blue order chits were lined on the butcher block at different angles like a huge game of solitaire. Liz was on the far side with all sorts of containers covering her workspace; it appeared that she didn't have time between orders to put anything away. Sweat dripped from all of their faces. They each had the expression of people who were lost. They couldn't see the forest through the trees.

In a professional kitchen it took just one thing, one moment, for everything to grind to a halt. A plate could be sent back, a server could forget an order, something could be dropped or burned, someone could get injured. All it took was that one moment and the weeds grew up around them and they couldn't see the light. Imagine trying to cut a field of hay with nothing but a butter knife. That's how it felt when you were in the weeds, as they say in a kitchen.

They were deep in the weeds.

"Where are we?" Spencer slid behind the others and reached for the order chits, the tips of his fingers moving at the end of the cast.

"Getting fucked up the ass with a giant pole." Gordie stated.

Spencer started sorting through the orders putting them together with the earliest ones first. "Did you get the ten top done?"

"We did, but they were missing an order on the chit, and I didn't count them so we had to stop and get that done. Then all these other orders arrived."

The one thing.

"Okay, I don't care how it happened. Let's just get out of the hole. I'll call and plate, Ranger can give me a hand and you cook everything. Liz, you still with us?"

She looked up. The strands of strawberry-blond hair sticking out from her knit cap were pasted to her forehead with sweat. "Yes, Chef."

"Take a minute to clean up your station and regroup." Spencer had to regroup himself. He quickly reviewed things to figure out where they were as far as appetizers and main courses. He tried to mark it down with a pencil, dropped it three times, then marked a backward check with his other hand.

The greatest part about working in a restaurant was that when you were really busy, so busy you didn't know if there was ever going to be an end to the night, everything else faded away. There were no thoughts about bills that needed to be paid or relationships tended to. Spencer didn't think about the woman in the hospital bed or Jessie staring at him every time she walked past or that he had to talk to Liz about being late, again. All there was, was the food. As food was being plated the server for that table was being called. As it slid beneath the heat lamps the next order was ready to be plated and the chef called out another order down the line.

This time Spencer thought about the food and the pain. Every time he lifted a plate to the pass he had to use his right hand. He tried to keep his left down at his side. It worked until he banged it against the butcher block.

109

Within forty minutes all of the appetizers were done. All Liz had left was to plate dessert orders as they came in, so she cleaned up her station and slid in next to Gordie on the hot side where she could easily get back to her own station.

"Excellent meal."

Spencer looked up at the man who had spoken as he walked past them toward the door. He didn't get a look at the man's face. All he saw was a purple mark on the side of it that looked as though it draped down onto his neck. The man's hand rested on the small of the back of a very shapely woman who walked like she wanted you to look. So Spencer did.

For a split second the chef remembered where he was and what was happening. He felt a chill through his body and pain shot from his wrist.

"Chef, those two steaks are ready."

Spencer watched the back of the man until the door closed behind him. "Let's plate it up. I need Wylie over here."

All thoughts were gone again and they were back alone in the kitchen. They could be seen by everyone in the room, but they were still alone in their own world putting good food onto plates. The only thing that remained was the pain around the Chef's wrist.

Chapter Eleven

"You owe me for this."

"I didn't ask you to come along, Chrys."

She rubbed crud from the corner of her eye. "And if I didn't who would put stuff in the truck?"

"I'm sure somebody here would give me a hand. Plus the big stuff gets delivered." Every Tuesday morning Spencer went down to the docks to hopefully get enough fish for the entire week. If they ran out, they ran out. The part he loved about his menu was that he could change it every day.

Chrys moaned. Both of her hands were wrapped tightly around a travel mug with her cell phone held between two fingers. "This is too fucking early."

"You were the one sleeping on the couch in the living room." She woke when he turned off the television. "I told you to go to bed."

"It smells like fish."

"It doesn't smell like fish, it smells like the sea."

When it was still dark the boats went out to catch their fill, then came back as the city was waking. As the fishermen unloaded their catch it was laid out where people could choose what they wanted. Spencer recognized three other chefs.

"And where do the fish live? In the God damn stinking sea, ergo, it smells like fucking fish." She started absently going through her phone. It was amazing how many texts she got through the night.

Spencer liked the smell of the ocean. He had gone out fishing with Hans, his main supplier, a couple of times. It wasn't the life for him, though he enjoyed it occasionally. The sound of the water lapping against the docks and the gulls calling out overhead was peaceful. The scent of saltwater calmed his nerves.

Last night had been a hard one. They eventually dug out of the hole the kitchen crew had been in with most customers leaving happy and satisfied. As usual they all left without any knowledge of how truly screwed the kitchen could have been. They had to compensate one table of three because the man complained about a long wait, but all it cost was a round of drinks. Paying for that and hopefully making them happy was much better than having them go home and complain to everyone who would listen. By the time Spencer hung his chef coat back on its hanger in his office and got upstairs his sister was waiting there ready to lecture him about how he was going to mess up his wrist.

He knelt down and ran his fingers along the skin of a halibut. The flat fish had the tiniest scales. The flesh beneath was white as snow and meaty like a good steak.

"That is the ugliest mother I have ever seen." Chrys's face scrunched in a look of disgust.

"This is a beautiful fish."

"Its eyes are all bug-eyed and it looks like someone smashed it with a bat or some shit." Halibut started their

112

lives with an eye on either side of their heads like every other fish. As they aged one eye migrated to the dark side of the body making them look like they had been tortured all to hell. They sat along the bottom of the ocean, their underside white and their top side dark to blend in with the sand.

Spencer looked at her. "This is a gorgeous fish. I'll take it to The Alcrest, fillet and portion it. Then I'm going to cook it in brown butter and top it with a delicate salad of baby greens. Maybe I'll serve it with a rice pilaf. No, a risotto. Asparagus risotto." The excitement seemed to vibrate from of him.

"You want dis one, Chef?" Hans knew who his customers were and called them by their titles. "Dis one eighty pounds."

"You can deliver it this morning?"

"Before lunch, yeah."

As Spencer rose he shook the man's gloved hand and rapidly avoided questions about his broken wrist.

Chrys stared at the parking lot. Her skin had gone pale.

"What's wrong?" He looked in the direction she was looking. When he got back to the apartment last night she practically screamed as he walked through the door from the restaurant stairs. She was never that jumpy.

"Have you seen that red truck before?"

Spencer barely glanced in the direction she was looking. "No."

Chrys was getting tired of having her nerves pulled so tight that every sound was making her jump. "I think he's following me."

"Who?" Spencer led the way down to the men unloading Pacific salmon.

"What?" She suddenly realized she hadn't meant to say what she did. She couldn't say anything. She didn't know for certain what was happening. There had been a red truck down the street from the dance studio after class, but maybe it had always been there. Just because she kept seeing one didn't mean anything. Maybe it was a case of not noticing things until you were looking for them.

Spencer took a moment from opening the belly of a fresh salmon to look at his foster sister. "Are you okay, Chrys?"

"You keep asking me that."

"You keep acting like a nut job."

"Oh, fuck whatever." Chrys slammed one hand in her coat pocket. Her heeled boots scraped the ground. She wasn't going nuts. She was paranoid maybe, but not nuts.

Spencer motioned to the fishmonger that he wanted four full salmon. Next he had to look at the lobsters, crab, and shellfish. They weren't a high-end restaurant, but often used high-end ingredients.

He looked back over his shoulder. There was a red truck three parking spots from his blue truck. It looked like somebody might have been in the driver's seat, but that could have just been the seat itself. *What did that mean? What did Chrys have to do with it?* Maybe it was nothing. She sure seemed jumpy.

~ * ~

"Where are we going?" Chrys searched the parking lot with her eyes as they walked back. All signs of a red truck were gone. She checked the back seat before getting in.

"Pawn shop."

"Why?"

"Maeve said she had a guitar when she was taken," Spencer said. "I called around to all the pawn shops. Do you realize how many there are in Middleton? I think I actually found her guitar too. It's only a few blocks away."

"Why would you even think to do that?"

His shoulders shrugged. "I had to do something."

"Why would you have to do something? She tried to kill you. Shouldn't the cops be looking for it, not you?" She looked down at her hands. She should have told the police about Kevin Bird, but if the bank didn't then why should she? She spent a couple of hours after dance class Googling the Linques trying to find where they were. She didn't find anything.

"I don't know. Maybe they are looking for it. They didn't really fill me in on their investigation."

Chrys turned to the side window with a slight smile to her lips. Her brother's actions justified what she had done, in her opinion at least. If he was looking for this woman's guitar, possibly a clue to who kidnapped her, then the fact that she looked for, found, and talked to Kevin Bird was okay.

"Did you drive my truck yesterday? When I got in this morning my legs hit the steering wheel."

"What? No." Chrys lied with a straight face. All those acting classes came in handy. "I drove it Sunday, remember?" Technically not a lie. Chrys slipped one boot off and brought her bare foot up to the seat. Her black pants slid up to mid-calf. She moved through applications on her phone before quickly typing something with both thumbs. "Hey, can you tell Jessie that Jen is covering my shift tonight? Thanks."

His head shook. "She's your immediate supervisor so you should be talking to her, not me. Why didn't you tell her yesterday?"

"Because I didn't fucking know about my damn practice yesterday." She looked out the side window with the thought, *I knew the day before yesterday.*

"So then call her. Text her. Why do you always have to leave it to me, so I'll get in a fight with her about it?"

"Tell her to kiss your ass. You're her boss you know."

"And yours." He looked at her.

Chrys wouldn't look his way. She didn't want to tell Jessie herself because she knew she would end up having to work. This way she got her way with minimal guilt and her brother had to take the brunt of it.

Spencer turned the truck into the Buy, Sell & Trade Pawn Brokers parking lot. This part of the city was midway between the docks and the downtown - nice people didn't go there after dark and tried to avoid it during the day. Almost any time of day or night you could get quick sex or a quick high for a price. Most of the buildings were run down. Across the street was a park with a children's playground which made headlines because of all the needles and other paraphernalia found around it. Spencer would be surprised to see any kids playing over there.

It might have been in their heads, but as the two of them stepped from the truck they could smell a foulness in the air that reminded them of the stale stench of a guy's apartment without windows ever being opened.

Chrys looked around. She wasn't really sure what she was seeking, she just had the feeling that she should look. Somebody could have been watching. There was nothing red.

She shoved her phone in a pocket and zipped up her jacket a bit more. On the back it said, *Elizabeth Frances Dance Studio* with the silhouettes of dancers behind the words.

"Are you wearing chef pants?"

"Yeah, so?" Spencer wore black pants and the shirt Chrys had helped him put on. "There are no ties, no buttons, just pull up and go." Since before he went to culinary school Spencer had been gathering chef pants. They were comfortable. The black ones were for day to day wear. He had a few with black and white checks and others with different culinary designs for the kitchen. "What about what you're wearing? Did you have enough paint to paint those pants on?"

"These are yoga pants, okay feneuter? They're comfortable and soft. Other guys here like it." Men inside the store were taking a look at the skin tight fabric clinging to her lithe legs and her behind. Years of dance and sport had been good to her.

"They're practically painted onto your," he lowered his voice, "ass cheeks"

"That's the point."

The two of them walked past a couple of tables with CDs and DVDs. Along one wall were glass cases displaying jewelry. A young couple was looking at a display of wedding rings. Further down there were video games and consoles inside the cases. Tables and shelves in the back of the long room were covered in tools, mostly of the power variety. Along the other side wall were television sets and DVD players. Just past the video games were a dozen or more hanging guitars and beneath them were drum sets and keyboards.

Spencer walked quickly until he stood beneath the guitars. Over his shoulder he saw Chrys had stopped at the jewelry. There were a bunch of acoustics guitars which all looked the same, then a few electric ones that were an assortment of styles and colours.

"You the one who called?"

Spencer's eyes fell on the man moving behind the counter. His thin grey hair was slicked back, you could see his scalp through it.

Spencer looked back up. "Yeah, you said you had the guitar I asked about, but I don't see it."

He moved behind the counter. "You said you was coming, so I took it down." His tone added the word *"jackass"* to the end.

From behind the counter he produced the guitar. It had the light brown base and blue pic guard like Maeve had said. On one part was the hand drawn design of a spiral growing outward. In another corner she had drawn something that looked like an ivy vine creeping along the edge. There were words written near the top, possibly some of the lines to her song, Red Island. Much of the writing was faded from where her arm had moved as she strummed the strings. Along one of the thinner side pieces were dozens of different flowers. Spencer reached out taking hold of the neck and turning it over. The strings made a noise. Maeve had drawn more pictures on the back, flowers, stars, geometric designs (again it was faded where her body rubbed against it) and there near one edge was where she wrote, Forever Love Elisa.

"So that it?" The man was chewing something. The chef was pretty sure it wasn't gum.

"This looks like it. How much?"

118

He chewed for a moment as if pondering what to charge. "A hundred bucks."

"So, did you find it?" Chrys leaned over the counter. She gave the man a smile as one leg kicked up behind her. "This is Maeve's?"

"Yeah, it is." Spencer nodded. He ran his hand over the wood. What was he doing?

Chrys looked up at the man with the slicked hair. Her bottom lip seemed to pout out farther than usual. Her thumb ring tapped against the glass counter. She asked, "Do you remember who brought it in? It would have come in somewhere in the last two weeks."

He looked at her for a while, his eyes moving over her body without any shyness. It made Spencer uncomfortable. "Maybe a guy came in just over a week ago with a bunch of stuff. I bought this guitar for thirty bucks and said no to this box of CDs he had. They was all of this singer I never heard of." He turned to Spencer, "You taking it?"

"Yes."

Chrys followed the two of them along the row of glass cases to the cash register. She walked like she had for a couple of fashion shows she modeled for – feet crossing in front of each other and ass swaying. The guys looking at the TVs noticed, the male half of the couple craned his neck and got punched in the shoulder, but *Mr. Slick* didn't really seem to look. Maybe he was a boob man.

By the time they got to the register she just stood straight and crossed her arms in front of her. "Do you remember what he looked like?"

"Sure I do. He was kind of memorable, you know?"

"You never thought of asking where he got the fucking shit?"

119

"What do I care?" He threw his hands out to the side. "Someone brings in good merchandise, doesn't complain about my price."

Chrys's jaw dropped. Didn't anyone get it? "This guy could be a killer and you didn't even think to ask? Do you have a name? Do you fucking know anything? You're not even worth the flesh you're printed on, are you?"

"Who the hell do you think you are? You ain't no cop. I don't have to tell you shit."

"What did he look like?" Chrys was getting loud. "What did he look like?"

"You know – screw you. Get the hell out of my place you squaw."

Chrys strengthened her stance. Her hands hit the glass counter as though she was about to fly over it.

"Chrys." Spencer put his arm around his foster sister. Her brown eyes burned right through him. She didn't know her native family and didn't really know much about her Aboriginal history, but she still hated that word. She hated it like African-Americans hated the N word or a woman hated to be called something starting with a C. *Something which Mr. Slick obviously was,* she thought.

Spencer made her look in his eyes. "Go outside." He briskly added, "Now," before she could protest.

She waited just a second then headed for the door mumbling to herself as she went. There was no swaying this time, just the stomping of a child sent to her room without supper.

Spencer had to think about this. Chrys was right. The guy who brought the guitar in may have been the same one who kidnapped and tortured Maeve. This was important. "Look, I-I'm sorry about my sister." He counted a hundred dollars from his wallet then another forty. "She gets a little excited sometimes."

"She has a foul mouth."

"Can't disagree with you there." He hoped smiling and being polite was going to do the trick. "Do you think you can tell me what the guy looked like? It'll drive my sister nuts that you told me." *Awkward laugh.*

The man stared at him for a while deciding if he was going to answer or not. He said, "He was tall, dark hair and he had this, like, purple birthmark thing on his face and neck. I had no reason to call the cops. In my business you don't turn people in. You do that and they stop bringing you good merchandise. It's best to just not ask."

Spencer didn't hear anything beyond being told about the birthmark. His mouth went dry. *Was that the guy in the restaurant last night? How many people could have that same birthmark?*

As Spencer placed the guitar in the back seat of the truck he kept his eyes on his sister who was sitting on the passenger side with her arms crossed over her chest, hands squeezing her biceps. He decided not to say anything about the birthmark guy. He didn't need her getting worried about something else. "You okay? You went a little crazy in there."

Chrys wanted to tell him what went on at the hospital and about how scared Kevin Bird seemed to be, but maybe it was all in her head. Maybe everything she feared of was just her over-active imagination playing tricks on her. She said, "Just take me home."

~ * ~

121

With one on each side, Chrys and Spencer dropped a large plastic container on the stainless steel prep table in the dish-pit. The pain in Spencer's wrist had passed the point where he needed drugs. He had only been stabilizing the bin with his casted arm, but that was enough.

"Good morning, Chef. Good morning, Chrys." Brian put his fist out and waited.

Chrys said, "I'll walk the dogs and then I'm going back to bed," and disappeared through the door to the apartment stairs.

Spencer bumped his first against Brian's.

"Bri, can you put these fish in the walk-in? Put a tray underneath and then put the whole bin on the floor for now. If you need help I'll be in here."

The plan was to sit in the office for awhile and get things organized for the day. He'd count the money from last night, write up the specials for the day, and talk about it with Gordie when he got in.

Last night he had popped too many pain pills. He took two more before sitting down.

His sharp intake of breath startled him. His eyes stared at what was on his chair. A white chef coat. His white chef coat. His name was there embroidered on the chest. *He hung it up after last night, didn't he?* He turned around to look at the hook. He knew he put his coat up there. He *knew* he did. Had someone been in his office? It actually looked like someone had folded it there and didn't just toss it like he would have. *Why would any of the staff move his chef coat? Was a stranger in there?*

The money.

Spencer got down on one knee and quickly went through the combination on the safe. He had to start over because his injured hand didn't do exactly what he told it to do. The black box made a beep as it unlocked. The money was there.

    Maybe he did put his coat on the chair.

Chapter Twelve

When Chrys entered the stairwell leading to the apartment all she could smell was fish. It wasn't the sea, it was fish. She didn't mind that smell if she went camping, but not from walking around a damn fish market before she was even totally awake.

"What the hell?" Chrys had to push to open the door at the top of the stairs. She gave it a hard shove. There were clothes behind it, and partially stuffed underneath.

Her eyes traveled around the room. Nothing was where it was supposed to be. Magazines had flown into a half-assed constellation across the floor from the coffee table. The couch cushions leaned against that. Books were knocked to the floor. Her candles had rolled away from where they had been. The mail was in a pile on the floor next to the table. "Damn dogs," she whispered.

She took a few steps expecting the dogs to come out with innocent looks on their faces.

Basically anything that had once sat on a surface was now on the floor. How could the dogs get up on the counter? To the book shelf? As she got near the kitchen she saw that food had been scattered over the tile floor. Most of it had been in cupboards. The dogs couldn't do that. The dogs wouldn't have left it there untouched.

Scratch.

What was that noise?

She flicked her foot and kicked a box of Special K that had been tossed from the apartment kitchen to the living room. It spun around sending out a spray of flakes.

"Breeze," she called out. "Bullet?" *Where were they? Someone had been in their apartment.*

A chill ran down through her body, the skin on her arms tingled. Her elbows felt weak. *Where were the dogs? Was it the same guy who attacked her? Maybe it wasn't his red truck at the fish market. Maybe he checked to see where they were then went back to trash the apartment. What if he was still inside?* Another chill went through her body. She was suddenly aware of every noise in the apartment from her quick breaths to a scraping noise. She quickly crossed to the kitchen and grabbed one of Spencer's chef knives.

There was that scratching again. Was it the dogs or was it him?

He had to have been watching the house. He knew the moment they'd left. *What would have happened if her brother went to the market alone, like he usually did?* She would have been asleep. *Would she have been killed? Raped? Taken and put in a dark hole somewhere?*

If he was destroying their apartment that couldn't have been him in the red truck at the fish market, could it?

The scraping came from down the hallway and was quickly followed by a yelp.

Chrys forgot about everything having to do with a stranger being in the apartment and headed toward the source of the sound. It was coming from the bathroom. As she opened the door the two dogs bound out quickly circling around the woman's legs. She knelt down, the chef knife forgotten on the floor beside her, and scratched each one behind the ears.

The three of them returned to the open area. Chrys stood at the end of the hallway. Bullet waddled around the kitchen floor eating whatever scraps had fallen from boxes and packages. Breeze scratched at her owner's leg wanting to be loved.

"Bullet, stop it."

Her brown eyes took in everything. She walked through the apartment opening doors, one hand pushing the door while the other held the knife at the ready. It was so stupid. Someone once told her never to carry a weapon unless you were prepared to use it and willing to have it used against you.

The bedrooms looked fine. Hers was a mess, but even she couldn't tell if that was from her own doing or that of someone else. Spencer's computer tablet was still on the coffee table, the pile of money she had pulled from her pockets before laundry was on the floor around the kitchen counter.

Her eyes stopped on the dry erase calendar stuck to the side of the refrigerator by magnets. She used it to keep track of where she was supposed to be each day. A circle had been wiped clean in the middle of the month. There in red dry erase marker were the words, *where are they?*

Where are they? The Linques? She wiped the words off with her hand. The red ink smeared onto her palm like blood. She grabbed the closest marker and started rewriting what she remembered had been on the calendar. Her hand shook. Her brother couldn't see it. It was crazy. *How dare someone do this?* Pulling her arms around her body, she hugged herself trying to dispel the fear. Chrys knew she should tell her brother. They had to call the police and get this settled, but she couldn't. She had to figure this out herself. She got into this mess, only she could get out of it.

~ * ~

Chrys surveyed the apartment. It wasn't perfect and Spencer was probably going to notice a few things out of place. He'd probably rub it off as his ditsy sister moving things around. The dogs were happy. They helped clean up the spilled food.

A knock on the door made her jump.

"You're dressed already," Chrys looked up and down Dawn's body. Over muscled legs she wore black tights with a rip on one knee. On top of those were cut-off denim shorts. Her black T-shirt was tied in a knot in the front exposing her midriff. Printed on it was a caricature of a busty woman shooting pistols in the air and wearing roller skates on her feet.

"Why wouldn't I be?"

"I need to go do something."

The only thing different between Dawn and the character on her shirt was that the real woman's hair was too short for pigtails. "So, no going downstairs for a pre-practice drink?"

"I'll explain to you along the way," Chrys said as she grabbed her duffle bag and ushered the other woman toward the door.

"What's up with Bullet?"

Chrys's eyes fell to the bulldog. "Shit." The tan and white dog had spots of raised fur over the bulk of his body. It had happened before and then she said it looked similar to the scene in the Gremlins movie after Gizmo had water splashed on him before multiplying. "I have to see Spencer for a quick sec. I'll meet you at the car."

It took until Dawn's car was parked at the curb in front of St. John's School before Chrys said anything else, other than giving directions. "I want to find the family from *The Creepy House*, okay. I really want to know what happened to them." It was half the truth. "Maybe I can get their personal belongings to them."

"Major Crimes is looking for them. You don't have to worry about any of it. I wouldn't even think about it anymore."

"I can't … I have to." She covered her eyes. Chrys hated censoring herself. This secret was taking on a life of its own. "I feel like I have to do something. I need to fucking try and find them." Her thumb started bouncing against the front of her phone, the thumb ring clicking on the screen. Chrys turned in the passenger seat to glance out the back window. "I don't want Spence to know." Also part truth. She turned back to the other woman. "Can you help me?"

Dawn stared back at her. Chrys knew that inside the other woman was fighting between the police officer she was and the affection she felt. "So this was the kid's school? They won't tell you anything you know. They shouldn't, anyway."

"That's why I brought a cop." Chrys brought herself close to her friend and took a quick snip at her ear with her teeth. She also brought a cop in case a red truck showed up.

"Look at the way I'm dressed. I can't go into a school asking questions. The back of my shirt says, Mount-Me." It was a play on her being a Mountie.

"Stay here then," Chrys got out of the car and jogged toward the school doors. She didn't feel good about

129

keeping secrets from anyone. What was she supposed to say though?

She could feel eyes on her. *Was that Dawn? Was it the nut job? Was it all in her head?* She turned to look down the street in both directions. Maybe some of it was in her head, but the apartment was real. The dogs could make a mess, they've done it before, but they could only get so high and wouldn't lock themselves in a bathroom. *Okay, they could probably lock themselves in the bathroom.*

It was just after lunch, so the children were heading back to class to finish the second half of their day. Chrys was one of those kids who always took the longest route possible through the school (taking hallways that she had no reason what so ever to utilize) just to prolong the pain of having to sit at a desk again. A couple older girls, probably in grade seven or eight, walked by with a conga line of little ones. She did the kindergarten helper thing for a couple of years too, until her teachers realized it was just another excuse to take her sweet time.

She closed her jacket after a couple of kids saw the roller skating cowgirl. On the back of hers was her derby name, Polka-Hotness. Her heels click-clacked on the floor.

"Hi," Chrys flashed her brightest smile at the secretary sitting behind a large open window in the wall. Behind the woman were two doors labeled Vice-Principal and Principal. "I'm wondering if you can help me out."

Fifteen minutes later Chrys popped into the passenger side of the car startling Dawn. "Got it."

"Got what? They told you where they went?"

"Ah, no." Chrys fastened her seatbelt. "The Principal wasn't there so the secretary couldn't give me specifics, but if they knew then she would know. She did remember the kids though. She said they often wore the same clothes all

130

week and used the school's free breakfast and snack programs every day. I feel so sad for those kids."

Dawn turned the key in the ignition. Heat wafted from the vents. "Did she know what happened?"

"She said they just stopped coming to school. They called to see where the kids were, but as far as she knew no one ever talked to anyone." Chrys's eyes flicked to the side mirror.

"What are you so happy for then?"

She smiled. "The secretary said the last time she talked to the boy he said something about being excited for the stampede. Do you think he meant the *Calgary Stampede*? Maybe they went to Calgary."

"There are a lot of stampedes, Chrys."

The car started to move. Chrys pushed open her door. Her foot skidded along the pavement.

"Chrys," Dawn hit the brakes.

Chrys almost lost her balance as she escaped the car. Her hand touched the ground and pushed her back to her feet. Dark brown eyes locked on the truck behind them. Rage and courage flashed through her body.

"Who are you?" Her scream echoed as she heard Dawn call her name behind her. "What do you want?" Her hand came down on the hood of the red truck that had pulled in behind them. "What the hell do you want?"

"Chrys."

The side window went down. The man on the other side was older than she expected and less intimidating. His eyes evoked surprise and fear. His hair had crawled back away from his forehead. Thin glasses were perched on his nose.

Chrys's hand stung as it came down on the hood of the truck a second time. "What do you …"

"Get your hands off my truck."

131

"What do you want from me?" She screamed so hard her throat hurt. Her fingers balled into fists down at her sides.

"Chrys," Dawn was there.

"He's been following me, Dawn."

"I don't know who the hell you are," his voice raised.

Her foot shot out and kicked the front tire. Her ankle felt like it twisted inside her boot. "Why were you at the fish market? Why are you here?" Spit flew from her lips.

"Do you want me to call the cops?"

"She is a cop. You're busted, you f…"

The other door to the truck opened and closed. Chrys stared through the cab at the young boy who had climbed into the vehicle. He stared back with innocence and confusion.

"Shit."

The man said, "I'm picking up my son," and that was all he needed to say.

Chrys let her friend tug her backwards away from the truck. Both women watched it back up then pull out and head down the street. Chrys looked at the tall blond woman who wore an expression of worry and confusion on her face.

Chrys felt tears run down her cheek. She quickly wiped them away. She was going crazy. Maybe it was a side effect of *The Creepy House*. It was haunted, she was haunted. But she was attacked at the hospital. The apartment had been trashed, searched. Those were real things that happened. He was out there. She flinched at her friend's touch.

"What the hell's going on, Chrys? You can't just attack someone like that."

"You don't understand." She looked around as more tears fell down her cheeks. She sucked back snot before it could come out. The flood gates were open.

"Get in the car then and we'll go somewhere to talk."

Chrys stared at her friend for a moment. She saw the compassion there. She knew this woman wanted more than she was willing to give, in more ways than one. *Why did everyone seem to want far more than she did?*

Chrys said, "I hurt my ankle," and carefully walked back to the passenger side with a slight limp. She didn't speak again for fifteen minutes until they were parked beside the Marina Park. "Do you know Liam O'Donnell?"

"The mobster?"

"What?" Chrys's mouth stopped. Her only thought was, *oh God*.

"Liam O'Donnell is the leader of the Irish Mafia. Every cop in and around the city wants to get him. He's responsible for probably hundreds of deaths. Nothing comes off a ship without O'Donnell knowing about it." Dawn looked out the car windows almost as though she was making sure nobody was around. "Why're you asking about him? This guy's like the villain in the Harry Potter books. You don't mention his name. He has ears and eyes everywhere."

"Have you gone after him?"

"Myself, no, but Major Crimes is always looking into his movements. He has lots of guys working for him and he always stays just out of things. His name comes up, but nothing can be proven. It sounds cliché but a couple of witnesses have disappeared. Why're you asking?"

What was she supposed to do? She couldn't go on with everything by herself. Chrys told her friend about everything from the attack in the hospital to the red truck and finding her apartment in disarray. When she was done she felt the weight fall from her shoulders. She opened the window and let the cool breeze caress her face. Finally she said, "He has some connection to the house."

"What? Did you tell the investigators?" She fumbled in the middle console and brought her phone out.

Chrys put her hand over Dawn's. "We can't."

"Chrys, you have to. If this had something to do with those women they have to know."

"He didn't. It was something to do with the Linque family that lived there, not the women."

"You don't know that, Chrys. Either way we have to tell them."

Chrys pulled the phone from her hand. "No. You're off duty. I told my friend, not the cop, all this." Panic ran through her body. She couldn't let them know, she couldn't let anyone know. She dropped her friend's cell phone on the floor of the car and quickly took the woman's face in her hands. Their lips pressed against each other's. Chrys's tongue searched for its familiar companion. She needed to let it all go for at least one moment.

As they parted she whispered, "This is between us. You can't even tell Spence." She kissed her again. "This is between us."

Dawn's fingers stroked the side of the woman's light caramel face. "This is a police matter, Chrys. We have to go to the police."

"I did. I told you." Chrys flashed her large smile brightening her face. Her eyes were moist again.

"No, we have to go to Major Crimes."

"Not today. Please, Dawn. We'll go tomorrow. Let's go to practice and then you can stay at my place tonight and we'll go tomorrow." Chrys stared at her friend until she nodded in agreement. She'd figure out how to avoid tomorrow, tomorrow.

Chapter Thirteen

Not often enough did Spencer remember to stand back and consider all that The Alcrest had become. It was part of the family before he was born. When he as ten his dad had him cooking on the line. He bought part of the business before his father passed away then his mother gave him the rest. His father fought the changes Spencer proposed when he came back from culinary school and had developed his skills. It was a different place now. The bare bones were still the same but the atmosphere, the décor, the clientele were all different.

"Oh shit, I smell like a halibut's ass." Gordie exclaimed as he crossed between Spencer and the stove range. His white apron was splattered with bits of white flesh and scales.

It was enough to bring Spencer back from his memories. "It's all portioned up then?"

"Yeah," Gordie squirted soap in his palm and started washing from his fingertips to his elbows. When he was finished he took off the apron. Underneath was a black Alcrest T-shirt and khaki cargo shorts. "We have enough salmon already, so I'll do that tomorrow."

"Leave two whole ones for the private party on Friday. We'll roast them whole with lemon grass and herbs. They didn't say what they wanted, just something different. Whole salmon is different. Liz," Spencer looked around Gordie to the cold side chef, "You're going to have to develop a special dessert, something we don't usually have."

"Alright," a nervous laugh escaped her. "What about an ice cream sampler? I can make three new ice creams."

"It'll be Friday night. How fast can you plate that for eight people when you're busy?" This was Spencer's way of trying to get her to do what he wanted without actually saying it.

"What about those lemon curd tarts you made a few months ago?" Godie pulled a pack of cigarettes from a hidden cubby hole within his station. One of his talents was remembering every dish they had ever served and how it was plated. "I'm gonna go have a dart."

Liz's face brightened. "Yeah, I can do those. Maybe stew some fruit to go with it." Nervous laugh. She pulled her wool cap down over her ears.

Spencer gave her his nod of agreement. "We don't have any reservations tonight, so if you're not busy see about getting some prep done for tomorrow. Can I talk to you in the office?"

He never really felt his age. Whenever Spencer spoke to people he felt like they were seeing a much younger version of himself. He was thirty-one years old, owned his own restaurant, was the governing power over his employees, was respected by them and his peers; yet he still thought people looked at him as the kid who took over Rene Alcrest's place. When he thought of himself he saw a young face looking back.

Spencer waited until Liz was in the room then shut the door. He walked around the desk but didn't sit.

"I'm sorry I've been late. My mom's been sick and she watches my daughter for me, so I need to …"

He held up his hand. Many people would have told him he treated the employees more like family than he should have. He could remember his father chewing him out in front of the staff for breaking a couple of plates. He said, "I can't let you be late all the time. I understand you have stuff going on, but this is a business. I mean, you don't even call to warn us. We need to know if you're going to be late or not even show." He was trying to speak as calmly as possible. He watched her face. She was trying to stay as stern and solid as she could, but her eyes betrayed her.

"I know. It's usually down to the last second and then …"

The door opened with a knock as Chrys poked her head in. She said, "I'm going out."

"Do you mind?" Spencer wasn't calm to his sister. "We're having a meeting."

Her brown eyes looked down at Liz whose eyes were quaking and ready to let go. Chrys looked back at her foster brother and repeated, "I'm going out. I'll be late."

"Chrys."

"Open door policy."

Under her jacket Spencer saw the T-shirt for the Annie Oakley's Roller derby team. Hers was torn slightly from the center of the collar downward to *draw attention to her humble breasts*, as she put it. She also wore slacks, but Spencer knew she'd be wearing something else with more rips in strategic locations by the time she was playing. He waved his hand for her to leave. Usually after one of their

139

practices the girls went out, still dressed in their get-ups, to see how many free drinks they could get. She'd crawl in sometime after he was asleep.

"Did you talk to Jessie?" He quickly asked as she turned.

Chrys turned back. Her hair flew over her shoulder. She let out a gush of air. "Did you?"

"That's beside the point. You still have to."

"Can you check on Bullet?" She blurted out. "He's getting those spots again."

"What? What did you feed him?"

"Fuck all," she responded quickly. "I have to go." She shut the door and then they heard a second door slam as she headed outside.

Spencer looked back at Liz. He slipped down into his chair. If his own sister wasn't going to listen to him then why should anyone else? "Sorry about that. You know Chrys."

"I'll call next time, Chef," Liz said with a nervous laugh at the end.

Yeah, he was Chef. He didn't encourage the staff to call him that, however. Some of the staff came from bigger restaurants where all the cooks were called chef and they were seen as higher up than the rest of the staff. Spencer didn't like to think that way, but he wasn't going to do anything to discourage it either. He did smile to himself a little when members of the staff corrected a new hire after they used his name.

Spencer didn't know how to finish the mini-lecture. He had it all thought out until hurricane Chrys turned everything upside down. He settled on, "We should get back to work."

"I was told Chrys was here," Jessie said as Liz walked passed her and she entered the office. The light sparkled off her gold watch.

"She was." He awkwardly tried opening an envelope with his right hand. He ended up just tearing it in half. The plastic window held. "She was late for her appointment."

"Right," Jessie frowned and her eyes shadowed over.

"What?"

Her hands went to her hips. "She can't keep doing this, Spence. She's using being your sister to run right over me. If she wasn't an Alcrest she'd be gone by now."

The last time he was asked about Jessie his response was that she was sweet and funny and random. She was also the least bejeweled of all the women he ever dated. The only jewelry she wore was the gold watch with etchings of old cars on each link.

Spencer licked his thin lips, said, "I'll talk to her," and flashed a bright smile. A dimple appeared on both cheeks.

"Who's that?"

"What?" Spencer looked down at the desk where he absently turned a CD case. "It's um …"

"I don't even remember the last CD I bought. Brittany Spears first one, maybe."

"Were you into the Catholic school girl uniforms too?"

"Shut up. I was like twelve. My point is, I just download now."

"Well I didn't buy this CD. I…" *What was a good word for it*, "…found it." Spencer rose and motioned that he was leaving the office.

"What do you mean?"

The dishwasher banged as Brian closed it over a new load. He crossed to where he was peeling potatoes.

141

Spencer put his hand on the small of Jessie's back ushering her forward. When he was a kid he noticed his dad always did that to his mom, so Spencer saw it as a gentlemanly thing to do.

Jessie never mentioned it to him, but even just feeling his fingertips on her back made her knees melt. She thought it was sexy old movie shit.

"There was a box of them at *The Creepy House*," Spencer said as the sound of the dishwasher faded away. For him *The Creepy House* was becoming something not so scary. He held up the CD, surprised it was in his hand. "This is the girl from the cistern."

"Oh," was all Jessie said.

The restaurant was pretty quiet. The lunch rush was over, so the only customers were those who happened to have the afternoon free. There was only one couple by the stage huddled over coffees. At first it looked like a mother and son (she had to be in her mid-forties and he in his twenties) but when Spencer looked closer each was playing with the other's fingers and she also rubbed his lower leg with her foot under the table. There were probably some others in the framed room.

The kitchen crew looked relaxed. Having a slow day often gave them a chance to recharge. Ranger was blanching French fries in the fryer. During service the fries would be fried again to order and would be crispy on the outside, soft on the inside. Gordie was doing a quick chop of onions and carrots to add to the other vegetable scraps in the fish stock being made from the halibut bones. Over the cold side table Liz had all the ingredients needed for a big batch of honey-lime vinaigrette. As for the front-of-the-house staff Sue was showing the new guy, Mario, how to reorganize the room. The other morning staff were gone and the evening crew would be in by four. They would be ready to go whether customers were there or not.

Spencer slipped down the line until he was next to the big man. His voice lowered. "I have to go out. Can you throw together a small pot of potato corn chowder? No cream or animal products."

"You want the potatoes roasted?"

"Yeah, yeah let's do that. There should be a bag of corn in the freezer. If you get busy though put it aside, okay?" Spencer tapped the butcher block with the CD and went back to the hostess stand where Jessie was pretending to look through the reservations book. "No calls?" he asked for something to say. She shook her head, but didn't say anything so he continued, "I'm going to take Bullet to the vet then I'll be back. Gordie's making me some soup to take to, ah, her." He held up the CD. "What?"

Jessie's face had suddenly darkened. She flipped through the reservations book again. Her shoulders shrugged. "Nothing. I'm tired."

"Well I'm going." Spencer squeezed her arm and headed down the hallway. Though everyone knew they were sort of a couple he never showed too much affection inside the restaurant. He was curious about her reaction.

She could be tired, but there was probably more to it. Spencer wasn't dense. He knew Jessie was insecure about whatever their relationship was. They had been off and on for years, both dated other people within that time, and lately it had been more of a casual sex thing. He guessed she had every reason to be insecure.

~ * ~

The guitar was still on the back seat of the truck, so Spencer lifted Bullet onto the passenger side floor. The bulldog had quarter-sized circles of raised fur all over his round body, looking like he had been attacked by atomic mosquitoes. As Spencer got in the driver's side the dog's face rested on the seat. His jowls spread out on the leather and his eyes twitched from Spencer to the seat.

"What? If you want up, climb up."

Bullet snorted a gush of air.

"Seriously, dog?"

Spencer pushed open his door and climbed out. Yellow leaves blew across the back parking lot. There were papers and plastic bags in the corners where the wind couldn't get to them. He made a mental note to have the dishwasher come out and pick up all the garbage. People's image of The Alcrest started the minute they pulled into the lot. Spencer opened the passenger door and lifted the bulldog onto the seat.

He turned and stopped. There was a red truck parked on the back street out behind the lot. *Didn't Chrys freak out about a red truck?* Spencer knew she was paranoid or something – *but she was never paranoid* – about a red truck and here was one. His eyes stayed on it as he walked back to the driver's side. He wished he could tell through the tinted windows if someone was in there, watching him. He felt like a hand squeezed around his heart. Spencer turned the key in the ignition and started moving forward. His gaze didn't leave the other truck.

It moved. As Spencer's truck started to move forward the red one pulled from the curb and drove away. It must have been nothing at all. A bad feeling took over his entire body. He looked down the direction the truck had gone. It was pulled up to the curb again as if it leap-frogged over the other cars and parked along the side. Spencer turned the other way and pushed down on the gas. He could see how falling into the cistern and finding Maeve and the dead woman could make someone frightened. He looked in the mirror. Chrys said a red truck was following her. Maybe *The Creepy House* affected her more than he realized.

Three more turns and Spencer saw a red truck in the mirror. It could have been any red truck though. He remembered being a kid sitting on the edge of a bridge counting each colour of vehicle that went by. You never noticed red cars until you were looking for them.

Outside the veterinarian clinic he looked up and down the street. He felt like someone was watching him. Nobody was except for the sad brown eyes looking up from the seat beside him.

He wanted to ask the good doctor about the Porsche parked in the veterinarian's spot, but forgot.

"Looks like hives," Dr. Ken took a close look at Bullet perched on a stainless steel table in one of the vet rooms. "I'll give him a shot here then you can follow up with Benadryl at home."

"Regular Benadryl?"

"Yes, sir. It sounds funny, I know, but it's an allergic reaction and that's the best medicine for it." He scratched around the bulldog's head. "Your arm okay?"

"It's fine. I'm making it work." Spencer looked through the vertical blinds.

"Something wrong?"

Spencer turned back to him. He said, "No, it's fine."

"Alright, just give me a second to get the shot and we'll get you going." The veterinarian looked bigger in his white lab coat than he did outside *The Creepy House*. "By the

145

way, we stopped by The Alcrest last night. You looked really busy, so I didn't say hello."

"You should come again then."

He smiled. "We will. I'll be right back."

Spencer turned back to the window. He saw two red cars drive by followed by a maroon truck.

During his drive he swore he saw a red pick-up with a shiny chrome grill a couple vehicles behind him just a few blocks from the restaurant. *Coincidence? Why would someone be following him or Chrys? "Because we fucked up some psycho mother fucker's secret torture chamber,"* his sister would have said. In fact he could picture her screaming those exact words while throwing her arms out. They didn't know what the whole cistern thing was about. It might not have been a psycho serial killer. It could have been personal. What did the dead woman and the singer have in common? He hoped Maeve wasn't into anything that would lead to being tortured. *And maybe he was long gone*. Spencer wasn't doing a good job of convincing himself.

"Here we go,"

Spencer jumped. He spun around at the voice. Dr. Ken re-entered the room, a needle held in his hand.

Spencer tried to hide that he almost pissed himself. "So what's the shot going to do?"

"It'll react with the allergy right away. The Benadryl is to continue getting the medicine. Are you sure you're okay?" He took a handful of Bullet's skin and put the needle into his flesh without any bedside manner.

"Do you remember any red trucks out at the creepy – the house with the cistern?"

"Red trucks?" Dr. Ken rubbed the spot on Bullet where he had stuck the needle. "The volunteer fire truck is yellow. I can't recall. I never really noticed the house out there before. Is there something wrong?"

Spencer took another look out the window. "Don't worry about it."

~ * ~

"You found it." Maeve tried to smile, but her swollen lips did their best to fight back. Some of the swelling had gone down. She was sitting up in her hospital bed facing the television, but Spencer could tell she wasn't really watching it. She sounded tired. He wondered if she could sleep without medication.

"I said I'd try."

Spencer smiled showing his deep dimples. He had taken Bullet home and picked up the soup from his sous-chef before heading to the hospital.

As soon as the woman had the guitar she barely knew he was there, giving him time to look around. It was still just a hospital room, only now there were vases of flowers on the window sill and around the sink. It still smelled like medicine though.

Maeve let out a moan as she maneuvered the guitar into place. She tried positioning her fingers. Her left hand found its place on the neck, her fingernails were cracked and worn down to the fingertips, a bandage covered the one missing digit. Her face cringed as she tried to play notes and the metal strings bit into her flesh. The broken fingers on her right hand were taped and held firm with a metal brace. She had to hold them out a bit to stroke the strings with her thumb. It wasn't the same sounds heard on the CD.

She rested the instrument across her lap. A hand stroked where she had written on its body.

"You okay?" Spencer took a step closer. In the bag hanging from his hand was a small plastic bucket with the soup.

Her blond hair fell, hiding the side of her face. It was wet and had been brushed. "It just doesn't feel right."

"What do you mean?"

She took in a breath that made her body quiver. Tears swelled in her eyes. She ran her fingers along the guitar strings. The metal splint made them scream. "When I was on the train I made some posters using pages from my journal, and taped them to doors all through the train announcing that I would be playing my songs in the lounge." She spoke down to the guitar as if this was her confession. "I did it just after dinner, so everyone would be finished eating and maybe they wanted to relax. I didn't charge anything. I just wanted to talk to the people and perform. That was what I did."

Spencer pulled over a chair. He placed the bucket of soup on the rolling food table beside an untouched tray of turkey, mashed potatos, gravy and corn. "So you perform for money? For a living?"

Maeve shrugged her shoulders and sheepishly dropped her chin. "I worked in a bag store." She laughed. "Handbags, backpacks, briefcases, suitcases; but my passion is in writing songs and telling stories. I saved for a year to make my CD and then I performed in bars and farmers' markets, wherever people would listen and perhaps buy them. I quit my job just before leaving home, then travelled across the country. When I did that mini-concert on the train I had to sit on a table because all the seats were bench seats, so there wasn't enough room for my guitar. I put my box of CDs behind me on the table next to the window hoping to sell a few." She had to swallow.

"You don't have to tell me."

"I nursed my beer," she continued as if Spencer didn't interrupt her, "and I told stories about how I wrote songs and sang. It was fun." She laughed a little. It went away like smoke in the wind.

"Do you remember who was there?" Spencer knew she had been through this already. The police had probably asked her the same question over and over. He couldn't help his curiosity. To him it felt like he was diving right into the world's secrets. This was like reading his sister's diary when he was younger, only that was about boys she liked and girls she was confused about. This was hard core Criminal Minds, Special Victims Unit, Castle shit.

She opened her mouth to say something, stopped and took a breath. "There was a man and his two little kids. He looked so tired. They only listened to a few songs then the daughter asked if they could go. Um, it was a small room. It was one train car with about six tables then stairs leading up to an observation area. There was one guy who sat on the stairs. Another guy at a table had tattoos down one arm; he drummed along. One lady bought me another beer. I can't, I can't remember any details about them. Nothing specific." Her face seemed to change ever so subtly with each remembered moment. Her breathing changed. Her eyes were nothing but tears ready to burst. "And that was just the first night. I did it the next night too. It was all the same people but there was nothing else to do.

Spencer wanted to hold her and tell her it was just a bad dream. He wanted to catch the tears before they fell.

He really wanted to see Jessie.

Cold ran down his spine and the hairs on his arms stood up. Spencer turned around quickly. He had that same feeling he got when he was a kid and thought someone was looking. There was no window in the door. It was open a little. *Did he leave it open?* No, he swore he closed it. He moved to the door, slowly opened it, and looked outside. The RCMP officer wasn't there. Maybe he looked in before heading to the washroom. *That was possible, right?*

Spencer returned to Maeve's bedside. This time he stood closer.

When Maeve started again her voice dropped. "I talked about Elisa. I gave birth to her twelve years ago and put her up for adoption. I was on the train coming to see her for the first time. Those flowers by the sink," she pointed at a green vase full with daisies, "are from her parents."

"Is she coming to see you?"

Maeve stopped talking. The room seemed to go cold. Spencer wondered if he had gone too far.

It took a few minutes before another word was spoken. Maeve said, "I don't remember much after I was singing in the lounge car. I woke up in a truck or something then I passed out again." Her eyelids couldn't hold any more, tears flowed down her cheeks. "Then I was put in that room."

Spencer barely heard those last words.

"Playing again doesn't seem right."

He was still locked on what she had said about getting into a truck. He ignored the fact that she wasn't sure if that's what it was. "Do you remember anything about the truck? A colour maybe?" He knew he should stop there, but this was important. This was about Chrys.

"What?" Her hand wiped the tears across her cheek.

"The truck, what do you remember about it?"

"I don't know. I just came to for a minute. I don't even know if it was a truck for sure. I was in something. It was a cage or something."

"Did you see any colours? Blue, black, *red*?"

Maeve pushed the guitar further down her body until it was over her legs. She wiped the tears again. "I don't know. I don't remember. Black, I guess." She repositioned herself and cringed from the pain. Her hospital gown slipped down over one shoulder. There was a bruise on her neck, but none on the bare skin of her shoulder. "Red maybe."

"Was the truck red?"

"I, I don't remember." She pulled the gown back over her shoulder.

This was important. He wanted to press some more. Spencer watched a tear streak down her face. *Did the police stop at this point or did they go on?* He had to be better than that.

"Why don't you tell me about your daughter?"

~ * ~

Spencer felt defeated. He wasn't sure if it was from his visit with Maeve or seeing the way Gordie was smoking his 'cigarette' and who he was sitting with outside the back door of the restaurant. It was both, but more the woman, he decided as he slumped out of his truck.

Maeve didn't know if the vehicle she had been in was red or if it was even a pick-up. All she recalled were flashes. Spencer gave up as they ate the vegan soup. She talked about her daughter. She was young when she had her, only 12 years old, so giving her up was the best plan at the time. She stayed in touch with the new parents and now that Elisa wanted to know where she came from they were going to meet, but Maeve didn't want the twelve year-old girl seeing her as she was. Spencer said, "You don't want to waste time. You're lucky to just be here. Maybe you can treat this as a do-over." She went silent after that, so he told her about his tattoos. A short time later he decided it was time to go. He wanted to help her and make things better. He just didn't know how.

When he left her room the police officer was back at his post. Spencer casually asked where he had gone. "I had a phone call," the RCMP officer said. "I had my eyes on the hallway and the room door the whole time. No one came down here who didn't have a white coat on, so don't worry about it."

"Grab a seat, Chef," Gordie slapped an empty plastic chair, another yard sale treasure. These chairs stayed under the back stairs no matter what the weather. Gordie held his self-rolled cigarette between finger and thumb with his hand cupped around it. Responding to the look on his boss's face he quickly said, "It's a regular cigarette. I swear. I don't smoke that other stuff at work."

Spencer let out a breath. "How has the night been?"

"Slow as hell. You know Charlie, right?"

The first anyone noticed about Charlie were the tufts of red hair sticking out from under a trucker baseball cap. One of his eyes was almost shut from swelling and a purple bruise.

"What happened to you?" Charlie quickly asked. He spat out a lump of something white that missed the coffee can between them and splattered on the pavement.

Spencer didn't sit. He knew the chairs were often damp and he really didn't want a wet butt. "I fell," he said. "What happened to you?"

Charlie was a line cook at MacGyver's – not known for its great food but well known for its low prices. As a side job he grew marijuana in his basement and crawled through cemeteries late at night looking for magic mushrooms. Spencer's rule was that Charlie was not allowed to come into the restaurant. He didn't care what his employees did when not at work. At his restaurant and home things were different.

"I sold stuff in the wrong place." He let out a laugh as if he didn't really care. "The Irish. Some purple-necked son-of-a-bitch slapped me around."

"Purple mark? Like a birthmark on the side of his face and neck?" Spencer was suddenly more awake.

Charlie spat on the ground again. He didn't even try for the can this time. "I guess I pissed off O'Donnell. I got the message anyway." He spat again.

"O'Donnell?"

"You don't know who O'Donnell is?" Charlie stared up at Spencer. Gordie looked confused.

"The birthmark guy works for Liam O'Donnell?" Spencer knew who he was. He knew too well. *Was the guy who had been at the restaurant the same one who hit Gordie's dealer? What was he doing at the restaurant?* Maybe they were looking into Gordie too. He'd have to give his dad's old contacts a call if anything else happened.

"Hey Chef," Spencer stopped halfway up the back stairs and looked over the edge. Gordie continued, "Gunther called. He said he has the last-of-the-season chanterelles and some pickerel if you want it."

Spencer waved at his sous-chef then continued up the stairs. He was too exhausted emotionally to deal with the restaurant and suppliers. Listening to Maeve, hearing her

153

pain, he could feel it. He wanted to find whoever did this to her. He just didn't know how.

As he opened the door Breeze bound across the room yapping at him. Spencer knelt down to pet her and she let out a growl. Bullet should have been there. He was never first to the door but usually showed up shortly afterward.

The bulldog was on the couch curled up beside Jessie. She scratched his head. The dark eyes of the dog looked at his owner asking, *is this okay?*

"What are you doing here?"

Jessie gave him a half smile. She wore the clothes from downstairs – black slacks and a shirt with the sleeves rolled to the elbows and top buttons open. A sky blue bra with a little lace was on the coffee table beside her bare feet. Whenever Jessie came up after work she wiggled around to take off her bra without taking off her shirt. She also wore no socks or shoes. "I didn't want to go home. I hope you don't mind."

Maeve's voice came out of the stereo speakers. The CD booklet was over Jessie's lap.

"No, I don't mind." He slipped his shoes off, crossed the room and dropped to the couch on the other side of Bullet. "Who's closing?"

"Wylie." She went back to reading the unfolded booklet.

"She," Spencer tapped Maeve's picture, "is afraid to play music again."

"That's too bad. She's good. So your talk with her was…"

"Exhausting."

Jessie flicked her head to get her bangs off her forehead. "She's lucky to have you around."

Bullet yawned. He slowly slid from the couch, walked a few steps, and dropped to the floor as though he could walk no farther. He started breathing heavily, almost snoring, but with his eyes open.

Jessie pulled her feet onto the couch curling them under her legs and turning her body to Spencer. She wiggled herself closer to him.

Spencer's hand automatically went to her foot. His thumb started rubbing the underside. "I don't know about that," he mumbled.

Jessie's hand cupped his face. Her fine lips pressed against his. For a moment he wasn't going to reciprocate then opened his mouth slightly and kissed her back. Her lips and tongue made his heart race and his cock start to get hard.

She pulled him toward her until she was leaning back with him on top. She sucked on his bottom lip. They smiled and laughed and kissed some more. The second he moved one of her legs so he was between hers she curled it up to be over his body.

His lips left hers and traveled to her neck where he hungrily sucked.

"Don't leave marks," she whispered.

Spencer leaned back and tried to get his fingers to work on the buttons of her shirt. His wrong hand fumbled trying to get them through the holes. Jessie pushed his hands away and quickly released all of them.

Spencer opened the shirt to expose her small breasts. He attacked her neck again with his mouth before letting his tongue travel down her skin until it could circle one red areola. He took an entire breast inside his mouth. As he let it out his teeth dragged along the skin then tugged on the erect nipple.

Jessie's fingers went through his hair and pushed him into her so that he took the breast in his mouth again. Her hand slipped inside the front of his pants. *Thank the heavens for chef pants.*

~ * ~

Hours later Spencer's eyes opened. He looked at the shelf of cookbooks along the wall of his bedroom. Jessie's body was curled perfectly into his. Her leg was wrapped over his to fit securely in between. He liked the way it felt to have her warm breath against his neck. Light glinted off her watch. He traced a finger over the words written along the inside of her arm. *Candle within the chaos*; she was his candle. She gave him some light amidst the chaos of the restaurant and his sister and what had gone on in past lives.

"Underneath my cast is a tattoo of a pig and words that say, suck the marrow," he said to Maeve after she had been quiet for a while. "It's a quote from Thoreau about getting everything you can out of life. Well, I took it from The Dead Poets Society. And this one," he showed her his right arm with the quote, God made meat – the devil cooks, written on it within lobster claws, "is from James Joyce."

"What does that mean?"

He shrugged his shoulders. "It reminds me to treat my ingredients with respect. Something I want to include in the rest of my life."

He wanted to treat Jessie with respect. He knew that he loved her. He knew that he should tell her and open himself to her. He ran his thumb along her smooth back trying not to touch her with the cast.

Jessie's lips pressed against his jaw line. "What are you doing?"

He licked his lips. "Thinking."

"About what?"

He could tell her right there. He could admit his feelings and change their whole relationship, make it better. He said, "Nothing. Did you move my chef coat and put it on my chair?" He wasn't sure where that question came from.

She let out a moan and pushed her body closer to his. "What?"

He felt her bare breasts squish against his side. "Nothing. Go back to sleep," and he kissed her.

Chapter Fourteen

"That smells good."

At the woman's voice Spencer looked up from the newspaper.

"Is there enough for me to have a cup?" Dawn placed her jacket over the back of a kitchen chair across the table from him.

He didn't want to be hospitable to her. She rarely was to him. He said, "You know where the cups are," and put his eyes back on the paper. He had been awake when Chrys and Dawn got in then lay there listening to their muffled giggles and voices.

"Thanks."

"It's just coffee."

"Well thank you anyway." She took a mug covered with pictures of cats from hooks under a cupboard. "I should say thanks for everything else too."

Spencer strained to hear if anyone else was up. He didn't want to talk about this with Dawn. It was all stuff that happened months ago. The two of them had been avoiding each other ever since. "We're not supposed to talk about that. We made a deal." He glared at her, but she turned her back to him as she made her coffee. She was in her roller derby gear so glaring at *Mount-Me* didn't have the same effect.

"I know, she's in the shower, so it's okay. She'd be pissed at me if she found out."

"Me too."

"I really like Chrys. I don't want her mad at me."

"That's enough," he snapped.

They both turned toward the hallway as Jessie turned the corner, her bare feet padding on the floor. She looked at Spencer then the tall blond woman. She said, "Morning," as if it were a question. She wore Spencer's white surfer shorts with the black and grey flowers on them and his culinary school sweater.

Spencer smiled at her. How much did she hear? He had too many people in his life that could go away with a moment's indiscretion. That's all it was. One moment's indiscretion months ago.

Dawn said, "Morning," then sipped her coffee.

Jessie sat down beside Spencer, one leg over his lap, and she drank from his cup. She didn't know why he disliked the police officer. He didn't like Dawn and that was good enough for her. She didn't have many dealings with the butch woman anyway, except when Chrys brought her into the restaurant.

Dawn quickly drank as much of the hot liquid as her throat could handle then said, "I should go. I have to go home and change before work. Spencer, make sure Chrys tells you her secret. She promised me she would, but I don't trust her to tell you."

As soon as she was gone Jessie asked, "What was that about?"

"No idea." Spencer got up to make more coffee.

160

"No, I mean when I walked in. Your conversation seemed a little heated." She pulled the paper around.

He knew having *Mount-Me* bringing up whatever happened between them was going to come back and bite him in the ass. He was glad Chrys was not there. He said, "It was nothing. The two of us just don't get along. I don't even know what my sister sees in her."

"See's in who?" Chrys came in with Breeze lying on her forearm. She wore tan shorts and a badly-wrinkled T-shirt. Her hair was wrapped in a pink towel. "Dawn? We have similar interests and she has a wicked tongue," she said matter of factly and grabbed an apple from a bowl on the table. "My room reeks of sex and candy. Well, Twizzlers."

Neither Spencer nor Jessie were surprised at her frankness. Chrys often sat around telling everyone the details about her sex life. It was those she didn't talk about that really mattered to her. Spencer thought about mentioning that it took her until Dawn left before she came out of the back even though he heard the shower stop before Jessie came in. It was before seven in the morning, so Chrys even being out of bed was something new.

"I'm going out to Gunther's. Anyone coming?" Spencer said after a long lull in conversation.

Jessie shook her head. "Not me. Some of us have to work. Are you working today, Chrys?"

Chrys put down her dog and went about the steps of making her chocolate coffee (half hot chocolate and half coffee) and ignored her boss. "Where's Gunther's? That's in Tulloch right? I'll come with you."

"How long are you guys going to be?"

Spencer poured his coffee in a travel mug. "If we leave soon we'll be back before lunch."

Chrys groaned. "I'll go change." She locked her feet on the floor, slipped the towel from her head and started whipping her head back and forth, her whole body going with it. Water sprayed out across the kitchen.

"What the hell, Chrys."

"What?" She spun and marched off to her bathroom. Her Chihuahua quickly chased after her.

Jessie waited until she was gone. "You better have her back by four or you're going to be in trouble. She can't get out of work today."

"We'll be back long before that." Spencer sat down beside her to finish his coffee. "Are you staying here till work?"

"Can I?"

"Of course you can. Can you walk the dogs though?"

She nodded and focused attention on the newspaper. Spencer watched her. As she read the paper her eyes seemed to take on that darkness that he found mysterious. He wanted to learn all of her hidden secrets, but was also afraid to go there. Right then would have been a great time to tell her he loved her.

~ * ~

He looked at his phone the moment it started ringing. The display showed it was his home phone - Jessie. He gave his thanks to Gunther before turning and answering it. "Hey."

"Your mom just called," Her tone of voice instantly changed. "She saw online that the police identified the woman you found. Your mom said she fostered her twenty-three years ago. Enid Bernadine?"

"Shit," he quickly told his sister the news.

162

"I don't remember her."

"No, she was with us just before you arrived. She wasn't with us long." To the phone he said, "Was my Mom okay?"

"Yeah, she was fine. She asked who I was though." Something in her voice said she was hurt by that.

Spencer looked up to the overcast sky. "What did you tell her?"

"Can I drive?" Chrys asked as they walked back to the truck from Gunther's little shop. She carried a cardboard box of bright orange chanterelle mushrooms.

Jessie laughed over the phone, "That I was a friend walking the dogs."

Spencer opened the tailgate of the truck to let Gunther load a plastic tub of pickerel fish in the back. He gave the man another nod. Gunther Buffalo had a quaint little shop beside his house where he sold Native Canadian artwork and foods that he foraged, hunted, or made. Spencer liked meeting the people who worked to bring in the supplies that he used to make good food and pay his bills. The guys back at The Alcrest liked it when Gunther had his wife deliver product. She was a tall, thin woman who never wore a bra, was very flirtatious, and didn't really care what was showing through her clothing. Gordie once talked about a four second nip slip for over a month.

Spencer took a bag of fresh beef jerky from his back pocket and handed his sister the keys. Without saying much more Spencer ended the phone conversation.

As Chrys stomped on the gas spitting up dirt and rock, he decided it wasn't worth complaining about and used his phone to search for Enid.

Most of the kids in the foster system were there because of some sort of abuse. It could be physical, sexual, mental, drugs, or alcohol and could be abuse against them or the parent doing it to themselves creating an unhealthy environment. From what Spencer could remember Enid had the "holy trinity." She was physically and sexually abused by an array of boyfriends her mother (who abused herself with heroin) willingly brought into their lives. She went into foster care when she was around eight, so who knew how long she had had grown men climbing and sweating all over her. She was also the cliché of foster kids going to bad homes that were barely better than her real home before landing with Mrs. Staples. Spencer knew the woman. She was one of the extremely good foster parents. He remembered that when Mrs. S came down with pneumonia all her kids were put into other homes until she got better and that was why Enid came to them. Enid ran away from the Alcrest house twice in her two weeks with them. The first time she made her way back to Mrs. Staples's house. The second time they found her sitting beside the sick woman in the hospital.

Who was Enid? Twenty years ago she had been an angry frightened kid. He didn't remember much about her. He couldn't even recall if they spoke to each other. All he remembered was that she was too old for her young age. *How did she end up in the cistern? Was it coincidence that he and Chrys found her?*

After reading a couple of articles online, it was amazing how fast reporters put things out there, he had the basic gist. Enid went missing seven months ago. According to one interview with her then-boyfriend, the police didn't care. She had a life that made people shrug their shoulders and give a silent prayer that it wasn't them. The accompanying photographs showed a tired woman who looked much older than her age. The boyfriend said she was turning things around, but authorities couldn't get past her history. The only response from the Middleton Police was that they had exhausted all leads at the time. The RCMP spokesperson couldn't comment on an ongoing investigation. The last article said that there would be an intimate service for family and friends of Enid Bernadine, Friday at 9:00 am at St. Michaels Church with cremation to follow at a later date.

Sure, Spencer thought, *when the cops are done probing and prodding her first.* He knew damn well who Enid could have been. If she had stayed with the Alcrest's she could just as easily have been his Chrys.

The web page he was viewing suddenly froze with a line asking to reconnect. The bars showing a connection to a cellular tower were down to nothing.

He sighed and put the phone down on his lap. He had other things to discuss anyway. He looked over at his sister. She was too busy driving to hide herself in her phone this time.

"So." There was no way to go but barrel right through. Spencer had already waited long enough for his sister to bring it up herself. "Dawn says you have a secret to tell me."

"What?" Chrys said pretending not to hear. She checked her mirrors.

"Dawn said you have something to tell me." Spencer popped a piece of jerky in his mouth. The pepper taste filled his tongue.

Chrys stared out the windshield. She thought about pretending that she didn't hear again. It would only prolong things and would piss off her brother. She was good at knowing what buttons to push. This time she knew the buttons had all been pushed and there was nothing left to do. She started with the attack at the hospital and moved on to what she learned from the bank lady and Bird the garbage man, leaving out the mob link. Her brother listened without comment, but that was normally something she would have done, not him. She finished by telling him about the apartment being trashed.

"You're kidding."

"No, I'm serious," Chrys quickly looked at him then back to the road, "the place was completely trashed."

"No I mean about you cleaning it up so well that I didn't notice." Spencer grabbed the arm rest as the truck swerved around a pothole in the gravel road.

"Fuck you, cock sucker."

"That explains my chef jacket being moved though. I'll call Hoyt when we get back and see if he can change the locks." He checked his phone, still very little signal. He wasn't sure how he should feel about all of this. Someone was in their apartment, in his restaurant. Sleeping at night was off the table. "What does he want?"

"I told you, he wants to find the people who lived there. Dawn and I have looked into it a little," she looked over at her brother and saw the way he was looking at her. "Okay, I've been looking into it. I can't find them."

"Jesus, Chrys. This guy could be a killer. Maybe he's not just looking for ..."

"He would have killed me already if he was the killer." Chrys swallowed. "There's more. Do you know who Liam O'Donnell is?" She didn't let her eyes leave the road. She had to stare ahead or she'd lose her nerve. Her brother made a noise so she continued, "Bird told me that the guy in the red truck, um, works for this O'Donnell." She suddenly felt extremely hot and pushed the button to open the window. Her long hair blew around her, some strands tried to escape to the outside.

Spencer fought the seatbelt to turn around and look out the back window. There was nothing behind them but open road and the dust cloud raised by the tires. His eyes slowly lowered to the back seat of the twin cab, it was still folded. The only thing back there was the tent he kept forgetting to remove. He felt fear tickle the back of his neck. The red truck. The guy with the birthmark. The killer who abducted Maeve. *Were they all the same man? Was Chrys just being paranoid? Did this have something to do with the Irish?*

"We have to go to the police," he said and checked his phone. There was enough signal to make a call, but not enough to guarantee it wouldn't cut out.

"I told Dawn."

"The real police."

"She is the real police, Fuck-hole."

He checked his phone again and started scrolling through his contact list. The number he was searching for didn't have a name attached to it. He said, "I mean put it on the record."

"Shit," Chrys pulled the steering wheel to the right. The tires bit where the grass of the ditch met the gravel of the road.

Spencer grabbed the door handle. His casted hand pushed on the seat.

Chrys's hands move quickly pulling the truck back on the road. The rancid stench of skunk spray instantly filled the cab. Her eyes flipped to the mirror as the black-and-white lump with its guts hanging out like a victim of a zombie disappeared in the dust cloud.

"Did you hit that," Spencer's voice went up a few octaves, "with my truck?"

"Someone else already speed bumped it a while ago."

A while ago? They didn't pass any dead skunks on the way to Gunther's. "Where the hell are we going, Chrys?" He knew the answer before he finished the question. There was only one place they both knew out this way.

"The Linson Ferry," she said, still unwilling to look his way. She heard him let out one of his trademark sighs. "What? I want to go back to *The Creepy House* to snoop around. Maybe the police missed something or maybe there's something the family left that will tell me where they went."

"You're a dance instructor and waitress. I'm a chef. What do we know about finding people?"

The truck crested a hill and there below was the Hillsborough River. It was a powerful wash which was responsible for many deaths over the years and destruction of nature and construction every spring thaw. The water had cut out a ravine with tall sides covered in brown grass and trees, their leaves stripped. The road continued down the side of the ravine stopping on the edge of the powerful river then picked up on the other side almost as though the road had sunk below the current. There were bridges further down where the highway crossed the river, but here there was only old-school ferry crossing. It was basically a raft that held up to four vehicles; an operator then pushed a button and cables pulled the ferry across to the other side. It always reminded Spencer of the river raft in the movie The Outlaw Josey Wales which Clint Eastwood quickly dispatched with a rifle shot to the rope connecting it to both sides of the river, sending the bad guys on a Missouri boat ride.

Chrys slowed the truck to a stop behind a small red sign jutting from of the ground at a precarious angle. She waited a moment until the man on the ferry waved for her to continue. Once on the metal raft the operator fastened a cable behind the truck. He went into a little booth on the side, pushed a button, and the engine whirred to action pulling them across the current. Chrys watched the water speed by. She wondered what would happen to them if the cable were to snap. *How far would they go before tipping or hitting shore?*

"I have to find these people, Spence. I'm not letting this ass-muncher beat me." That was all that needed to be said.

Spencer checked his phone every few minutes. At the top of the hill on the far side the signal seemed to get stronger, so he pushed send. It was answered on the fourth ring. "Ah, hello," he cleared his throat, "it's Spencer Alcrest. Yes, I know."

Chrys looked at him out of the corner of her eye.

"I need to talk to you. Can I buy you dinner tonight at The Alcrest? Eight o'clock sounds good." He pressed "end" and put his phone back in his inside pocket. He looked out the side window at what was passing by.

Chrys waited a few minutes before asking, "What the fuck was that?" She had never heard him be so cryptic before. The only time he did anything like that was when he was planning a surprise for her. She hated it.

Trees from the other side of the river and this side of the ravine gave way to farmers' fields.

Spencer looked at her. He wanted to smile and blow it off, but couldn't bring himself to do it. He hadn't told her about the birthmark guy at the restaurant. It was probably nothing anyway. He suddenly felt like he was in way over his head. He quickly dismissed her enquiry.

169

"Who the hell is this?"

A yellow Sunfire sat on the dirt road opposite *The Creepy House's* driveway. Chrys slowed the truck and engaged her turn signal. She held her breath as they got closer. The car pulled onto the road. As the two passed both drivers looked at each other.

"Fucking tourist," she mumbled.

"Who do you think that was?"

"Cheese dick tourist. Moustache freak is probably a death groupie."

"Is it the hanging out by *The Creepy House* that you don't like or the moustache that bugs you?"

Chrys turned the truck into the driveway of *The Creepy House* and a blanket of dread fell over her. It wasn't about what had been inside the house, but concern for the missing family. *What could have been so bad that they left so much of their life behind?* "Moustache," she mumbled.

"So Moustache Man doesn't have a chance?" Spencer didn't want to look at the house. Instead his eyes stayed on the grass that had been trampled by emergency services. There was a small bird bath in there that he did not see the other day.

"No moustache cunt is going to touch either of my lips." She slammed the truck into park.

"How come you can say cunt and men can't?"

Chrys's head slowly rolled to look at her brother. Without any expression she said, "I have one."

Outside the truck the air was comfortable. The trees held back all the wind. Even the paper ghosts hanging from the evergreens didn't move. The kiddie pool and trampoline were still there. Everything reflected a moment in time stopped a year previous. The greatest indication that police had been there was the red tape sealing the front door to the frame. Chrys walked right to the door and smacked a hand against the tape. If they cracked the tape the police would be asking questions.

Spencer walked slowly through the tall grass around the side of the house. His eyes stayed on the pile of garbage at the corner. Something twisted in his stomach and chest. He wanted to leave. There was just a bad feeling in the air. He wondered if it would disappear if someone bought the house and land. Or would the sense of evil always be there like a feeling you just can't put your finger on?

"Spencer."

His heart raced. He stopped in his tracks and turned to his sister. Spencer wasn't sure what his mind expected, but it wasn't his sister looking annoyed.

"We can't go in."

He shrugged his shoulders and continued walking. Pathways had been trampled in the grass where police had searched. The news said they had the police dogs out looking for more bodies.

The shed behind the house had black-and-grey weathered walls which seemed to sag outward. The roof was covered in dead leaves and broken branches from the trees behind it. There was also green moss growing on the corner. Behind the house was a rusted swing set, minus the swings. Garbage had been strewn about.

Spencer looked along the tree line. An overgrown driveway was there somewhere beneath tall grass and low hanging branches. Grass had grown between two packed down tire marks like a Mohawk haircut. Through the trees he saw something red.

He stopped moving. One foot was in mid-air and hung there as if putting it down would send out a signal. Aquamarine eyes stared at the red through the tree trunks.

Was it a truck? It looked too big to be a car. *What was it doing there?* It could have absolutely nothing to do with them. There were lots of red vehicles out there.

He held his breath as he lowered his foot to the ground. His eyes stayed locked on the red behind the trees, moving only to see where his feet were stepping. He knew they shouldn't have been there. If they had gone back after Gunther's, they would have been almost home. His teeth ground together. *Where was Chrys?* He fought the urge to call out to her. He had to find her. The driver of that truck could be a killer. At the very least he worked for the mob.

By the time Spencer side-stepped his way back to the front of the house, keeping his gaze on the red, a cold sweat dripped from his face. His blood pulsed.

Chrys was over on the front deck with her hands cupped around her face trying to see through the window. Broken blinds still hung inside, so she probably couldn't see anything. Maybe bits of the wall that looked like blood.

Spencer called her name in a whisper that came out more like a grunt. She didn't acknowledge him at all. He looked back to the overgrown driveway and the tree line, but couldn't see the red any more.

"Chrys," he called a little louder.

She flicked her eyes in her brother's direction. "They didn't put tape on this door."

"Come here," Spencer looked to her then back to where the red had been.

"What?"

"Come here."

"What?"

Spencer waved his arm, "Get over here."

Chrys didn't like the tense tone of his voice. "What the hell's wrong with you?" She stood there a moment staring

172

at him. An engine started. Spencer was climbing into the driver's side of his truck. *What was he doing? Whose engine started?* Something moved behind the truck, behind the trees. *Something red.*

She exploded off the deck. Her feet hit the soft ground in a full run. Her toe tripped on folded grass making her stumble across the driveway in front of their vehicle.

The red truck turned into the main driveway behind theirs as she opened the passenger door.

Spencer rammed his foot against the gas pedal. The tires spit up rocks. He saw the other driver's eyes in his mirror.

The truck bounced over grass and whatever was hidden underneath. It rocked side to side through ruts. The red truck followed.

Spencer drove up the small back driveway and onto the road. His good hand turned the steering wheel with the palm open. The back end of the truck fishtailed side to side. His casted hand hit the wheel. Pain shot up to his shoulder.

Chrys's knuckles were white on the door handle. She turned in her seat. "He's chasing us."

"I know," Spencer grit his teeth. In the mirror the red truck was barely visible through the dust cloud. It was like a phantom chasing them.

The two trucks sped down the dirt road. The dust streamed behind them.

"Put your seatbelt on." Spencer didn't have his on either, but his safety was nothing. His temples pulsed with blood and pain. *What the hell was happening?* At the end of the road he made the choice in the last second. Left. The front tires desperately gripped the road as the back tires drifted across toward the ditch. The chef's foot never left the gas pedal.

In seconds the sides of the road were lined with trees. Spencer cut corners where he could, saying a little prayer to the road gods that no one would be there. They came over the top of the hill. For a moment the tires seemed to leave the earth. Spencer held his breath. Chrys let out a murmur of fear and excitement. The red truck had fallen back a bit. *Was the driver unsure on the windy roads?*

"Is he still back there?" Chrys's voice shook.

Spencer stared at the ferry. It was still on their side of the river. A white sign said slow to 10km. His eyes flicked to the speedometer – 85 km/hr. His eyes flicked to the mirror. All he saw was his dust cloud.

"Slow down, slow down," Chrys held herself back in her seat with her arm locked, hand on the dashboard. Her eyes were wide. She saw the river and the ferry coming toward them. "Slow down." She felt something swell in her throat. She wanted to push back, as if that would help. The man on the ferry waved both arms wildly. Chrys wanted to yell at him to get out of the way. "Slow the fuck down, God damn it!"

Spencer hit the break with his foot. The wheels skidded through the loose earth. The rear of the truck slid to one side. Spencer compensated quickly. He held his breath. In his mind he visualized the truck speeding right across the ferry, breaking through the cable barrier and flying into the river.

The front wheels bounced up onto the ferry. The tires caught traction. The truck suddenly stopped.

The ferry driver threw his hands in the air yelling as he did. Spencer knew the words he was using. His sister used them all the time.

The two Alcrests looked at each other. Both had beads of sweat running down their faces. They started breathing again as though their brains just remembered how. In one move they turned to look out the back window. The dust they had raised was moving down the ravine as the wind took it and it dissipated into nothing. There was no red truck. He had stopped or turned or maybe there never was one. Maybe it was just some random guy in a red truck. Maybe it was a serial killer. Spencer knew he'd have a couple of answers in a few hours. That or he'd be dead.

Chapter Fifteen

"Where are we going?"

Spencer stared out the windshield at the road ahead. It had taken a good twenty minutes for his body to calm down. He had parked on the other side of the river where they had a view of the hill they'd just descended. There was nothing red there. Spencer wondered if it was like the TV show *Mantracker* and the psycho was hidden in the tree line watching them. He brought the truck to a stop at a red sign. Cars zipped by on the highway. He said, "I have to go see Mrs. Staples."

"Who? Now?" Chrys shifted in her seat. "Why?"

"Mom asked if we could check on her," he lied.

"And we have to do it now?"

"I do." He sounded as serious as he ever had. "I want to find out what happened to Enid. You've been afraid for days; I've been looking over my shoulder; Maeve's terrified. I want it to stop."

"We're not the police, Spence. You're not fucking, fucking Dick Tracy."

His phone started ringing and he ignored it. "Says the one who's been trying to find the missing family." His phone stopped ringing.

Chrys's started ringing. She looked at the number, sighed, and pushed the button to silence the phone. "You don't think this guy killed the family do you?"

"Who was that?"

She knew he was avoiding her question. "Work. Probably Jessie trying to find you. We were supposed to be back by now." She turned and watched the countryside go by. Forest with occasional houses turned to farmers' fields to houses lining the highway as they got closer to the city. She looked at the big houses with their multi-car garages and manicured lawns and wondered what those people's lives were like. *Did they have someone chasing them?*

The foster parents that seemed to work, according to Momma Alcrest, were the ones that leaned on other foster parents for help and support. She helped develop a support group for them that still had meetings and provided assistance. Once a year they even met at The Alcrest for a lunch put on by the Alcrest family. It had changed to a barbeque in the park, but the tradition remained. Spencer's mother didn't foster any more (hadn't since before his father died.) But he still felt the responsibility to give a hand to foster families and kids.

When he was younger and Mom was needed at the restaurant Spencer and the foster kids (they always seemed to have two) went to Mrs. Staples for a few hours. She had four or five kids at a time. Nights at her place meant board games, popcorn, and hot chocolate with mini-marshmallows.

As soon as they were back in the city he followed along the river until he got to the park. Across the street was a two-story brown house with a second-floor balcony wrapping around two sides. A rusted mini-van was parked in the slanted driveway. A kid's bike leaned against a leafless hedge. Stickers of ghosts and bats were stuck to the large bay window.

"You don't have to come in," Spencer said as he climbed out of the truck.

"I'll come." She really didn't want to stay outside by herself.

It wasn't Mrs. Staples who answered on the second ring of the doorbell. A teenage girl with dark hair leaned against the door. She cocked her head to the side and let out a, "Yeah?"

"Is Mrs. Staples in?"

"Yeah."

"May we see her?"

The girl groaned, spun around, and walked away leaving the door open. There were voices in the back room before someone came out. This new person was much older. The skin under her eyes seemed to sag. Mrs. Staples looked up at them and smiled. She looked very tired.

"Is that Spencer Alcrest? And Chrysanthemum, oh, you're so lovely." She rubbed Spencer's arm and reached up and touched Chrys's cheek with her fingers. Her eyes were red. She lurched forward, her hand grasped Spencer's arm, and tears started to fall.

Ten minutes later they sat at a dining table. Faye Staples sipped a glass of water. The teenaged girl was in the attached living room watching a television show about pet emergencies. Three other children came and went. On two walls of the dining room hung dozens of framed photos of children. Chrys lost count around fifty.

"I'm guessing you've been told Enid was found," Spencer said when he thought Mrs. Staples was ready.

She nodded and took another sip of water. "I didn't even know she was missing for a few weeks." She stared deep into her water as if there might be an answer there. "I've lost touch with most of the kids I've mothered over the years. Some were here for a couple days or weeks. Enid stayed here a couple years and then came back for two months after she'd gone home for a few years." Mrs. Staples pushed up from her chair with a groan. She took down a picture near the first row and one further through the wall of faces. Both showed the same girl at different stages. The first was a younger girl who looked angry, but still innocent. The second was a pissed off teenager with dark make-up and old eyes. She looked very much like the young woman watching television.

Chrys said, "She looks, um ..."

"She had a rough life." Mrs. Staples caressed the wood frame around the older girl's photo. "She wasn't lucky like you were, Chrys."

Chrys knew she was lucky. When her mother disappeared the Alcrests took her in and gave her a great life. She had talked to other foster kids and knew they had gone in the system for things she couldn't, or didn't want to, imagine.

"When was the last time you talked to her?" Spencer looked at the picture of the younger Enid that he could barely remember.

"A year ago. I ran into her at *Wal-Mart*. She had a boyfriend who she said treated her right. She was finishing a course at the college. She had high hopes. Then she went missing and then this." The tears started to streak down her face again. "What do you think she went through for seven months? You found her, right? What was she like? What happened to her?"

Spencer's eyes dropped. He remembered the hand grabbing him as he hung offer the trap-door edge of the cistern. He recalled falling and his face going into the wet mush that was Enid's body. He couldn't tell this woman about that. He knew some of what had happened to her from what Maeve told him. She was tortured and made a fun plaything for this guy's sick games. He couldn't tell Mrs. Staples that. He couldn't say anything.

Chrys looked at her brother. Her hand touched his arm and to Mrs. Staples she said, "Remember her the last time you saw her."

Mrs. Staples's hand covered her face as her body lurched in sobs. She knew what Chrys's words meant. The girl had been horribly mistreated life through most of her life and it ended all the same way.

~ * ~

"Where the hell have you been?" Jessie blared out as she stormed from the front to the dish pit. The two Alcrests had only walked through the back door thirty seconds earlier. "You said you'd be back before lunch. Lunch is almost over. Don't you answer your phone calls? Check your messages?"

Spencer didn't like the way her eyes burned at him. He said, "There wasn't much service out there and then my phone died. Relax already." He reached out.

She slapped his hand away. "Don't tell me to relax." Jessie turned and stared at the sister.

"I didn't take mine." Chrys's arms folded over her chest.

Jessie turned her face to the wall. "Bullshit," slipped through her lips.

"And … and we got lost," Chrys said defensively, but she didn't believe the sound of her own voice.

Jessie's eyes snapped to Spencer. "How could you get lost? You go to Gunther's all the time."

Spencer didn't say anything. He wasn't even too sure what was going on. He noticed Brian sheepishly looking over his shoulder. Okay, they were a couple of hours late, but was that it? "We took a detour." Hell, it was his damn restaurant. "What's going on?" He leaned against the metal prep table. Behind him was the bin of pickerel and the box of chanterelles. Dee walked in from the dining room, dropped a handful of dirty plates next to the dishwasher and left with only a glance in the boss's direction.

It was almost a full minute before Jessie put her hands on her hips and said, "Besides one cook not showing up, at all, and another cutting the end of his finger off? Quite a bit." She stared at Spencer.

"Who cut their finger off?" He thought about Maeve and the pruning shears.

"Ranger," Brian said as he turned from the sink. Water splashed from the bowl he was holding onto his shoes and the floor. "Blood everywhere." He saw Jessie staring at him, dropped his head, and returned to the dirty dishes.

She pushed both sleeves up her arms until the cuffs were over her elbows. "Ranger cut his fingertip dicing tomatoes. Sue took him to the hospital, so I'm short a server too."

"Liz didn't show?"

She shook her head. "She didn't even call."

"Shit." Spencer hated firing people, but sometimes it had to be done. Yes, she needed the job, but he needed a cook who was going to show up. And he just gave her the damn lecture about the whole mess.

"Um," Chrys slinked between the two. "I'll go upstairs and change. I'll be in the restaurant in ten." She looked at one, then the other, said, "I'll be right back," and went through the door to the stairs.

As soon as the door closed Jessie stepped closer to Spencer. She smelled like vanilla. "Did you go to the hospital?" Her hazel eyes stared up at him. Her voice was completely different with this question. There was some sadness there, and jealousy?

"No," Spencer looked at his wristwatch. He started walking out to the restaurant knowing she would walk with him. "I need a table tonight at eight o'clock. A corner one would be best. Set it for four people, I guess."

"Under what name?" Her tone of voice said their conversation wasn't over.

"Mine." He stopped at the opening into the kitchen and watched Gordie plate a burger and fries before saying, "I leave for one morning and you get rid of all the cooks?"

"Not my fault, man." Gordie quickly scraped the char broiler grill with a wire brush.

"Why don't you tell Spence how it happened." Jessie leaned against the small barrier wall beside Spencer. Her voice sounded calmer. She smiled at a customer and pointed the direction to the washroom.

Spencer thought the sudden change in her demeanour was just because they were out front.

Gordie looked down at the floor before looking back up at his chef. There was a giant grin inside his beard. "Okay, Ranger was dicing tomatoes with his tongue sticking out, you know, and I yelled out about a world class MILF walking by. Ranger looked up, smiled, and screamed all at the same time."

"A MILF?"

"You know, a Mother I'd Like to Fuck."

"I know what a MILF is. And you let him go to the hospital when you were already down a cook?"

"I had to. He was bleeding like a stuck pig. He went all pale and shit."

In restaurants there were two kinds of cooks. There were those who wrapped cuts in paper towel and duct tape, put on a glove, and got back on the line. Then there were others who left work to get medical attention. When Spencer burned his arm (the hot oil burns under his tattoo) he took some pain meds and kept a bottle of cooling bacterial spray on the line as he cooked. Gordie once cut off the tip of his little finger, which he cauterized by pushing the bloody tip into a cup of salt. It didn't work and just gave him a lot more pain. Whenever Ranger got back he was going to be tortured.

Spencer looked at the reservations book. There weren't many on the list, but it was Writer Wednesday, so there would be a few. His *guests* didn't always like crowds.

Jessie ran her hand down Spencer's arm. "She called for you."

"Who?"

"Maeve. She asked if you were going to come see her. Are you?"

He flashed her a smile, "I don't know. You're welcome to come with me if I do. This Dr. Ken Stewart table at seven, give him fifty percent off." He gave her a nod. He wanted to touch her, but they had their rules. *He had his rules.* He left her and crossed to the kitchen. Gordie was checking things in the Lowboy fridge. "Let's add chanterelle cream sauce to the chicken. Do you want to do a pan fried pickerel tonight?"

As Gordie stood he let out an old man's moan. "You getting me another cook? Jess helped at lunch, but I'm going to be screwed if we get busy tonight."

Spencer took a look around the room. There wasn't much going on now, but that could change at any moment. He wiggled the fingers sticking out the end of his cast. "I'll be here." Chrys walked past them dressed in black, ready to start work. "I have someone coming at eight though, so I'll need to talk to them. I'll see if I can get a dishwasher to come help. Let me make some calls."

Spencer closed the door to his office cutting out the sounds of the dish pit. His chef coat hung on its hook, as it should be. The more he thought about the morning's events, the more he wondered if the red truck chasing them was more hysteria than reality. It could have been some kid having fun or even some form of rural neighborhood watch. *Why else would the driver stop?* Unless it was like Chrys said and he just wanted to frighten them. The whole thing could just have been overactive imaginations. The cistern thing could have made his sister get more creative with her thoughts.

The first number he dialed was Liz's cell phone. There was no answer. He left a message telling her to give him a call. He knew he wouldn't be able to get in touch with any of the night dishwashers because they were all high school students and there were still almost two hours before they were finished classes. It was a safe bet that they all had mobile phones or iPods set to Facebook, so they would get his message right away, but he hoped they had more respect for school than that. He shook his head at the thought. Next he called Hoyt to inquire if he could change the apartment locks. He said he was booked for the rest of the day but could do it first thing in the morning. Spencer called a couple other chefs to find out if they knew of any cooks looking for work. Maybe it was wrong to be looking for a replacement before hearing from Liz, however the weekend was coming. He needed a full roster for those busy days and it was time to admit to himself that the pain in his wrist was becoming too much for him to be much help.

Finally, Spencer dialed the number for the hospital. He was bounced around three times before he heard Maeve's voice. She sounded somewhat groggy.

"Hey, it's Spencer. What are you up to?"

She let out a moan before answering, "Catching up on the soaps."

"Lots of time for that I guess, eh? What about your guitar?" Spencer's eyes stayed locked on the door. *If Jessie entered would he quickly end the conversation or lie to her about who he was talking with?*

Another moan, that sounded more like a groan, came through the phone. She said, "I've tried playing a little. My hands don't feel right though. My finger ..." there was a hitch in her words, like something inside her was trying to fight it.

Spencer wondered if she would ever return to the way she was. He wanted to talk to the woman on the CD cover. That woman, he would have liked to have known.

"They found out who the other woman was."

Spencer blinked. He had been staring across his office daydreaming of the blond woman from the front cover of the CD with only the thin white strap over her tanned shoulder. Most of the images disappeared instantly from his mind, though he felt the creature stirring between his thighs.

Maeve continued, "The police came and asked me about her. I knew her first name, but I never heard her full name before and even the pictures they showed me didn't look like her. The woman in the, in that room …" she had to clear something from her throat. "They said she was missing seven months. Do you think he would have kept me that long?"

"I don't know," was all he could say.

"I don't either," was what Spencer barely heard over the phone. Enid survived seven months and came out looking like a different woman, food for the next. She had already been through a tough life and was a survivor. Maybe what Maeve was saying was that she wouldn't have lasted that long.

They sat there with nothing but their breaths going back and forth over the phone line. He remembered long conversations like that with girls when he was a teenager. Both he and the girl were too afraid to say anything and didn't want to end the call. This was one of those times. Though in high school, the calls usually got interrupted by his sister picking up the other line.

"Well, I have to work in the kitchen tonight so I should …"

"Can you come see me?" Maeve sounded hopeful.

Spencer looked at his chef jacket and the door. "I can't. Some of our cooks are …" the word "missing" would have freaked her out, "sick, so I'm cooking cast and all. I'll try to come tomorrow." That didn't sound right. It sounded like it was a burden. He said, "I will. I'll come tomorrow."

Maeve was quiet for a few breaths then asked, "What about later tonight then? I can't sleep anyway."

~ * ~

"Two pickerel, two fries."

When Spencer left his office he was already in his chef coat and went right into the kitchen avoiding everyone else. Chrys watched him come out and awkwardly start helping to prep food while avoiding eye contact. He focused on his work. Whenever someone asked him a question he looked up, gave them a quick answer, and went back to work.

Maybe he was mad at her for taking him to *The Creepy House* and for all the secrets she kept from him. Maybe he knew this Enid better than he said.

Whatever, was her only thought. Her foster brother liked to keep things inside until it had no place to go. She kept things secret. He kept things inside, there was a difference.

"Do you need anything, Spencer?" Chrys tapped her thumb ring on the hot tile under the heat lamps.

He looked up at her for a second then looked around the room. They weren't that busy yet; only about six tables had customers. He said, "Can you make sure Dr. Ken is okay?" His head went back down.

Chrys let out a sigh and spun on her heel. Her boots clicked on the floor. "Dr. Ken, how are you?" She flashed her white teeth.

Kenneth Stewart flashed his own. "I'm ah," he looked at the woman sitting across the table from him, "good, really good. How are you doing after all this," his hand made circles in the air, "cistern craziness?"

She shrugged. "I'm trying to forget about it."

"You're stronger than me," the woman said.

Chrys had to admit the two made a lovely couple. He was the rugged dark-haired doctor with chiseled features and she was the tall "girl next door" with a wave of dark hair falling over her shoulders. He wore a casual suit and tie. She was in a slinky red dress with a scooped neck and a scarf around her neck. "If there's anything you need, please just ask."

"I noticed the menu's different from the last time I was here."

Chrys cocked her head to the side. "Some of our cooks are away sick and Spencer has his cast, so they had to limit things. Plus he likes to change things up depending on what our local suppliers have available." It was their assigned speech whenever anyone asked about the menu.

"I see they're short-handed," the scent of his cologne was tasty. His companion sipped at her wine leaving a red lipstick mark on the rim of the glass.

"Will you excuse me?" Chrys turned away from them and rolled her eyes. Back at her spot on the restaurant side of the pass she said, "There, you fucking happy?"

Spencer looked up. For just a moment his hands stopped mid-action.

Jessie walked around Chrys to the hand-washing sink. "Who do you want serving your table?" She turned on the water.

Chrys had forgotten about her brother's mysterious call. *Did Jessie know who was coming?*

Dropping his gaze from his sister he went back to his sauté pans; he had three pickerel cooking. "I need Chrys to sit with us, so let Hanni do it."

"Seriously?" Jessie didn't watch where the water was splashing. "We're getting busy and we're going to lose another cook and server?"

"This has to be done." Spencer's hands moved with the pans. His cast hit a handle and spun the pan around.

"You're the owner," Jessie glared at him. Her eyes had taken on that dark shadow they revealed on when she was moody.

"Ranger," Gordie was as loud as always.

Ranger walked through the door. He shoved both hands in his jacket pockets and shrugged his shoulders, "Yeah?"

"What did they do? Cut off your dick and attach it to your hand?" Gordie gave his tongs a double click like Spanish castanets. "Or was that too small to replace your little finger?"

The young guy's cheeks flushed red. His eyes dropped. "I got three stitches."

"That's it?" Gordie let out a laugh. He looked from the chef to the fry cook. "What took you so long?"

Ranger looked up at the big man. He looked to Spencer, then Chrys, before his eyes fell. "Sue had to go home after to shower." He looked up quickly. "What?"

Hanni tapped Chrys's shoulder. "Table six wants you."

"No shit," Gordie grabbed Spencer's chef jacket and shook him back and forth. "Do you believe this guy? What did you do?"

"What?" A sheepish smile formed on Ranger's lips. His cheeks almost glowed.

"You working?" Even Spencer was smiling.

"What? Yeah," Ranger replied.

Chrys missed whatever else was said between the Three Stooges as she went to visit her table.

Spencer never told her who he called after leaving *The Creepy House* and being involved in a car chase. She asked him on the way back to the city; however, he didn't respond. After a few long minutes of silence he said, "Don't worry about it," and that was it. It wasn't it for her.

190

Chrys gave Dr. Ken her brightest smile. Thanks to acting classes and modeling she could fake just about anything. "Are we ready to order?" Two minutes later she slipped the order slip across the pass, "Order in."

Her brother was back to not smiling and keeping his eyes on his work with occasional glances at the door. Ranger came down the hallway stopping to ask Jessie to help with the buttons on his coat. The finger of his left hand was wrapped in gauze.

Spencer looked up.

Chrys turned as the front door to the restaurant opened. Two men stepped in from outside and the feeling in the air changed. The first was dressed very casually. His slacks had been pressed and his turquois shirt was open at the collar, a little chest hair showed through. His hair was longer on top, flowing to his jaw line, and was the perfect mixture of salt and pepper. His trimmed goatee was the same. He had soft eyes and a face that looked warm. The man behind him looked colder. He wore a dark suit and his eyes darted around the room.

As Chrys's eyes jumped to her brother she saw him nod in familiarity. He looked to Jessie.

No time like the present. Chrys quickly crossed to the men. "Hi, you must be Spencer's guests."

The first man looked at her. His eyes were kind with crow's feet in the corners. "And you must be Chrysanthemum."

Her smile dropped. *Who was he? How did he know who she was?* She never used her full first name.

"I haven't seen you since you were little. You're gorgeous." As he nodded his hair flowed back and forth along the sides of his face. A hand went up and pushed his hair straight back. Chrys noticed the gold ring. When the hand came back down the black and silver hair fell back into place.

"Thank you so much. I didn't know we ... I, um ... Spencer's cooking right now, so I'll take you to your table." As she turned around she looked at her brother.

He glared back at her. His head nodded upward, "I'll be over there as soon as I can." He slapped the pass and turned back to the stove.

Chrys led the way through the tables to the far corner. She could feel eyes on her. She wasn't sure if they were from the men behind her or others in the restaurant. She noticed Hanni watching as she dealt with another customer. Chrys raised an eyebrow and shot her a look that she hoped said, *fuck you*, before returning to her happy demeanour.

"Here's your table, gentlemen. I'm sure Spencer will be with you soon."

"Thank you, Chrysanthemum." There was a faint accent when he said her name.

She gave him another smile. Her face was starting to hurt. "Please call me Chrys. I never use the long one. And I didn't get your name."

He looked her right in the eyes. "It's Liam."
What?

She had to control every emotion exploding inside her. Chrys said, "It's nice to meet you," and turned away. *Holy hell, what the fuck was going on? Liam O'Donnell? What the hell was Liam O'Donnell doing there? How did Spencer get in touch with him? How did Spencer know him?* Her body tingled from the inside out. She had to go somewhere. *How was this happening?* Her eyes stayed on the floor as she walked brusquely across the restaurant. She looked up at her brother in the kitchen. *Who was he?*

"Chrys, order up." Spencer stared at her over the pass. The plates for Dr. Ken sat beneath the heat lamps.

Her hands hit the tile beside them. "Do you know who that is?"

Spencer looked right through her. "Your food's here."

Chrys leaned over the pass. The heat of the lamp warmed her cheek. "Spencer, I think you have a problem with your brain missing." She checked behind her to make sure no one was there. "This guy could be a serial killer."

Spencer stared at her with a stern expression. "He's no serial killer."

"He has someone trying to kill us."

"Chrys." Spencer leaned over the butcher block until he felt the heat lamps against his forehead. "If he wanted us dead, we'd be dead. Take your food."

Her face burned, but not from the lamps. She wanted to ask him how he knew the Irish mobster, but everything about the moment made her feel wrong. It was all so crazy.

~ * ~

It took Spencer twenty minutes before he could step away from the kitchen. His hands shook so much that plates went out sloppy. His stomach twisted. Some news reports called Liam O'Donnell a modern day Al Capone. Others called him a great and generous man. He only met the man a couple of times and knew very little about what his father and the Irishman discussed. He knew they spoke a few times, but his father was very secretive and Spencer never thought to ask his mother. He wasn't even sure if she knew anything.

"Do you have free time to join us, Spencer?" Liam asked as the chef reached the table.

Spencer nodded. "I asked Chrys to sit with us, too. This has to do with her as well."

Liam sipped from his tumbler of whiskey. "It seems I'm the only one in the dark. We haven't spoken since your father's funeral and now you call me out of the blue." The eyes that looked up at Spencer were a solid green.

He looked over his shoulder as he heard his sister's boots on the floor. The two of them sat across from the two men. Spencer nodded at the bigger man.

The man in the suit glared across at them, searched the room with his eyes, and brought his gaze back onto them. There was a bulge under his jacket. Neither of the Alcrests wanted to see what it was.

"So," Liam took another sip of the brown liquid, "why am I here?"

"Um …" Spencer wasn't sure how to start.

"Do you have someone following me?" Chrys blurted out. Her forehead glistened with perspiration.

"Excuse me?"

Spencer put his casted hand on his sister's arm. He said, "I'm sure you heard about the two women found in a house out in Hillsborough." As he said that the Irishman sat back in his chair. "We found them and since then someone in a red truck has been following Chrys. He trashed our apartment."

"And he fucking attacked me."

Spencer squeezed her arm.

At that Liam sucked in his bottom lip and bit down. You could see the muscles of his jaw tighten. He let out a breath. "And how do you know this has something to do with me?" He took his glass in hand, but did not drink.

"Chrys was told that this man was looking for the Linques for you."

"Who is the man who attacked you?" He stared at Chrys. His brow was furrowed.

She tried to keep her eyes on his. "I …" they dropped, "I didn't see him."

"He has a birthmark." Spencer stared straight at him. His father once told him never to give the gangster an inch. "It goes from the side of his face down his neck. He drives a red truck. Who is he?"

Liam put his glass down beside his bowl of mussels. He looked at his bigger companion.

For the first time the bodyguard spoke, "Gaylen."

Liam sat back in his chair. "I hire Gaylen from time to time to find things and get them back."

"Like people who owe you money?" Chrys blurted out.

Liam smiled. The seriousness melted from his features. "Sometimes. My associate here, Mr. McGregor, will give Gaylen a call and tell him to leave the two of you alone." The two men nodded to each other and the bigger one immediately rose. As he headed for the front door he took a cell phone from his pocket. Nothing was said again until he walked back and gave another nod.

"Anything else?" Liam O'Donnell's expression was; identical to the one you saw smiling from the newspaper under headlines about charitable donations.

Spencer wasn't sure he should ask what he really wanted to know, but if he didn't he couldn't go further. "Any chance this Gaylen hurt those women? Maybe he got a little rough."

"I can make some inquires, but I really don't think that's his style. He likes intimidation. The things that have been done to you, I can see him doing." He looked at Chrys with sad eyes. This man told stories with his eyes. "I apologize

195

for anything done to you. If you ever need anything, please ask."

For a moment Chrys looked like she as going to ask something. She looked down at her hands. When she looked up again her face was calmer. She said, "I should get back to my tables." All three men watched her get up from the chair and walk across the room, then turn toward the back.

"How is she doing?"

Spencer turned back to find Liam staring at him intently. He wondered in what sense he meant. "She's fine. This guy has her scared, but otherwise she's fine."

Liam used the shell of one mussel to pluck the meat out of another.

Spencer looked over at the bar and kitchen. Hanni and Wylie talked over the varnished wood bar. Both took turns looking at the corner table. The kitchen boys were busy doing their thing, probably trying desperately not to look. Customers looked over at the three men then leaned across their tables and spoke quickly. Spencer knew it was probably more in his head. People knew the name Liam O'Donnell, but not everyone knew the face.

"What about her family?" Liam asked.

"What?"

"Does Chrysanthemum have questions about where she came from?"

Why would this man be mentioning where Chrys came from? What did he know about it? Spencer turned and just at that moment his sister walked out from the back with a smile on her face. He said, "I don't know. Why are you asking?"

Liam shrugged his shoulders. "Something for another day perhaps. Thank you for the appetizers." As he got to

196

his feet his bodyguard rose in unison. "Mr. McGregor will find out if Gaylen had anything to do with the women and will be in touch. You can call me about anything, Spencer. Rene, your father, did, so I offer you the same courtesy." The two of them walked away.

Spencer had more questions than when they first sat down: *What did the Irish mobster have to do with where Chrys came from? Why and how often did his father ever call him? What sort of relationship did they have? If birthmark guy wasn't the killer, then who was?* So many questions that would have to wait to be answered. For a few minutes he sat at the table thinking about the questions and the possible answers. He could ask his mother, though he believed there was a lot his father didn't tell her.

The kitchen had just a few orders, nothing Gordie and Ranger couldn't handle. Spencer walked around scanning what was going on in the restaurant. He stood in the frame room and listened to one of the writers read her work. He tried his best to avoid Jessie. Chrys did her best to avoid him.

He went to the veterinarian's table and asked, "How was everything?"

"Excellent." Dr. Ken smiled up at him. His black hair glistened in the dim light. "That man you were with, was that …"

Spencer rolled his eyes and interrupted, "Yeah."

"Interesting."

"Not really. It was all a misunderstanding." He gave a little nod to the woman at the table. Perfectly sculpted eyebrows made her look like she had something to say.

Dr. Ken let out a little laugh which really sounded fake. He said, "I hate those misunderstandings. Everything gets blown out of proportion." He paused for a moment staring up at Spencer the entire time. "This was a fabulous meal," he went on. "The cheesecake was a great finisher."

For some reason Spencer wished the woman would speak. She looked different wearing an elegant dress and make-up, much different than when he had seen her at the animal clinic wearing a lab coat. "I'm glad you liked it. I don't know if you've been told, but I'm going to take fifty percent off your bill tonight."

"You don't have to."

"You helped Bullet, so ..."

"Well thank you so much. How is Bullet?"

"Good, the hives are gone. I'm about to go upstairs and check on him."

"You live upstairs?" This was from the woman. Her voice was soft, almost musical.

Spencer tripped over his tongue. "Yeah, my sister and ..."

"Any idea what's happening with that woman you found?" Dr. Ken interrupted.

"She's doing better. She can't remember anything. That's a good thing, I guess." He smiled. His dimples appeared. "I should go check on Bullet. Have a good night."

~ * ~

Spencer looked up at the sounds of the door opening and his sister's voice. After talking to the doctor he slipped upstairs, changed into shorts and a Middleton Mad Hatters' sweater (the cities professional soccer team) and sat on the couch with the dogs watching whatever he could find on *Netflix*. He decided to watch the show *Firefly* again. He felt spent. His arm ached and his head seemed to swim with a million thoughts and questions. He absently rubbed Breeze's ear with one hand and scratched between Bullet's wrinkles with the other.

"Jessie's asking about you. She wants to know if you're okay."

Breeze flew from the couch to her owner's feet. Chrys squatted and rubbed the Chihuahua's head.

"I'm tired. It's been a long day." *Did he dare tell her?*

"Well," she crossed the room and dropped to the other corner of the couch with a bounce, "Your fucking girlfriend …"

"She's not my girlfriend."

"- is curious if you went to see Maeve. I have to head back down, so what should I tell her?"

"That I'm asleep," he said as he leaned back and closed his eyes. He heard his sister emit one of her famous sighs and leave. Her heels clicked on the floor then faded away down the stairs. Telling Chrys about what an Irish mobster said would help with nothing. It was something that could wait for another day, as he had said. At least he didn't have to worry about the birthmark guy. Things were good.

Chapter Sixteen

Spencer's eyes opened.

What was wrong? Something was wrong? A feeling of dread crept up inside. *Was it just a dream?*

He was still on the couch stretched out with Bullet pressing against the back of his knees. The bulldog snorted at the feeling of movement. It was dark. The television had been turned off and a blanket placed over him. He smelled something sweet in the air. The scent must have come from downstairs, so it was morning already. Sandra was making something tasty for the morning visitors.

It was just a dream. He could go back to sleep.

A scream speared through the floor.

In one move Spencer threw off the blanket and was on his feet. Bullet barked.

Spencer pushed open the door to the stairs, it wasn't locked. The smell was instantly stronger. It was different than baked goods, sweeter. His bare feet moved from step to step.

Another scream echoed up the stairwell.

His foot slipped. The cast hit the railing sending shockwaves of pain up his arm. He missed the last few stairs and slid down. His body hit the bottom door, hand fumbling with the handle. That door wasn't locked either. He had to talk to his closing staff about that.

The scream started again.

Spencer's feet padded on the cold floor. The air was hot. He held his breath. He didn't want to continue. The sweet smell was stronger. It was like the richest of meats. He could almost taste it.

Few lights were on in the restaurant. Sandra was there backing away from the far opening to the kitchen. Her backside pushed chairs and tables out of the way. They scratched on the floor. The scream rolled out of her opened mouth.

"Sandra. Sandra."

She looked at her boss. Her mouth closed tight, cutting off the yell.

Spencer looked down the kitchen and saw nothing out of place. Muffin trays were on the butcher block. Everything was still clean. "What's happened?"

Sandra's skin was as white as her hair. She looked like she was ready to either fall or run and just hadn't made up her mind yet. "The fans and ovens were still on," she started in a monotone voice. "I thought Gordie forgot again." She stared up at Spencer. Her eyes had glassed over. "I could smell something burning. It wouldn't be the first time things were spilled in the oven." Her voice was flat and dry, as if she was struggling to get out every word. She said, "I was running late, so I wanted to mix the muffin batter first. I didn't know." Sandra sunk down into a chair. The legs teetered for a moment.

Spencer looked down the kitchen line. Everything was clean and in its place. On the floor down the line was a long, black, rubber, honey-combed mat. He stepped across it. Nothing seemed wrong. It was as though the kitchen crew cleaned up and left with the oven still burning; it happens. Then the front-of-house closing crew missed it; that's possible. The only things that shouldn't have been on the butcher block were the muffin trays. The sweet charred smell was strong. *Was Gordie making pulled pork?* That would explain the oven and exhaust fans being on and the sweet meat smell. He could have seasoned the pork, put it in a covered pan, and put it in the oven with too little liquid. All the liquid dried up and it burned. *But they didn't have any pork*.

His fingers curled around the oven handle. It was like a band aid that had to be pulled off fast. He quickly opened the oven door. Smoke curled up over the stove top. Heat flashed on his face. This was no pulled pork low heat oven. The large thing in there was charred dark. It crackled like bubbling pork fat. There was burnt fabric. There was skin. An arm. Fingers.

"Fuck." The door slammed shut. He stumbled back. The corner of the butcher block dug deep into his buttock. His cast hit the tray of muffin tins. A finger went in the batter. His heart raced. *That was a body.* There was nothing on the shoulders. There was a body in the oven with no head.

Chrys.

Spencer took off running. Sandra called out his name. *Why hadn't the door to the stairs been locked? Because there was no need to be afraid?* He took the stairs two at a time. His heart pounded in his chest. His pulse raced.

What if she was in the oven?

He crossed the living room, jumping over the arm of the couch. His hand grasped her door handle. *What if she wasn't there? What was he going to do if she was dead?*

What would he tell his mother? He realized he wasn't breathing. Spencer pushed his sister's bedroom door open.

She had thrown off the blankets and her bare ass shone up at him. She barely moaned the first time he called her name.

"Chrys," he called again. She started to move. Suddenly Spencer was very aware his sister was naked. He dropped his eyes and spun around. His forehead bounced off the door.

"What?" her voice was groggy from sleep and pissed off at being awakened.

How the hell was he supposed to say anything? He said, "I need you to get dressed and come downstairs." Spencer shut her door and let out a breath.

"Did you see me you fucking perve? What's that smell?"

~ * ~

Spencer was the only one who left the frame room. He paced out of it to see what was going on then went back. Chrys sat on one of the love seats beside Sandra trying to get her to drink some tea. The poor woman still looked like she had seen a ghost. Her body literally shook. Megan had shown up for her morning shift shortly after the police arrived and instantly went about making coffee and tea for them. Jessie came in the moment she got Spencer's text about calling the staff and telling them to take the day off. She called the staff then started cancelling any reserved tables.

The City Police had taken over The Alcrest. There were already reporters outside taking pictures of all the activity.

Spencer looked at the front doors as Dawn came through. She showed her RCMP identification badge to the first officer who stopped her and told him that she was a friend of the owners. She walked right past Spencer and went to his sister.

"Mr. Alcrest, can I have a moment?" Constable Eric Wright had introduced himself when he arrived, asked a few questions, and sent them all to the frame room to wait. He had the most perfect posture Spencer had ever seen in a man. On top of hard wide shoulders was a round jaw and a perfectly trimmed white crew cut. He looked like he should be in the military, not the police. He walked, expecting the chef to follow, until he was standing next to the table where the head of the Irish Mafia had been sitting just twelve hours prior. "You're positive you have no idea who that could be?"

Spencer didn't even want to look in the direction of the oven. When the police arrived they quickly realized they would have to wait for it to cool before they could remove anything. He said, "No, no idea. I hope I don't know who it is at all."

"You live upstairs, right? You didn't hear anything last night?"

"It had been a long day and I was exhausted. I passed out with the TV on." Chrys had apparently turned it off when she went to bed, so why hadn't he heard anything? There were no screams, no bangs. The dogs would have barked if there was something. Perhaps whoever the crispy critter was had already been dead before things happened. He hoped so.

"Did you lock up?"

"No. I went upstairs before closing."

"Who would have locked up then?"

"My front-of-house manager, Jessie Husk, and bartender, Wylie Wade locked up last night. Jessie's here. She said they locked up just after midnight and swears the doors were locked." His mouth was dry. There was panic rising inside him that he knew he had to supress. Someone had been inside his place. "Are there any marks or jewelry on the, um ... That you can see?" Part of him wished he had taken a better look inside the oven. Most of him was glad he didn't.

Cnst. Wright looked at the chef. He looked behind himself before saying, "We haven't really gotten in there yet. It's still too hot and without a head it's going to be hard. What type of security system do you have?"

"I don't have one." Spencer checked his phone then slipped it in his pocket along with his hand. He didn't know what to do with his other hand. His forearm was suddenly itchy inside the cast.

"No?" Wright had that tone people who talked to younger people got when they think they are being stupid.

Spencer let out a breath. "We live right upstairs. My sister comes and goes without a schedule and we have dogs, so we don't have an alarm."

"Did your dogs make any commotion last night?"

"No."

"What types of dogs are they?"

Spencer bit his lip. He shouldn't have said anything. He said, "A bulldog and a Chihuahua."

A smile cracked the cop's exterior, "So real attack dogs then."

The stench of burnt flesh still permeated the room. It had gone from sweet to something nasty. Just the thought of what it was changed everything. The taste of it was somehow in Spencer's mouth. He wanted to get out into the fresh air for just a moment to have something different touch his senses. It was something he was never going to forget.

He wasn't saying anything, so the Constable asked another question, "You didn't walk the dogs at all last night?"

"Chrys took them out before going to bed."

"When was …"

"She said one o'clock. Then she went to sleep and she's a very sound sleeper." Spencer checked his phone again. He looked over his shoulders at the others watching him.

"So you didn't hear any noises?"

"No."

"No screams?"

Spencer's jaw dropped as he looked up. He hadn't thought of how it went down. He turned to the kitchen; luckily he couldn't see the oven. The grim faces of the police officers said it all. He asked, "You think that person was alive when they got here?"

"I don't know if she was alive then. There's no blood though. I'm thinking she was killed before being brought here, but we have to consider every possibility." He tapped a pen on his flip notepad. "Who has keys to the restaurant?"

"You're sure it's a woman?"

He nodded. "Keys?"

"Me, Chrys, Sandra the morning cook, Jessie, and Liz. She's garde-manger (the cold-side) but sometimes does the breakfast stuff or comes in early to bake."

The police officer looked to the frame room and did a count. "And where is she?"

Spencer's mouth opened to say "asleep at home," then his eyes were drawn to the kitchen. "She, she didn't show

207

up for work yesterday. Jessie's calling everyone," his voice faded away. It all clicked together in his mind. He saw a hand come out of the darkness of the cistern, heard Liz scream, felt the heat of a hand as it clasped over her mouth, tasted the killer's sweaty palm. That was Liz in the oven. Somewhere in the back of his thoughts he heard her baby crying. *How did she get in there?* His heart sank. Something solid suddenly shot up his throat. He swallowed it back down. Stomach acids burned his insides. The taste of bile replaced the taste of burnt flesh on his tongue.

Cnst. Wright waited a few minutes before placing a hand on Spencer's shoulder. "I'll need her address."

He bobbed his head. Spencer felt overwhelmed. *Was it his fault?* "Jess can get it for you," he mumbled. "I know how to get there, but I don't know what it is."

"Constable Wright." Another officer moved rapidly across the room. His eyes wouldn't go to the oven. His voice was panicked. He looked as white as Sandra. "We," he looked at Spencer, "found something in the staff washroom. It's …" He looked at the chef again and seemed unsure if he should say anything. There was fear deep inside his eyes. Perspiration seemed to erupt from his pores. Spencer saw that same fear earlier in his breakfast cook's eyes. "We found the victim's head."

~ * ~

Chrys hugged Breeze close to her body. The tiny chocolate dog greedily licked the woman's chin. Her bother had moved them all upstairs, going outside and around to the back stairs, to get away from the burnt smell and commotion. Megan had taken Sandra home. The police were still downstairs looking for evidence. Dawn sat beside Chrys with her hand on the other's thigh. Jessie was in Spencer's favorite chair, one bare foot on the hardwood and the other curled up beneath her body.

Spencer paced across the room. At first Bullet paced with him, then when he realized the man wasn't going to stop, the bulldog waddled to the chair, dropped onto Jessie's foot, closed his eyes, and started snoring.

"You should sit down, Spence." Jessie said as she started rolling her toes under the dog's soft belly. Her eyes were red. She had done her job of calling everyone to tell them not to come into work before letting the emotions take over.

"I don't think so, Jess. I've got too much to think about." His left arm itched deep inside the cast.

"Like what?"

"Like that I'm going to have to close the restaurant." He moved things around on the coffee table. There had to be something there. Spencer grabbed a pen and shoved it down the top of the cast.

"Why?" Chrys asked. It was the first word she had uttered since being told the body was probably Liz and that her head was in the tank of the staff washroom toilet. The cistern.

Spencer threw the pen down on the table. It didn't help any anyway. He said, "Who's going to want to eat food from an oven that cooked someone? I can't use that oven any more. And, and, and the staff bathroom. I can't ask everyone to shit where her ... where Liz's ..."

"Really, that's what you're thinking about?"

He stopped and stared across at her. "It's better than thinking about my burnt-up-friend, isn't it?"

"Get a new bloody oven then."

"Oh yeah, Chrys. A new oven and stove would cost twenty grand, easy. Used ones are unreliable. And once people know, once they know what happened …"

"It was your," her hand flew around the air as she tried to find the right word, "*friend* who did this. Get him to fork over the money."

"Excuse me?" Spencer crossed his arms over his chest. That lasted three seconds before he started scratching all around the top of the cast.

"You're best friends with a God damn monkey-fucking mobster."

Dawn pushed forward on the couch. "Wait. What? Who?"

"We're not friends." He picked up the pen again. He already had blue streaks where he had scratched before.

"God's balls! You've got him on speed dial." Chrys's voice went up a little.

"Who are you guys talking about?" Dawn didn't know who to look at.

"Liam has nothing to do with this. I've already talked to him. We wouldn't even be in this if you didn't have us go to *The Creepy House* like it was some frigging storybook adventure."

As Chrys stood, she and her brother stared at each other with eyes that burned.

At that moment Spencer wanted to take back his words. He knew he couldn't. It wasn't Chrys's fault, it wasn't anyone's fault. They just happened to be on the same path as some psychotic.

"You think this is my fault," she screeched, "then you can just kiss my firm caramel-coated ass, buddy. Liz is not my fault." Chrys flung her hands around as she yelled and slapped her ass to make a point. Breeze jumped back and forth beside her owner's feet yapping her annoyance. "I was the one trying to do something. I was out there looking for this guy."

"You were looking for the wrong guy." Spencer stepped closer to her. He abandoned the pen still half in the cast.

"What?" Chrys asked.

"You were looking for the guy following you, who had nothing to do with any of this."

"So you and Liam O'Donnell say,"

Dawn grabbed Chrys's pant leg. "What? Spencer, you can't be talking to that guy."

Chrys ignored her girlfriend. "At least I was doing something. How was I supposed to know the guy following me and trashing MY place was the wrong douche bag? If he even was."

"It's *our* place," Spencer demanded.

"Oh whatever," She dropped to the couch.

"And you don't even know if Liam's guy trashed our place. Maybe it was the killer instead. Maybe he's after us. Maybe this isn't even the same killer. There could be another one out there."

"Oh that makes me feel so much safer, you …"

"Chrys." Dawn grabbed and squeezed Chrys's thigh.

Everyone went quiet. They looked around the room without catching the eye of each other. The brother and sister fought, once in a while, like they really hated each other and it was usually done in front of everyone. That was part of their relationship. They may not have been siblings from birth, but they had grown up together and were very close.

After a long time Chrys asked, "Why did he cut off her head?"

"To make her fit," Dawn said. She was staring at Spencer. "At least that's what Wright said he thought was the reason."

Spencer pulled the pen out of the cast and tossed it down again. "And then he put the head in the cistern of the toilet like some kind of joke."

"He was giving us a message," Chrys whispered.

Spencer walked to the window and looked out at the front of the building. There were large flakes of snow falling. Luckily none of it was staying on the ground, for the moment. Most of the police vehicles were gone. Only a truck from their Crime Scene Department remained. The CSI of the Middleton Police Department was downstairs dusting for fingerprints (of which they would find too many) and looking for particles or clues like in all the crime TV shows. Wright said he was going to contact the RCMP Major Crimes Unit and the Missing Persons Department of his own police force (they were the ones who dealt with Enid's disappearance) to see if there were connections. The Constable wasn't willing to admit that Enid, Maeve, Liz, the cistern, the oven, and the cistern of the toilet were all connected. The chef thought that was going to be the problem. The various parts of the crime were crossing too many desks, they couldn't see where it all began.

Began.

He turned back to the others. Only Jessie was looking at him. Spencer said, "What if Enid wasn't his first?"

All the women looked up at him. Nobody seemed to want to be the next one to speak.

"What do you mean?" Jessie looked tired.

"Enid disappeared seven months ago and died not long before we found the cistern, right?" He looked at all three hoping one would speak his next thought. He couldn't wait

212

any longer, "Does that mean he got lucky and was able to keep her that long?"

"Or did he have practice?" Chrys finished. Her eyes were still red from having cried about Liz, but her lips showed a wide sinister grin. She looked at her brother and all the arguing was forgotten. That was their usual routine.

"Enid wasn't his first victim," Spencer said and looked at Dawn.

She looked up at him. Her green eyes went wide. She looked around and realized everyone in the room was now looking at her. Even the two dogs were looking up at her. "What?"

Spencer was getting excited. "What does Major Crimes have on past murders? There has to be a pattern, right? Isn't that what they always look for on TV?"

"I don't know. I'm not with Major Crimes. And don't go thinking about what they do on TV. You're a cook. You're just a waitress. There's been enough Sherlock Holmes-ing around already."

"Just a waitress?"

Spencer let being called just a cook slide. "Can you find out?"

"What?" Chrys wasn't going to let being called *just* a waitress go.

Dawn looked at her sad and hurt brown eyes. She knew she was in trouble. To Spencer she said, "I'll see what I can find out. I make no promises though. I'm not risking my career over you two playing Nancy Drew and the lone Hardy Boy."

Spencer shrugged. "I always had a preference to Frank, myself. Joe was always too impulsive."

Dawn's eyes did a massive roll. "I have to get ready for work." She placed her lips close to Chrys's ear. She was close enough that the other felt her warm breath against her lobe. "I'll call you later." A little louder she added, "Don't go getting into trouble," and headed out the door.

"I guess I can look online," Jessie said when it was just the three of them. She wore blue jeans and a baggy knit sweater instead of her all-black work clothes. She had been playing with her gold watch for awhile, but that was forgotten as she pushed up her sleeves and took over Spencer's computer tablet. She was just glad to have something to get her mind off everything else. "I'll search newspapers and news sites for, what?" She looked up. "Women who went missing and were found dead? I can start general and see what I can find."

"Yeah, do your best. I'm going to go visit Liz's mom."

"I'll come," Chrys started toward the bedrooms.

Spencer said, "Why don't you stay here?"

Chrys stopped and turned back. Jessie didn't lift her eyes from the computer. Spencer was already getting his coat on.

"What the fuck you talking about, Willis?"

"You have to call Hoyt and get him to change the locks."

"Jessie's right here. She can call Hoyt."

"I'm going to see about an oven," Spencer said. "I'd like it if you two would stay together, so I know you're both safe." He didn't want to tell her his real reason for not wanting her along. She was going to be safer where she was, even with a psycho killer out there.

~ * ~

Hidden behind a pair of towering blue spruce was Liz's mother's weathered bungalow. It had seen better days. The

214

pale blue siding, with wood flower boxes beneath the windows, were all faded. A collection of wind chimes hung from the overhanging roof. As soon as Spencer got out of his truck he heard the musical tin sound of hollow bars and carved metal pieces. By the time he had walked from the street up the stone path to the house, he was annoyed with the cacophony of musical noise.

"At least I got here first," Constable Wright said as the two men passed, the cop having exited the house. "Why are you here?"

Spencer shrugged, "Condolences, I guess." In front of people of authority he felt like there were chores he forgot to do and Dad just walked through the door.

Wright looked back at the house. The woman who owned it stood behind a storm door watching through the dirty glass. "I don't know whether she's strong or a heartless. She didn't seem that upset."

"Everyone reacts differently, Constable." Spencer continued on his way to the house without looking back. The woman behind the door opened it for him. "Hi, Mrs. Palmer, how are you doing?" He realized that was a stupid question.

She didn't say a word. She stared at him for a long time. Somewhere in the house a baby was crying. She wasn't strong and she wasn't heartless. She was in shock.

"Stupid question I guess, eh?" he said with a nervous laugh at the end.

Spencer had only met the woman a few times when Liz brought her to the restaurant or her mom came to get the baby. As far as he knew the two did not have the best relationship through Liz's entire life and it got worse when she got pregnant.

"Well?" Mrs. Palmer said suddenly.

"Do you need help with anything? I know it's a shock right now …"

The baby cut him off with another wail.

Mrs. Palmer groaned and spun around. Over her shoulder she asked, "Do you know any babysitters?"

"I might." He had a sudden image of Hanni in her five-inch hooker heels coddling a baby. He followed the woman through the house. It was the home of someone who didn't give a damn or didn't have the time.

As they passed through the kitchen/dining room the table and counter were almost completely covered with papers, mail, and odds and ends. One sink was overflowing with dirty dishes, food stuffs caked to them. Spencer noticed an empty potato chip bag on the floor under the table. He stepped over a dirty sock. In the center of the living room was a mesh playpen. Stuffed animals and plastic toys were on the carpet around it. A little girl stood inside the topless prison grasping tightly onto the edge and screaming her head off.

It made Spencer think about Maeve. She missed all of the screaming baby stuff. He wondered if she had heard about the body in the oven yet.

Mrs. Palmer bent down (a moan passed through her throat and a little air escaped her ass) and picked up the bottle that had been thrown after the toys. The little one didn't want it at first. Then Grandma picked her up and the baby hungrily sucked on the rubber nipple. "She's a cuddler. Liz made her that way. She'd cuddle this thing every time she cried. Probably why the baby's father took off, men don't like to cuddle. So now I have to figure out what to do. I'm working midnights this week."

"Your daughter was just …" he couldn't finish the sentence. "Wouldn't they understand and give you time off?"

"I can't. I can't afford that." Her words were choked back. A literal flood of tears ran down her face. She squeezed her granddaughter to her chest and buried her eyes in the baby's hair.

Ten minutes of texting and Megan responded saying she would take the little one for the night.

"Can I ask you some questions, Mrs. Palmer?"

"You a cop now too?"

"No, just curious."

She sniffed as she laid the baby down. "You know what they say about curiosity."

Thirty minutes later Spencer knew all that Mrs. Palmer knew about the last time she saw her daughter. Yesterday morning when she left for work at The Alcrest. They had argued about the baby teething and how she had been up most of the night. Mrs. Palmer told Liz she was going to have to start paying for daycare and Liz didn't know how she could afford it on top of everything else. She took her knife kit and left without a goodbye to either of them. Mrs. Palmer didn't know what she was going to do with a baby.

Spencer looked up and down the street as he reached his truck. It was a family neighborhood. There were houses with swing sets in the back yards and toys across the front lawns that hopefully wouldn't be forgotten by winter. He stared down the route Liz would probably have walked and tried to imagine her going that way. *What stopped her from getting to The Alcrest?*

He got in his truck and slowly drove in the direction she would have walked. There was a tree marked with red paint for removal, an old RV camper with two tires up on the curb, a house with a wheelchair ramp. In the front yard of one house three men worked on a fence. Spencer pulled over to the curb. On TV police shows didn't they call this canvasing? Did Wright talk to the same workers?

"Hey guys, can I talk to you for a second?" Spencer crossed over to them. "Were you guys working here yesterday?"

All three of them looked at each other. The ground beneath the fence line had freshly dug dirt where posts had been put installed. The cleaner looking of the trio stepped forward.

"We've been here three days. Why?"

Spencer rapidly went through the pictures on his phone. He stopped at one of Liz and Gordie. "You ever see this girl?"

"I'm the boss, so I'm not here that often." He turned to one of the other guys. "You see her?"

The youngest one leaned in and looked at the phone. "She said she was going to bring us cookies."

"So you saw her? When?"

"Yesterday. She was walking by and asked how we were doing. Rick said he was hungry and she said she'd bring us cookies today."

"So she came walking by."

"Yeah, then she got in a car."

"A car? What car? Are you sure it was a car?" *Not a red truck?*

"It was a blue four-door Ford, I think."

"Did you see the driver?"

"No man, sorry. She talked to us and then started walking away. I was getting back to work and when I looked up a car had pulled to the curb beside her. When I looked again she was gone."

Spencer dropped his gaze before looking back at the young man. "You didn't actually see her get in the car?"

"She either got in the car or she had a rocket up her ass."

~ * ~

"Isn't meeting in Marina Park kind of a cliché?" Spencer asked as he looked away from the *Angry Birds* game he had been playing on his phone to the man who walked slowly toward him. Since leaving home Spencer had over a dozen texts from his sister asking where he was and what he was doing. The one phone call he got was a woman's voice that told him to go sit on a bench by the amphitheater in Marina Park. He didn't know who he was meeting until he saw Liam O'Donnell walking down the path. Mr. McGregor stood outside their parked car, his eyes on everything. There was a chill in the air and since leaving Liz's snow had begun to fall. There didn't seem to be anyone else around.

"There is a reason for clichés, Spencer. No Chrysanthemum today?"

Spencer didn't like the way the man said his sister's name. "What's with you and her? What do you know that I don't?" He stared at the older man. It was strange being with him. He felt guilty. The chef wanted to know more about the notorious man and how he related to his father, but a part of him didn't want to know. He was certain there was a point where he wouldn't be able to go back.

"I would have stopped by the restaurant," Liam said, "But I heard it was closed."

Spencer let out a breath he didn't realize he'd been holding. "Do you know why?"

Liam nodded.

219

"Did Gaylen do it?"

"No," he said flatly. He pulled in his coat as a gust of wind came off the ocean.

Marina Park was a lovely green place in the summer. The lawn was manicured, the perfectly placed trees and bushes offered shade, there was a small beach for swimming, the local theater group did plays in the amphitheatre, and walking paths crossed over the seaside hill that protruded beside the private docks. In early autumn the leaves took on a golden and fiery red colour, but in winter the land became just a blob of snow and ice. Some die-hards went there for exercise, though it was left mostly to the elements. On this cool autumn day there were a couple of people walking dogs.

"Do you know what I do, Spencer?" Liam asked after a long silence.

Spencer wasn't sure how to answer. Liam O'Donnell was a matter of opinion. Killer, criminal, philanthropist, savior. He had been called all. Spencer went the safe route and said, "Not really."

"I'm a business man. I own a couple of restaurants and a real estate business. I am part owner of a successful construction contractors, several apartment buildings, a shopping mall on the west side, a tax company and yes, an import and export business located on the docks. Sometimes I have to deal in bad things, however, I do a lot of good."

"Do you sell drugs and kill people?" Spencer wasn't sure where that question came from. He tried his best to keep his eyes on the dangerous man.

The response was, "I don't. None of my people are responsible for anything that happened at The Alcrest or that house. Gaylen was in your apartment, but that had to do with the Linques."

"Did he see anyone at *The Creepy House* besides the garbage guy?"

"He wasn't there twenty-four-seven."

Spencer looked at his watch. It was almost the end of the business day. He said, "Thanks for your time. I have to see about getting new ovens."

"What's wrong with the ones you have?" The two of them started to stroll toward the parking lot.

"I can't cook food in an oven that cooked one of my cooks. Once this hits the news I don't even know if customers will come to the restaurant. They might be too disgusted by it."

"They might be fascinated by it." A small grin crossed Liam's lips.

"Well I can't do it."

"How much is a new oven?"

"You can't get one piece, so the two ovens and ten burners brand new cost about twenty grand. I might be able to get one for a third the price slightly used."

"Slightly used?"

"A lot of restaurants close down. Their equipment gets sold cheap. Only you have no guarantees on how good the stuff is. Plus you have to pay for delivery and someone to install it and the gas company to check the connections. It all adds up." Spencer's stomach lurched and twisted with the thought of all the money he would have to spend. Not to mention how much he would lose while the restaurant was closed until he got the new equipment.

At his car Liam stopped and turned to the younger man. "Do you need a loan?"

Was that how his father got involved with the mobster?
He didn't want to think about whatever Rene Alcrest and
Liam O'Donnell had going, nor how it involved Chrys and
the restaurant. He was not his father. He also knew he
didn't have the money for what he needed.

~ * ~

Spencer nodded to the police officer outside Maeve's
door. He was the same officer as the last time Spencer was
there. He knocked and entered.

The flowers he carried looked like a handful of weeds
compared to what was in her room. The vases of colourful
flowers had multiplied since his last visit. They had moved
from all of the surfaces to the floor. Sitting on the bed
amidst the garden was a woman who looked close to the
woman on the Maeve Campbell CD cover. She had the
guitar on her lap and papers were scattered around her. She
looked up at him and smiled. "Elisa came today," she said
and waved for him to come over. "She's so gorgeous. Her
parents brought her by. They're amazing people. Elisa's
dad plays guitar. I started writing again." Her words came
out fast as the excitement overwhelmed her.

"That's awesome." He knew right then he wasn't going
to tell her about Liz. There was no point. She would hear
about it soon enough. He didn't want to be the one to tell
her, her bogeyman was still out there.

He *was* out there.

Chapter Seventeen

"Where have you been?" Chrys sat on the living-room floor with her back against the couch. Bullet laid on the cushions behind her, breathing heavily into her dark hair. There were two pizza boxes on the coffee table.

Jessie sat in Spencer's chair, still with his computer. She looked at him with the same question in her eyes, though she didn't speak a word. She knew how to work him. Staying silent made him uncomfortable which gave her power. Spencer wasn't sure if she did it on purpose, but it worked.

He walked straight through the apartment and took a beer from the fridge. He said, "I was taking care of things."

"What the fuck does that mean?"

He really did not want to say that he had done everything he could to stay away from the apartment. "Liam swears none of his guys did this."

"Dawn says he's a killer, drug dealer, pimp, and arms dealer all rolled up into one. Can you really believe anything he says?" She took a huge bite from a slice of pizza.

"I found out Liz might have been picked up by someone in a blue car," Spencer said changing the subject. He sat on the couch. His eyes popped up to Jessie and she held them. He surely didn't want to say anything about going to see Maeve. It was nothing; she talked about her daughter and showed him the new songs she had been writing. He hasn't answered the texts and calls from both women he was now with though.

Chrys made a noise, moved the mouthful of pizza to one side and asked, "What about the driver?"

Spencer shook his head. His choices of pizza were a supreme or the special one Chrys always had the pizza place make her. It had a basil pesto sauce, ham, tomatoes, green peppers, feta cheese, a few black olives, and a thin sprinkling of bacon. He took a slice of the first one.

"I found three possible victims." Jessie stated. "They go back a couple years. Jessica Lamb, a student at the vet college, went missing over a year ago. Her body was found a month later half buried in the woods. The police said her body showed signs of trauma. That's all the newspapers reported. I also read a bit about the body of a woman found just over two years ago out near Hillsborough. All the paper said was that the police believed it to be a street walker. There wasn't enough to make a positive ID."

In a large city with a high percentage of homicides and other crime deaths, many stories just slipped away. The homeless man killed in a hit-and-run at 2 am barely had a chance in the news against rising fuel prices and the weekend weather. A dead hooker was lucky to get page three.

"The earliest case I read about was four years ago. Miki Harris's body was found with ligature marks. She had been beaten, raped, and tortured. She had been reported missing almost a week earlier."

Chrys said, "I texted Dawn about them and she said because the first one was found in city limits it was a City Police case and the others were RCMP cases, so they may not have been bundled together. They may not be connected anyway. That's what she said." Chrys stopped to go through her phone messages. She found what she was looking for. "She also said the victimology was so different, one being a hooker." She really didn't want to think about how screwed up a world it was that certain people went forgotten just because of where they stood in life. "The girls looked different. The first was a student, the second was in the work force. All were from different areas."

"So what do we do now?"

"Do you have addresses and names of living relatives or friends or anything?"

Jessie nodded and handed him a piece of paper where she had written down names and addresses. She had been busy.

"I'll talk to them tomorrow."

"We will," Chrys jumped in. The two of them stared at each other for a while.

Spencer wanted to fight her. This was his thing. This was something he had to do for Liz, for Enid, and for Maeve. He knew fighting her wasn't going to solve anything. Chrys would yell about how she needed to get in there. He opened his mouth to say something. The thought vanished with the glare of her brown eyes.

~ * ~

Breeze stretched out to the end of her leash. She was a dog that would jump into something first before checking out what is there, much like her owner. Bullet plodded along beside Spencer's feet sniffing the sidewalk carefully checking everything out. The night air was cool. There was a scent to the air, something fresh.

"It's going to snow more."

"That what *Enviroguess Canada* says?"

"No, I do." Jessie bounced her hip against him. She gave the leash a little tug to bring the chocolate Chihuahua back from the road where she was sniffing an Arby's cup someone discarded along the curb. "My mom always said you could taste the snow in the air. I can taste it."

Spencer smiled and let out a little laugh. He looked up and down the street. He wasn't sure what he was looking for this time, just that he had to look and check for anything. There were no trucks or blue cars, but that didn't mean someone wasn't watching them. The killer could be staring right at them, studying them, sizing Jessie up, deciding what type of container she would fit in figuring out the best time to get her whenever she would be alone. He reached out and took Jessie's hand. He wanted her to be close to him. Spencer looked back at the restaurant. Chrys was all alone. There was nothing but a door and newly replaced lock to stop whoever was out there.

"So what did you do today?" Jessie squeezed his hand.

"I told you, I talked to Liz's mom and went to see about a new oven." He didn't want to lie to her. He cared about the woman. Her jealousy, though, was irrational in his opinion. "I also went for a meeting with a mobster."

The dogs twisted their leashes around until it was one braided leash holding two dogs. It took a few moments to untie them from each other and from one of Jessie's legs.

"You were gone for a long time, Spence."

He knelt down to pick up a present Bullet left. "That's what I did."

"You didn't go to see Maeve?"

"Really, Jessie?"

"What?"

"You have to trust me, Jess. I'm not fooling around. I, I, you know." Spencer felt a chill run up his spine.

"I never said you were cheating on me."

"You're hinting at it."

Jessie swept Breeze up with one hand. "I'm not hinting at anything." They walked for a little while without saying a word. They were almost done the second trip down the street when Jessie asked, "Do you think she was alive when she was brought back here? Liz."

"Probably not." Spencer hadn't seen any blood where the beheading could have taken place, but there were enough sharp knives around to do the job. *And how else would the killer have known that her body wouldn't fit in the oven without removing the head if they weren't already there in the restaurant? Blood didn't flow from a dead body, did it?* Maybe the psycho was a neat freak as well. "We shouldn't think about it." He took her hand again and gave it a tight squeeze.

~ * ~

Friday morning brought on the first real dusting of snow, it was going to stay a little while. As the day broke the white dust hung in the cool air touching Chrys's cheeks as she slipped from the passenger side of her brother's truck. Her dark eyes fell on the yellow Sunfire parked in front of them. Her brother slowly walked around the car looking through the windows. Some of the snow covered the hood as though it had been there awhile.

"Is that the same car from *The Creepy House*?"

"Looks that way."

There were not many cars around the small church. It was not what you would expect for a funeral service. You hope that when you pass you can at least fill a room with mourners, people who may think of you once in a while. It looked like Enid Bernadine was going to be lucky if her mourners filled a pew.

Chrys started wishing she had worn pants instead of a dark green mini-dress and black-on-top stockings with a triangle design. She also wore grey work socks and brown boots. The footwear didn't exactly go with the outfit, but her feet were warm. It probably wasn't the best thing for a funeral either. Her view was that black was too depressing. She needed colour. Dark colour, at least. As she entered the church she slipped off her coat. The dress had long sleeves down to mid-palm with buttons from cuff to elbow.

"Isn't that skirt a little short?"

"It's a dress," was all she said.

They stopped at a notice stating the time for the Enid Bernadine service. There was no guest book to sign. The inside of the church was no bigger than the restaurant. A handful of people sat in the front pews. The two of them slipped into one of the back ones as a priest came out. He said a few words about how life was fleeting, read a couple psalms, said a prayer and that was it. Chrys didn't want to go that way. She could have been Enid. She could have had a life forgotten.

Sometimes she felt like her life could have gone so many directions. Her mother had been forgotten. She never showed to pick Chrys up from daycare one day and went away like smoke in the wind. Was that what was going to happen to the memory of Enid?

That was not happening to Chrys.

Chrys let Spencer go to Mrs. Staples in the front row as she pulled her dress lower on her thighs and waited in the back. Moustache Man was in the front of the church. He hugged people and thanked them for coming. From the similar hair colour and facial features she guessed that they were mostly his family. Maybe Mr. Moustache was the guy who treated Enid right. Curiosity got to her and she walked toward the front to find out.

"Hi," she said when she reached him. "I'm sorry for your loss." It seemed the thing to say at that moment.

"Thank you." He noticed her for the first time. His eyes studied her face trying to determine out who she was. "Did you know Enid?" His voice was soft and sombre, but not overly sad. He was in control of his emotions.

"I was a foster kid, too," was all she said and guessed that was a good enough reason to be there since he didn't ask any more. Chrys was glad that he turned to a picture of Enid instead of keeping his eyes on her.

The photo showed a young woman in a graduation gown. *Was that from the course she had been finishing in college?* She had a long thin face with some lines around her eyes and mouth making her look older than she was, a product of a tough life. Her smile was crooked; it looked incomplete. Long dark hair draped over her shoulders, bangs curled down hiding her forehead. Chrys thought she was pretty. She probably wouldn't have hung out with her in her high school days, but now that she was an adult things would be different. Enid appeared happy in the photo.

Chrys looked around for other photographs. There were none. When Spencer's dad died they had to sort through plastic containers and albums full of photos of him and only picked the best to put on three large boards. Maybe Enid didn't have any or they just wanted to remember her in happy times. From what Spencer told her there weren't that many.

"I'm Chrys," she said with a little too much enthusiasm and thrust her hand out.

"Brian." He barely touched her hand as they shook.

Brian had one of those full Chuck Norris - Magnum PI - Ned Flanders sort of moustaches. It looked like a comb under his lip.

"You were her boyfriend?"

"Fiancé. We would have been married by now."

"Big wedding?"

"No. We were going to go to Vegas. I bought the tickets two days before she disappeared."

"I'm sorry," Chrys said. "I don't really know what happened."

Brian stared down at his hand. For a moment it seemed as though he wouldn't tell her, then said, "She liked to run. She said it cleaned out her old demons. Sometimes she'd run for hours. She would drive to Culpepper Road and run along the dirt roads breathing in the clean country air and breathing out her past. That's how she described it. I guess you can't run from everything though. On that day she didn't come home. The police found her car and they found her cell phone in a ditch five kilometers away. I guess that's as far as she got."

"There was no ransom or anything?" It sounded strange the moment she asked it. *Did people really kidnap others for ransom in this day and age?*

He shook his head.

"No witnesses?"

Another shake. "Nothing until she was found. I had to identify her body. She was so …" He took a deep breath as he tried to find the right words.

"Fucked up?" Chrys whispered thinking about when she saw the body.

~ * ~

"Why are you asking about Jessica?"

"We, ah …" When Spencer looked at his sister he looked like a deer in headlights. The only thing he could think to say was that he wanted to stop a serial killer from cooking his sister or girlfriend. That seemed like a crazy thing to actually verbalize, even in his thoughts.

Let me do the talking, he had said. Chrys grabbed his arm to shut him up. "We're in the journalism course at the college," Chrys spoke up as she scowled at her brother. "We're doing a story on unsolved homicides and how the police are not really doing their job."

"Well, that they're overwhelmed and can't keep on top of everything." Spencer quickly added and stared at his sister. He still looked like he was ready to panic.

She turned her head, so only he could see, and gave a look that told him to go fuck himself. "What can you tell us about her?"

The young woman, Lori, looked at both of them. Her long hair was tied back. She sat at a dining table covered in open textbooks and binders of loose-leaf paper. The man who opened the door for them went back to a grilled-cheese sandwich he had waiting next to the kitchen sink.

"I don't know much about her," Lori started. "I mean, we didn't know each other long." She stared at Chrys for a long time, almost challenging her. She was in her early twenties with mousy hair and average features. She had been Jessica Harris's room-mate and was the only one they thought might give them information. "She moved in here because I had advertised for a roommate on a bulletin board. We didn't really talk. I met Tom two weeks later. If I had met him sooner he would have moved in and I would have only seen her in classes."

"I don't know what to tell you. She came from Saskatchewan to vet school here. She didn't go to the vet school at the University of Saskatchewan because she wanted to get away from home. I don't think she had many friends. She stuck to her room mostly."

"Did she have a boyfriend?" Chrys felt like she should have a notepad or something.

Lori looked at her boyfriend. He shrugged his shoulders. "I don't know. I don't think so. She went to class, went to work, came here, that was it." She shuffled papers around on the table.

"Where did she work?"

"Beacon Street Pizza, that little corner dive place by the college." The apartment was on the third floor of a large house. Chrys and Spencer stood just inside the door not having been invited any further inside. The kitchen smelled of toasted bread and smoke.

"What happened when she went missing?"

Lori reached across the table for a pack of cigarettes. As she lit one Chrys noticed her two fingers were stained yellow. "She told me that Friday morning that she was going away for the weekend and would be back Sunday. On Sunday she didn't show, so I figured she'd come back home after classes on Monday. She didn't." She took a long drag from the white tube then handed it to her boyfriend.

"Is that when you called the police?"

"I didn't call them. I thought maybe she left school and went home. Other people did. Then her mom called wondering why she hadn't heard from her." Lori looked up at the two of them. "Jessica usually called home every couple of days."

"Did the police have any suspects?" Spencer asked.

Lori took the cigarette back and sucked on it before saying, "Not that I know of," as she exhaled.

"Fucking cops investigated us and let the trail get cold." It was the first thing Tom had said since he opened the door.

"You moved in after she was gone?" Spencer stared at the younger man. He had seen how he was looking at his sister. *Did he look at Jessica like that with desirous eyes*?

"A couple weeks, yeah. Nobody knew where she was or if she was coming back. For all we knew she could have been-" Dead was the word he couldn't find.

Lori took out another cigarette. "That's why the police suspected us."

Chrys looked at Tom and realized his eyes kept moving up and down her body. Women wore sexy clothes so they could feel good about themselves, not so men could leer at them. She had to admit she liked men checking her out, but not this one. It was creepy. "Do you know anyone who didn't like her? Did she have problems with anyone?" *Would Jessica have said anything to Lori if she had troubles with Tom?*

Lori pushed the end of the cigarette into a full ash tray. Three butts tumbled to the table. "I barely know anyone

233

who knew her. If she had problems she kept them to herself."

~ * ~

"Would you like some coffee? Tea maybe?"

Chrys used the line again about how they were journalism students finding out where the cops went wrong to get invited into the home of Beverly and Nick Harris. They all sat in the dated living room.

Miki Harris's father snorted. He sat in a big comfy chair facing the television. He had the remote in his hand with a mug of beer beside him and a smoldering cigarette next to that.

Both of Miki's parents were in their mid-sixties, both retired. Nick had worked for the city and Bev – "everybody calls me Bev" - was an accountant. She still did the books on the side for some small businesses. On Wednesdays Nick played poker with his buddies. Bev made knitted crafts all year for the Christmas craft show circuit starting in November. Otherwise the two of them watched a lot of television. All of this was quickly explained to Spencer and Chrys between knocking on the door to ask if they could talk about Miki and being seated on the sofa.

"She was a miracle baby, you know." Bev's hands quickly took up her knitting needles, going back to her project. The needles clicked together. "I was told in my teens that I would never have children, something to do with my ovaries, and I was fine with that. Nick was fine with that. Weren't you Nick?" She didn't wait for an answer, but did get a snort. "We both didn't really want children. Then I'm forty-two and go to the doctors because I was throwing up every morning and what do you know?"

Click, click, click.

"Are you sure you don't want any coffee? I can make a pot, you know."

"No thank you," Spencer said while thinking this older woman spoke faster than his sister.

Chrys threw her fist sideways, hitting him on the edge of his knee. She knew what he was thinking because she thought the same thing. "I'll just stick with the water." She was sitting between the lady and her brother. The couch was lower than most making her cross her ankles and carefully squeeze her thighs and knees together. Even with her effort her skirt almost showed the "promised land." Not only was she wishing she had worn something different, but she wished she'd worn something underneath.

"Do you know what the doctor said? He said, Bev it's a miracle." *Click, click*, she put the needles and half made scarf down on her lap. Her eyes started to glisten.

"What did Miki do?"

Bev cleared her throat and went back to her scarf. "She was in school to be a veterinary assistant. She was top of her class, you know."

"She wasn't in school. She was done school." Nick stared at the television as he slowly went through channels. "She worked at the clinic on Second Avenue."

"The Middleton Vet Clinic?" Spencer asked. His body pushed forward on the couch.

Nick responded with a nod and a snort.

Beverly stared at him for a moment.

Chrys wondered if that was hatred she saw in the woman's eyes. Maybe it was embarrassment at getting something wrong.

The lady's lip curled up as she looked away from him and back to her knitting. "I sometimes mix details. Old age, you know."

Chrys patted her leg. "You're not that old yet." She slid her hand back between her thighs.

Ideas ran through Spencer's head. Jessica was in vet school. Miki worked at the clinic. Dr. Ken was at *The Creepy House*. "I know this is hard, but can you tell us about when she went missing?"

"Not really, no."

"Why not?" She wasn't going to tell them about how her daughter went missing?

"Nobody knows anything. The police seemed baffled. Is that the right word? She went to work, when was that? Four years ago now? And there were witnesses who saw her get in her car after and that was it." *Click, click* "No sightings, no phone calls, nobody used her bank card or credit cards. She just vanished, you know." Bev adjusted how she was sitting. She was knitting with a new vigour. *Click, click, click, click*

"And the police didn't find anything?" Chrys asked. Dawn had already told her the answer to that one.

"They told us she must have taken off. The police detective said, he said, people didn't just disappear like that. That she must have gone somewhere and didn't want to be found." *Click, click, click.* "Not my Miki. She wouldn't go off like that. She loved her old mom and dad."

Chrys saw tears run down the woman's face. Her stomach lurched. She didn't want to do it anymore. The old man did not say a word, but she could tell he wasn't watching the program on the television either. She was terrified when Bev suddenly got up and crossed to an armoire along the far wall. She brought back some photo albums.

"You know, those are lovely earrings," Beverly said as she rested her hands over the first book. It had the title Family Memories.

Chrys smiled with a polite thank you. She had forgotten about putting the earrings on. They were wire dream catchers with beads of smokey blue amongst the web and a single silver feather hanging down the middle. She absently tucked her hair behind her ear to show the matching magnetic bracelet. She thought the earrings brought her luck. As she watched the woman open the photo album she started to wonder. Chrys ignored her brother tapping her leg. They were torturing these two by asking questions about a lost child, so the least they could do was indulge the woman. It was only ten minutes before both women were crying.

~ * ~

Spencer parked his truck beside a white Nissan in front of the Middleton Vet Clinic and turned the engine off. He saw a woman go through the door with a small pet carrier.

"You can ask the questions this time," Chrys's voice was blank. Something caught in her throat. As she slipped down from the truck she wrapped her arms around herself. A chill blew up under her dress.

"You okay?" Spencer asked as he opened the clinic door. All his sister did was shrug her shoulders. After leaving the Harris's she went quiet. She just stared out the side window. Spencer was sure he saw tears on her face.

The inside of the clinic was alive. The woman with the carrier stood in line behind a short man with a balding head and an uncontrollable impulse to check his watch every few seconds. Another man sat in a chair to the left. His golden retriever stretched its leash and sniffed at the cat inside the case. A little boy stood on a chair facing a large glass case behind the seats. A snake inside ignored him. Phones rang and were answered with a, "Middleton Vet Clinic, can you please hold?" It was much busier than when Spencer brought Bullet in. The two ladies behind the front desk seemed frazzled. A lady wearing a white lab coat scratched her head as she flipped through charts. Unsatisfied she flipped through them again.

Chrys went directly to the chairs and slowly lowered into one near the boy. She crossed her legs and pulled her jacket in. As the eyes of the golden retriever's owner finally made it up to hers, he caught her browns staring at him with indifference and forcing him to look away.

As Spencer finally got to the counter he was greeted with a smile, "Hi, how can I help you?"

Spencer smiled back flashing his dimples. From his pocket he withdrew a paper Jessie had printed off for him showing the faces of Jessica Lamb and Miki Harris. There was a third picture there, but it was just a sketch of the unidentified woman. He asked, "Have you worked here awhile?"

"About seven years. Why?"

"Do you recognize any of these women?" He handed her the paper. Her eyes were automatically drawn to one.

"This is Miki. She worked here years ago before she," the woman leaned forward and covered her mouth with a hand, "was murdered."

"How long did she work here?" Spencer retrieved the page and shoved it in the pocket of his cashmere coat.

"A few months."

238

"Was she close to anyone?"

"At work? Maybe Tara. Why are you asking?"

Time to change things. "Is Dr. Ken available?"

"He's with a patient right now and we're very busy. What is your visit about?"

"My dog. My bulldog. He saw him a few days ago and I have some questions." *Yeah, sure.*

She stared at him with a slight sneer. She didn't believe him at all. For a few seconds he wasn't sure if she was going to answer. "Have a seat and I'll get you a few minutes as soon as he's done."

Twenty minutes later Dr. Ken walked out from the back. "Spencer, I have only a minute or two. What can I help you with?" He put his hands on his hips flaring out his white coat.

"Can we talk in private?"

"Ah, yeah, follow me."

Spencer looked at his sister. "You coming?"

She stared up at him for a moment. She pushed herself up with her arms as if she were pregnant. There was nothing feminine about it.

Spencer waited until they were in the small exam room with the door closed. He looked at the man in front of him and couldn't see it. Just hours ago he began to think this veterinarian was a serial killer. Looking at him now, Spencer couldn't see how it was be possible. "Do you remember Miki Harris? She worked here about four years ago." He handed over the paper with the photos.

Dr. Ken's tongue flicked out to moisten his lips. "Yes, I remember her. She was fresh out of school, so she worked with Tara more than me. She could probably tell you more."

"Can we talk to her?"

"What is this about, Spencer? Are you a private detective now?" He let out a laugh and looked at each of them.

Chrys didn't like the way the veterinarian's eyes lingered on her. Maybe she was seeing things, just like seeing a red truck everywhere. But the red truck *was* following them.

"Tara's not here," His eyes went back to the brother. "She never showed up for work today," he said with a twinge of annoyance.

Spencer caught his breath. His body tensed. *Another woman gone missing? Another victim?*

Dr. Ken's face broke into a smile. "Well, she called in sick. Same as not showing up, right?"

His eyes were strange, Chrys thought. They looked *into* you.

So many things went through Spencer's mind. *One of the women worked here.* Another was in veterinary school. Dr. Ken couldn't be a killer. He'd helped Spencer after he fell into the cistern. The chef blinked. Dr. Ken Stewart was part of the volunteer fire team out in Hillsborough. He had to live out there. *How did a dead hooker connect to the clinic? What did Enid have to do with it? Maeve wasn't even from the city. What if the other two were just coincidence?*

"So what was happening at the restaurant?"

"What?" Spencer realized he was staring at the doctor without seeing him.

"There was a picture in the paper this morning, but the story didn't say much. It just said police were there and speculated about it having something to do with the cistern body. Did you know they're calling it *The Cistern Killer* now?"

Were they in the room with The Cistern Killer? Was Chrys thinking the same thing? He avoided the question and asked, "Do you ever teach at the university, Dr. Ken?"

He leaned back against the counter, arms crossing over his chest. His white coat folded in the front, almost like a chef coat and fastened with buttons. It wasn't like a real doctor's coat, but it could pass for one at a distance, maybe. "No I don't."

"Have you," Spencer felt his face flush. *What the hell was he doing?* "Have you taken a train lately?"

Dr. Ken's smile slipped away. He said, "No. What is this about?"

Spencer felt Chrys's hand on his back. He kept his eyes on the man in front of him. "I'm just asking quest-"

"Tara took the train a couple weeks ago. After you found that woman in that house Tara told me she heard her sing on the train. Frightening, right? It could have been her instead."

So he wasn't the killer? Was he the killer? He could be lying. Spencer's head was spinning. He wasn't becoming paranoid because he was already there. He looked at his sister. She was staring back at him teetering on the brink of panic. Spencer asked, "Did you call the police? Maybe Tara-"

"She's my wife. We're separated."

"…saw something."

"I don't think so. She said she listened to the girl sing an hour or so then went back to her cabin and took a sleeping pill. She slept most of the trip. When Tara sleeps she really sleeps." He let out a laugh that sort of faded away. "I'm sorry, Spencer, but I really have to get back to actual patients. This was fun though, interesting. Dinner was great the other evening, by the way. Tara loved it."

"That was your wife you brought to dinner?" Chrys asked. They hadn't acted like married people in the restaurant, not married people who were separated.

Dr. Ken opened the door and kept his hand on it indicating the pair should leave. "We might be talking divorce, but we still have a pretty good relationship.

~ * ~

"Dr. Ken is the killer." Chrys stated as she grabbed a bottle of water from the fridge.

"I was thinking so at first, but I don't know. He's not the killer type."

"And what the fuck's the killer type, Spence?"

"I don't know. He wasn't shady."

"What the ape's balls is shady?"

"What are you guys talking about?" Jessie had tidied the apartment a little while they were gone.

Spencer rubbed the sides of Bullet's round belly. "I don't know. A killer should be evil or sinister or something. What about his wife? Maybe she's the killer. I don't know who it is."

"So what did you guys find out?" Jessie looked from one to the other. The dog's head followed the same movements.

Jessica Lamb was a veterinary student. She said she was going away for a weekend and just vanished. Miki Harris worked at the same clinic where the doctor who patched up Spencer outside *The Creepy House* worked. She just disappeared like smoke in the breeze. Enid went for a run in the country and ended up dead in a cistern. *Did she connect to Dr. Ken? How was the hooker involved? Was she involved?* Maeve was on a train with his estranged

242

wife. The lines were all there connecting together but didn't quite meet up. Three of four women were attached to the one man. He had been in the restaurant. He had seen Liz. Maybe he was the killer. Maybe it was somebody else. Chances were they didn't even know who it was.

"We need to call Dawn," Spencer said as he finished telling Jessie everything.

Chrys came walking back into the room from the bedrooms. She had changed into tight yoga pants and her dance studio's T-shirt. She said, "You call Dawn. I need to go to class."

"You're not going to class." Spencer rose from the couch. "We might have just confronted a serial killer, Chrys. He's not going to be happy."

Her arms went up. "I don't care. I'm going to walk to the studio and sweat a little. I need to burn off some energy."

"I'll drive you."

"No. Thank you for the thought, Spence, but I need to be alone. I've had enough of this shit."

"No, I'll drive you."

"I said, no." Chrys raised her voice. Her cheeks were red and her eyes glared. "I want to be alone."

Spencer ran a hand back through his hair. He looked at Jessie who just shrugged her shoulders. That wasn't any help. He dug in his pocket and handed Chrys the keys to the truck. "Take this. I'd rather you drive than walk. It's safer."

"Oh fuck, whatever." She took the keys anyway.

Chapter Eighteen

Leg warmers.

Ankle wraps.

Towel.

Water bottle.

Chrys was sure she had everything she needed. She had already changed and planned on wearing the same clothes home, so she had everything.

Music. She had been listening to some songs the other night she thought would be good for a dance routine. The girls had a Christmas recital coming up and then there was a competition in late January to which they had been invited. She wanted them to have a new routine. She tossed her *iPod* into her bag as she stormed out. Chrys heard her brother yell at her to be careful as the door closed.

The cold bit right through her tight pants as the wind swirled up the stairs. Through the door she heard Breeze yap her unhappiness about being left behind. Chrys zipped her jacket up, flung her bag over her shoulder and headed down the stairs. Her boots crunched the light dusting of snow that had collected on each step. Soon she'd have to break out her mukluks. The days were getting shorter and the moment the sun went down the temperature dropped. The sun was setting.

She tried her best not to think of all that was happening, but as she quickly took each step, her mind wandered over the recent happenings. She looked around for a red truck. Her brother and his mobster bum buddy said the guy in the red truck had nothing to do with any of it. He was a mobster. He wasn't going to admit to anything. She knew what he was. *And why did he use her full first name the other night?* She didn't like how he said, Chrysanthemum. It was too familiar. *Who the hell was he?*

Then there was this thing with Dr. Ken. He seemed so nice and genuine. *How could he be the killer? Wouldn't he have done something to them while they were in his office?* That would have been stupid. There were too many people around for him to really do something. She stopped halfway down the stairs and looked around the back parking lot. The only vehicles there were Spencer's truck and Jessie's *Volkswagen Beetle.* She even leaned over the railing, knocking the snow from it, to check beneath the stairs. There was nothing there. More snow had softened the tracks leading from the doors of the truck and from around the building. Neighbourhood people always cut through the back of the restaurant building, but there was no indication of recent activity.

The other thing that wouldn't leave her mind was the smell of Liz's charred body. The restaurant smelled like roasted meat. The smell had even wafted up to the second floor. When Chrys took a quick shower before going out she tilted her head back so that the flow of water went into her nostrils. She was more than glad she didn't see the body, see her, see Liz. She was curious though, but if she had looked into that oven or the toilet tank those images

246

would never leave her mind. She was still innocent in a way.

A smile burst across her lips. *You're far from fucking innocent, Chrys,* she thought as she pushed the unlock button on the truck key. Her brother had a lot of extras on his truck, like runners that came out from underneath when a door was opened. It made it easier for her when she had been wearing her dress. As she opened the door this time she slipped back slightly to avoid the runner.

She tossed her bag across to the passenger side and climbed in.

Chrys looked at herself in the rear-view mirror. Her skin was red around the eyes. She brushed her hair back behind her ear. She still wore the dreamcatcher earrings. *Damn it.* She forgot to take them off when she was changing. She'd have to make sure to put them in her jacket pocket before hitting the floor at the studio in case any of her students were there. It was barely supper time, so kids were certain to be there.

She turned the key in the ignition. Loud music blared through the speakers.

"What the ..." The radio wasn't that loud when they got back from the veterinarians. Chrys leaned over and turned down the volume. As she sat up, her eyes flicked to the rear-view mirror. There was a shadow there, a shadow behind her.

Oh my God!

Hands reached out of the dark.

Chrys turned to the door. She had to get out. She had to scream. *Spencer.*

A hand clasped down on her mouth. Another grabbed the side of her head.

Fuck.

There was a smell. *What was that?*

There were stars and flashes of red in her eyes.

She had to run.

Chrys lurched forward. Something hooked her earlobe. There was a ripping pain. *What was it?* A sound that she couldn't understand escaped her throat. She felt heat on the side of her neck. Her head hit the door frame. The world spun. Chrys felt like she was falling. *Was she falling?* Pain. Something cold touched her face, her body.

The world turned rapidly. Things faded around the outside. Dark replaced light.

Chapter Nineteen

"What are you thinking about?" Jessie flopped down on the couch beside Spencer and curled her feet beneath her. She reached out and started massaging the back of his neck.

Spencer squeezed the bridge of his nose. He liked the feeling of her fingers against his skin. He moved a little so she had a better angle. "What am I not thinking about?" he said and moaned. "I have to find money for a new oven and a toilet for downstairs. We're closed on a Friday night. We're going to be closed tomorrow night too. That's thousands of dollars in lost revenue."

"You can't think about it like that."

"What if customers don't come back? Would you eat at a place where a person was cooked?" He let his head drop back flattening the woman's hand behind his neck. His head rolled until he was looking at her.

Her eyes were warm. You couldn't tell if she had been crying or not, even though she had. She was a tough lady, so she had probably gone through that stage of grief and moved on. She said softly, "We'll think of something."

"Will we?" Spencer liked thinking of them as "we." It scared him too much to tell her, but he still liked it.

Jessie put her other hand on the side of his face and brought her lips to his. Their thin lips fought with each other. She sucked on his lower one. Moist tongues caressed alongside each other. As she pushed back a thin line of their joined spit strung out between them. "We should go out. When do we ever have a Friday off? We should go out to dinner."

Spencer ran his hand along her thigh. "Where do you want to go?"

"What about that new tapas place?"

"It's not even six o'clock yet."

"Then we go to a movie afterward. Let's just get away from here."

He thought about the money it would cost for a night of entertainment. Everything seemed to come down to dollars and cents. If he sat there in his apartment he'd be tempted to go downstairs and clean things and he really didn't want to do that. Not yet. "Let's go then."

Spencer helped Jessie with her jacket as best he could with a bum hand. As they stepped onto the top landing of the stairs, the cold smacked him in the face. He'd swear it got colder since they had been home. The snow had stopped falling. "My truck's still here."

"Maybe Chrys walked. You know how she gets."

"Yeah, maybe." There was a pain in Spencer's chest. *He told Chrys to take the truck, so why was it still there?* He took the steps two at a time. His shoes slipped on the snow. This wasn't right. Something was very wrong. The snow around the driver's side door had been disturbed. *Was that her getting into the truck and then changing her mind?* There were too many tracks. There was something red. Blood.

"Oh my God, Spence."

Spencer tore open the driver's side door. There was blood on the seat. He reached in and picked up a dreamcatcher earring with smoky blue beads and a piece of flesh hanging from the earlobe hook. He stepped on the runner and looked behind the seat. The camping gear was still there. There was an empty spot behind the driver's side. *Had someone been there? How could they have gained entrance without anyone seeing? Chrys had been here. Was that Chrys's earlobe? Where was she now?*

"What happened, Spencer? Where's Chrys?" Jessie tugged at his coat.

There were no other cars around. The tracks in the snow were scattered at best. Something was dragged away toward the curb. *Chrys?* The doctor.

Spencer grabbed Jessie's shoulders. "Go back upstairs and lock the doors. Lock the door to the restaurant and call Dawn. Tell her what happened. Then call Gordie and Hanni and everyone else and get them to come to the apartment. You'll be safe in numbers." He climbed into the truck without another word, shut the door and started the engine. As he drove away he saw her, in the rear-view mirror, running up the stairs.

His phone rang. He knew it was illegal but he pushed the button to answer it and brought it to his ear. "Chrys?"

"No, it's Dawn. Where is she?"

"I don't know. There was some blood and a struggle." He quickly looked down at the speedometer. He was going way too fast. The police were going to stop him before he got anywhere.

"Blood? What are you talking about?" Dawn's voice was harsh as though she was trying to keep it low enough not to be overheard.

Spencer slowed for a stop sign then pushed the gas to power around the corner. "What?"

She grunted in frustration. "Where's Maeve Campbell?"

Where's Maeve Campbell? What did she mean? She was at the hospital. She had to be at the hospital.

"What?" His eyes fell from the road. He looked back up, braked and steered around a car that appeared out of nowhere.

"Maeve Campbell's gone, Spencer. She had a visitor and then just disappeared this afternoon. You've gone to see her. Where is she?"

Maeve? Dr. Ken had been at the vet clinic, he saw him there. How could he have taken Maeve? Did he have Chrys? Did Gaylen? Did Liam O'Donnell? Who the hell was he after? "He, he has Chrys. Someone took Chrys. There's blood …"

"What the hell are you talking about, Spencer?"

"I don't know what happened." He threw the phone onto the seat.

The Middleton Vet Clinic closed at six. It was five after as Spencer slammed the truck into park and jumped from the seat. He expected the door to be locked. It opened on the first tug. The woman behind the front desk looked startled.

"We're closed."

"Where's Dr. Ken?"

"He left a few minutes ago."

"A few minutes ago? He's got his Porsche right?" Spencer didn't wait for an answer. As he climbed back behind the wheel he grabbed his cell phone and shoved it into his pocket.

He had to guess which way Dr. Ken would go. *If he had Chrys where would head?* Out to Hillsborough. A couple of turns and it was a straight stretch out of the city to the country where he could be all alone. On a low traffic day he could be out of the city in ten minutes. It was rush hour; even with the powerful engine in his car it would be closer to thirty minutes for him to be out of the city, even with the powerful engine in his car. But he couldn't have both women with him. *Was one of them dead?* Spencer saw the grey sports car in front of a bus. His heart raced in his chest. His mouth was dry and his head spun. The bus turned. He pushed down on the gas pedal staring straight ahead at his target without a simple glance at his speed.

Spencer didn't really know what to do. He didn't want to try running him off the road, *Bourne Identity* style, in case he was wrong. *Wrong?* He didn't have a clue what was right. He wailed on his horn. He saw the man in the Porsche look in his mirrors. Spencer expected him to push down on his gas pedal to leave the blue truck behind. Instead he signalled and turned off the street into the parking lot of a motorcycle show room. Dr. Ken stopped in the first parking space. Spencer cut off the front end of the man's car with his truck and leapt from the driver's seat.

He marched toward the driver's door. Anger rose deep inside him. He didn't know what to do. He wasn't sure what he was willing to do. The door opened. "Where the fuck is she?" Spencer yelled channeling his little sister.

Dr. Ken got out of the fancy car. Everything about him looked calm and set, just like when he was in his office. "What the hell, Spencer?"

"Where's Chrys? Where's Maeve?"

"What are you talking about?" Dr. Ken did a fine job of keeping his door between the two of them.

"Look," Spencer held up his right hand which had tried to wipe the blood from his seat, "This is Chrys's blood.

Someone took her and ripped her frigging ear half off. You did this."

"What? Who the hell do you think you are? I didn't do anything to your sister." His nostrils flared. His eyes glared at the chef.

Spencer's shoulders dropped. "Then where is she?"

"Spencer, I don't know what you're talking about."

"We found five women in total who've disappeared and ended up either dead or beaten and dead. One worked as a vet assistant for your clinic, one was in the vet school, another was on a train with your wife. I don't know how the Jane Doe hooker and Enid Bernadine are connected, but there has to be something."

"Enid Bernadine?" Dr. Ken stepped around the driver's door and closed it. "Who was she?"

Spencer's adrenaline was threatening to run out. He said, "The dead woman from the cistern."

"I remember that name." The doctor's eyes showed an immense amount of emotion. He was being honest. "Enid's a hard name to forget?"

Had Spencer asked him about Enid or just showed him her picture?

Dr. Ken continued, "She interviewed to be an administrator at the clinic. Tara interviewed her once and then she never showed for her final interview."

"Dr. Ken, I'm going to ask you something and I want you to really think about it and be honest. What type of person is your wife?"

"What?"

"I mean," Spencer went on, "is she stable? Would she hurt people? She's the only one right now that seems to be connected to most of these women." He scratched his scalp through his hair. "I don't get it, but I don't know her."

Dr. Ken sighed, "Maybe I don't either." He fell back against his car. Other vehicles slowed as they drove around the awkwardly parked truck and took a look at them, but they didn't really notice. "She was always jealous." His fist hit the car. He looked at the street then up toward the sky. He looked everywhere but at the man in front of him. "I had an affair with Miki Harris. I didn't realize Tara knew, but she must have. She always said she'd torture and kill anyone if I ever fooled around. I thought it was just an idle threats."

"Where would she take Chrys?" This was crazy. *Why would she take Chrys?* Spencer watched Dr. Ken shake his head and lift his hands in frustration. "*The Creepy House*. I'm going to *The Creepy House*."

"I'll take you," Kenneth said quickly. "If this is Tara I can calm her down. If it's not, I'm a big guy. And my car's a lot faster than your truck." He opened the driver's door as if the decision were already made.

Spencer's mind was everywhere at the same time; nothing could become a solid thought. *A woman did all of this? How did she kidnap these other women?* He supposed a woman could get the confidence of another woman a lot easier than a man could. *How did she get Maeve off the train? What if it wasn't her? Who had Chrys?* He looked at his truck and wondered if it would be safe to leave it in the parking lot. *Did he have a choice?* Something had to be done. He had to do something. He had to find Chrys. He had to find Maeve. *Where were they?*

Dr. Ken asked, "Are you coming or not?"

Without another thought Spencer returned to his truck. His hand touched the earring. Chrys was hurt. He moved the truck to a proper parking space then slid out and got into the passenger side of the Porsche. The roads were awash with melting snow. He didn't know how well the sports car's tires would hold up. He didn't care. Shit, he didn't even know if he had just climbed in to a car with a killer.

Chapter Twenty

Pain. She felt pain. Chrys knew that if she felt something then she was still alive. She also felt something sticky. It was on the side of her face and down the front of her throat. Her hand wiped at it. *Had Kyle brought something to bed again? Kyle? No, they broke up a long time ago. She was seeing Dawn now.*

She touched her ear. Pain popped through the side of her head. *What the hell was that? Why did her ear hurt so much? Why wouldn't her eyes open? Earrings!* She had been wearing earrings. She should have taken them off before leaving the house for the dance studio. She had been going to the dance studio. *Did she get there?*

Earrings. She was wearing her favorite dreamcatcher earrings. She touched the left side of her face. Her fingers found her ear, her earring still dangling from the earlobe. She touched the right side of her face. *Was it her cheek or her hand that was sticky? Why couldn't she see?* She touched her ear. It was wet, sticky. Pain. *Where was her earring? Where was her earlobe?* It was there, but it felt like some of it was missing.

Oh my god. What the hell is going on?

The truck. There was snow. She was going to the dance studio. There was a shadow. Hands reached out from the dark behind her. The cistern. Spencer had fallen in the cistern. *Where was he? Where was she?*

Panic rose inside her. It sat in her chest ready to burst. There was a foul taste in her mouth. It was something chemical that she couldn't place. *Had she'd been drugged? No, something had gone over her mouth. What had happened to her?*

Her eyes were open, but she couldn't see anything. She quickly moved her hands over her body. Any woman's greatest fear was being sexually violated. She couldn't imagine what it would be like to wake up and realize you had been raped and there was nothing you could have done. She had bad things happen to her in the past, but she was lucky that it never went that far. Her hands moved over her body. Her yoga pants and shirt seemed to be in place. She still wore her sports bra underneath and her jacket over top. Her side hurt and was wet, however nothing else on her body hurt as much as her ear. She took that as a good thing.

Why couldn't she see? Her eyes were open. There was nothing there but darkness.

Her hand touched water, cold water. It recoiled back. She had to think this out. She had to shake the webs from her brain.

Where am I?

Chrys pushed herself to a sitting position. Whatever was underneath her was damp and cold. As she felt around she discovered there was water around her. Her body was raised up on something keeping her out of the water. Her hand reached into it. It was just a black sea around her. Underneath the liquid was a hard bottom, rough to the touch. It was solid. The cistern. She was in the cistern.

But then she should see things, shouldn't she? It smelled different. It wasn't as stale and foul as before. It didn't make any sense. She stretched her hands out to either side. One touched something solid. The wall. She ran her hand along the rough surface. Her fingers traced the indented lines. Cinderblocks. She was back there.

She was in the cistern. *Oh Go!*

Wood creaked. *Where was it? Above her head? Around her head?* She couldn't tell. Chrys wasn't even certain what was up any more. It felt like her brain was sitting in *Jell-O* that hadn't solidified yet. She couldn't see anything. Logic said that up was above her. *Was it?*

"Are you awake?"

A voice? Who's voice? Where was it coming from?

"You should be awake by now." It was a woman's voice. *That was a good thing, right?*

Chrys still couldn't tell where the voice was coming from. Pain spider-webbed through her skull. Something was walking on the roof. There was another sound. Metal against metal. Wood creaked. Something above her lifted. Light suddenly shone down on her so bright she had to squeeze her eyelids shut.

"You awake?"

Chrys pushed herself to stand. Her head spun like she was on an amusement park tilt-a-whirl ride and her brother was trying to get her to throw up by spinning it faster and faster. *Spencer, where was Spencer?*

"He's coming, you know," the voice in the light said as if the owner of it read her thoughts. "He'll be here soon. The games will start then."

Spencer was in trouble.

259

Chapter Twenty-One

"None of this makes any sense," Dr. Ken said as he switched gears. The car sent up a cloud of soft snow.

Spencer stared out the window. It was a fast car, but he felt like he lacked the control he had driving his truck. He looked at his watch. Time was ticking away.

"How could Tara do this?"

Spencer lost track of how many times Dr. Ken had asked the same question. He started ignoring him around the sixth time. The whole thing kept repeating inside his head. None of it was making sense. *Why would this woman take other women?*

"I never believed she would actually hurt anyone."

"You said that already."

"I know, but I can't believe it. We've known each other since we were kids."

"Then why would she?" Spencer asked. "I don't get why she would do this to these women. Some she didn't even know. What could Maeve have done to her? What did Liz do? And some random hooker?"

He looked away from the road in front of them. "I don't know." His eyes returned to the road as he signalled the final turn. "She's an angry woman. I know when she was younger she had violence issues. Something to do with animals."

"And she's a vet?"

Dr. Ken smirked. "Veterinary assistant. She said it was a phase she went through. She told me she wanted to redeem herself by going to veterinary school."

"How did you two meet?" Spencer looked at his watch again. *What was happening to Chrys?*

"We were neighbours. We played together a lot, went to the same elementary school, then high school. I'm a few years older so I graduated first and went to vet school. Six years ago she came to the clinic in a school work program. One thing lead to another, as they say. It had been years, but we still had so much in common. We had similar interests."

"So what happened?" He didn't really care.

Dr. Ken looked across the small interior. He said, "Personal issues. Wanting different things."

Spencer checked his watch and saw the date. It was hard to believe that just six days ago he and Chrys saw *The Creepy House* for the first time. They found Maeve and Enid's body in the cistern and began this journey that brought him back to the same horrible place.

He held his breath as he saw the front light of *The Creepy House* breaking through the cracks in the tree wall. He couldn't remember how it got so dark. The days were getting shorter. He didn't really notice it in the city since it was always light there. Fear made his body tingle. His muscles twitched with nervous energy. He observed tire tracks of other vehicles that had been on the road. As Dr. Ken turned into the driveway the headlights washed over the trees and down the driveway.

"There are no tracks here," Dr. Ken said reading the chef's mind.

Nobody's been here.

"They, they could have gone around back or something." Even Spencer didn't believe himself. The snow around the front of the house was pristine. Nothing had disturbed the white except the tall dead grass whenever the wind was able to touch it. The only light was the one outside the door. He had the car door open before the it came to a stop.

"Spencer."

The temperature had dropped since the sun went down. His foot slipped on the fresh snow. His eyes searched everywhere. There was no movement. He didn't hear any sounds. His hand circled the doorknob of the front door. It didn't turn. The door didn't open. He pushed and tugged it a few times rattling the square window. There was no one there.

"Maybe we should try somewhere else," Dr. Ken stood by his car. "It doesn't look like anyone's been here."

"Where do you want to try? We don't have anywhere else to go." Spencer had to decide what to do. He had to find his sister. He started walking toward the deck. There was the large window there. Maybe he could see something.

"I don't know, but there's nobody here. We could go to my house. Tara lives there by herself now."

Spencer looked back over his shoulder at the man. They had a house nearby. That's how Dr. Ken was on the volunteer fire team.

His foot hit something and he nearly stumbled. It was a large ceramic flower pot. The plant that had once grown in it was long dead, only a gnarly brown stem remained. The brown grass had woven around the pot obscuring it from sight. He stepped around it and climbed the stairs onto the deck. The snow was untouched here too.

He took his phone from his pocket. It was still engaged in a call. *Who had he last called?* He shook his head, pushed the "off" button, and looked for his flashlight app. The screen burst into a white light. He put his face and the phone up to the big window. Again there was nothing inside except for what they had seen six days before. The far wall, the one with the torn wallpaper, still looked like it was bleeding. Chrys could be in there.

What was Ken saying?

Spencer had to get into the house.

He jumped off the deck. Spencer took the ceramic flower pot in both hands. His fingers went instantly cold. Pain shot through his left wrist as he pushed and pulled it back and forth trying to break the hold of the grass and frozen ground. It barely budged. He took a step back. His foot shot out hitting the top edge of the pot; it rocked.

"Spencer what are you doing?"

Spencer didn't know what he was doing. He just knew he had to do something. He heaved the pot into his arms and walked back onto the deck. The large bay window shattered as the flower pot crashed into it. It hit the floor inside with a crack.

If anyone was in there they knew he was coming.

The chef was in the living room in seconds. His shoes slipped and cracked on the broken glass. With his phone he looked around. Nothing seemed to have been disturbed. He was certain the police had taken things, but he couldn't really tell what. The case with Maeve's CDs was gone.

Maeve.

Chrys.

Spencer ignored the protests coming from the man who reluctantly followed him into the building. He had to get downstairs.

It was just as creepy as before. His phone cast eerie shadows down the walls as he quickly. His shoes slipped, making him go faster. If someone was waiting at the bottom there was no blocking. He stumbled into the room at the base of the stairs. There was nobody there. He rapidly cast the light around. In his mind he was certain that if he moved fast enough he would see someone in the shadows, hiding in the corners, watching him. There wasn't anyone. The fan continued to oscillate.

He knew where to go. He had to go there, but he didn't want to. He entered the furnace room and saw the cinderblock walls.

"Chrys. Chrys are you in there?" His voice cracked like the glass.

He moved between the outer wall of the cistern and the outside wall of the basement. *Was Tara going to be waiting? How much damage could she do to him? Did she have a weapon? A gun?* The makeshift ladder was still there. With his phone in his left hand, he pulled himself up with his right. There was nothing on top. The trap door was open. He slowly peered over the edge. The last time he had done this hands grabbed out at him and pulled him into the wet dark tomb.

Nothing. There was nothing in there. Even the water had been drained by the RCMP. Spencer dropped himself back down the ladder. His back slumped against the outer wall. *Where was Chrys?*

"She's not here," Spencer said with defeat in his voice as he made it back to the kitchen at the top of the stairs. The lights were on. The top floor was already cold from the broken window.

Dr. Ken tapped his hand on the stove top. "I searched up here. There's nobody. These people just left all this stuff here, eh? Your, hand's bleeding."

Spencer looked down at his right hand. There was a gash across his palm. A tiny piece of shining glass still sat there in the blood from when he pulled himself through the window. It wasn't until that moment that he felt pain. "I'm going to search outside."

There were no human tracks around the back of the house, but an animal (possibly a dog or coyote) had crossed through. Something small had made tiny prints in the snow from one tree to another. The police had secured the shed out back with plastic ties after having broken the lock on the door to search inside. The ties were still there, secure. Spencer searched the ground for a rock, something he could use to break the latch that held the ties together. He started kicking at the snow and grass. There had to be something there he could use.

"What are you doing?" Dr. Ken asked.

Spencer didn't even look at him. "I have to get in there. I have to search everything." Chrys had to be somewhere. *If she wasn't here, if Tara hadn't brought her here, then where was she?* He didn't want to give in to the fact that he didn't have a clue.

"They're not here, Spencer." Ken grabbed his sleeve, but Spencer pulled from his grip. "We have to look somewhere else. Our house is right near here. Tara's been staying there since we separated and I've been renting a place in the city. Let's see if they're there."

If they aren't then Chrys and Maeve are dead, was Spencer's only thought.

266

Chapter Twenty-Two

A shiver ran through Chrys's body. She tried to focus as a ladder, or stairs maybe, unfolded from the open hole in the ceiling. It sparkled and floated in front of her eyes, much like the haze of summer that sat atop paved roads on the hottest of days.

Drugs. That foul smell she remembered from when she was in the truck. *What had that been?* Her head was spinning.

A foot landed on the first step.

Chrys dipped her face into the cold water. The chill stung her skin. She pulled her head back and the water cascaded down her front. It didn't taste foul. It didn't have that disgusting stench as when they found the women in the cistern. She tasted fresh mud as the water ran over her full lips.

Boots clicked down the stairs from the bright light above the box she sat in. "Maybe we should start before he comes," said the voice. At first there were lithe legs in tight jeans. As she got further down Chrys saw it was the woman who was with Dr. Ken when he came to dinner. Waves of dark-brown hair fell over her shoulders. She was a good-looking woman. Her eyes stared across the horrible room at the young woman who still couldn't see straight. "What should we do first?"

Chrys tried to stand up. Her legs failed her and she crumpled on top of them. Her feet ended up underneath her and her hands on the small landing. "What did you do to me?"

The woman laughed. "I made a little mixture of some medicines from work. Just something that made you sleep and makes your head spin around. Perfectly harmless, but you'll feel like a drunk for a while. Not bad, eh?"

"You bitch." She spat.

The woman's boots splashed into the water covering the floor. "Do you remember me?"

Chrys wobbled to one side and then the other. Her knees were bent tight to her body. "You were at The Alcrest with ..."

"My husband. And there you were flaunting your tight young body in front of him."

"I didn't."

"Oh shut up. You all do. Why else would you wear those tight clothes at work? It's not like it makes your job any easier. I saw you strut your little ass in front of him." She kicked at the water as she walked toward Chrys. She held a metal rod in her hands. "He talked about you when you and your fucking brother let our other playmate out. He mentioned you by name." She shouted the last. "Kenny's got the hots for you."

"Why did you kill Liz?"

Tara tapped ringed fingers against the metal rod one after the other. Chrys saw she was still wearing all the rings from the other night. "I saw the way she looked at Ken. I just wanted to play with her a little."

"What? She wasn't there the other … when did you see her?"

"Monday night. Kenny so wanted to go see you again. Too bad you weren't there. Maybe your little baker would be alive. Do you know what killed her?"

Chrys used her hands to move her body a little. She rested her weight on the balls of her feet. She wanted to tell the woman that cutting off Liz's head was probably what killed her.

The woman said, "She spat on me." Her foot flicked a spray of water up toward her prisoner. "Ken called me and told me about that little dress you were wearing today. Who were you trying to impress?"

Chrys's muscles tightened. Her arms and legs were like elastic bands pulled taut. It felt similar to when she and her friends protested in high school and joined the football team just because they said girls couldn't play. She was ready.

Her body exploded. She shot forward with all the muscles she had working together. She speared her shoulder into the other woman's stomach. Tara's breath left her. The metal pole flew from the woman's fingers. Chrys's hands clasped behind her legs as she half lifted the woman's body. It was all muscle memory from her year in football.

A loud crack echoed through the room as Tara hit the stairs. The woman growled and fell.

Chrys's head spun wildly. The room was turning. Her hand grabbed the stairs. Her feet slipped backward. She felt slivers dig into her fingertips as she pulled herself up the stairs. She had to go. She had to run. Her feet stumbled under her. The light up top made her eyes hurt. It was false light. A strong bulb swung from a pole. She turned, or the world spun around her, she wasn't sure.

There was a house with lights burning inside the windows. There was machinery. She saw lights moving.

Headlights.

There was a road in that direction and headlights were heading toward her. In her mind she tried to get her feet to move. They didn't want to listen to her. The drugs she had in her system were too strong. Chrys leaned forward and suddenly her feet shuffled beneath her.

A scream echoed from the hole in the ground she had just escaped. She couldn't go back there.

Chapter Twenty-Three

Twenty years ago.

"Can I see?" The little dark-haired girl sounded so sweet.

The boy's fingers flexed around the handle of the knife. Mommy was always looking for it. She didn't know he kept it under his mattress. Sometimes he went into her bedroom at night, the knife in his hand, and watched her sleep. She awoke once. He put the knife behind his leg and said he had bad dreams. She told him to get a drink of water and go back to sleep.

"Okay, Mommy."

As the girl came closer the boy kept his arm down, hand and knife behind his leg.

Mrrreeeooooowwwww

She smiled at him. Her dark curly hair bounced over her shoulder. She stepped up to the box and let her eyes fall. Her smile seemed to grow at the corners. Her hair draped along her cheeks.

The boy's hand tightened. *What was this going to be like?* He continued to grow. A warmth filled him.

"You're doing it wrong."

271

The muscles in his arm eased.

"You can't tell them it's gonna be okay while hurtin' em. You gotta be nice."

"What?"

She sunk down onto her heels beside the box.

Meeeewwwww. The cat wailed at the newcomer.

The boy watched as the girl suddenly produced a thin copper wire, looped like a balloon, from her sleeve. His eyes followed the wire until he saw the other end twisted around a belt loop on her jeans.

"This is a rabbit snare," she said as if there had been a question. "My Daddy taught me." There was a mark on her arm below the wrist where a long sleeve would normally cover it. The mark was about the same diameter as a cigarette. "My Daddy's taught me lots of things."

She leaned over the box making the loop a little bigger.

The cat tried to roll to its side. It took a swipe at the wire.

The girl pushed on the block with her other hand.

Meeerrroooowwwww

The loop slipped around the cat's neck. The girl pulled back so it tightened just enough that the cat couldn't slip out. "Watch this," the smile covered her whole face. She rolled the cinderblock onto its side.

The cat sprung from the box. The boy lurched as if to catch it. The knife fell to the ground. Two feet away the cat's body suddenly flew into the air. It's hind end shot out from under it and the animal crashed to the ground. The cat got to its feet again and tried to run. The wire around its neck got tighter and tighter.

The girl's laughter filled the air and danced around them. She was delighted with what she had done. "See? If

272

you're nice they'll hurt themselves." She looked at the boy. "I'm Tara. What's your name?"

"Kenny."

Chapter Twenty-Four

"It's just down here," Dr. Ken said as he turned the car onto a narrow side road. It had a thin line of grass down the middle that stood through the snow. "Our place is nice and private down here. That was Tara's idea too. I guess I know why now."

Spencer felt a rising in his chest. It was fear and excitement all bubbling together. He needed to get out of the small car. He needed to know where his sister was. *What was he going to tell his mother if he couldn't save her?*

"It was just a fixer-upper when we got it. We added new windows, new roof. I built on a two-car garage with a large office above it. I repaved the driveway and brought in professionals to beautify the grounds. All the improvements we've made have cost a lot, but the sick puppies, kittens, and horses keep me able to afford it." He brought the Porsche to a stop in front of the garage. "Just a few months ago we saw something in another house and thought it would make a great addition to our back yard."

Something hit the side-window. Both men jumped. Spencer's fists came up.

Chrys.

Spencer pushed open his door. "Chrys." She collapsed against his body as his arms wrapped around her. She was suddenly heavy as if she couldn't hold herself up any more. He turned and leaned her against the side of the car. His hand pushed back her wet hair which stuck to the sides of her face. Blood smeared across her forehead.

"She's after me," Chrys said. Her brother seemed to be weaving back and forth as if swaying to some music. *Was it his body swaying or her own?* "She, she drugged me. She was waiting for you to come."

"You've got blood. Your ear." Spencer pushed her hair back. Her earlobe was torn open. The blood had dried and crusted.

"We have to run."

Dr. Ken walked around the car and said, "We should find her. I know I can calm her and get her to give up."

"She's crazy. She thought I was flirting with you or something. She was going to beat me."

"We have to stop her." Dr. Ken started off around the side of the house without looking back at the two of them.

Spencer looked at his sister. He knew she was in pain, he knew she was frightened, but he couldn't let that other woman stay out there. She still had Maeve. He took Chrys's hand and followed the other man into the dark.

The light flowing from the house windows lit the way around the building. There was a large deck at the back that stretched around the side. Further out in the darkness was a tall mechanical dinosaur. Its powerful scoop was dirty from digging the earth. Spencer didn't know what that was for. Chrys had a clue. She didn't want to go back there. She didn't feel good. Her feet were numb in the snow. They couldn't see the doctor. *Where was he?*

He appeared from the dark. "Watch out."

Something moved. Spencer turned and saw the two-by-four swinging through the air. It struck against his ribs. The cracking sound erupted in his ears. Pain spider-webbed through his body. He let go of his sister's hand. His eyes were wide. He couldn't breathe any more.

Tara was there. She swung the board again. It connected with Spencer's back sending him to his knees. He yelled.

Chrys swung. Her fist hit skin and jaw bone. Teeth flew from the woman's mouth.

"No," Ken yelled. His arm flew out. The back of his hand crossed Chrys's cheek.

She stumbled back. Her body flew through the air. The ground came up fast and slammed against her back. Her air was gone. She closed her eyes and hoped for the pain to go away.

Chrys opened her eyes. She was wet and cold. She could breathe again. Black stretched all around her except for the hole of light above. She rolled over, groaning in pain, and pushed onto her knees before shakily getting to her feet. Her body felt week. She knew she could fall any second, but she had to stand. She had to keep fighting. She wasn't going to let anyone rape her or play games with her.

"Still standing are you?" The voice was far away. It wasn't the same voice as before. This was a man's voice. "How are you at catching?"

Chrys looked up as something came down the stairs towards her. She put her arms out. The heavy body of her brother collapsed against her. She staggered back. Her feet slipped under the water sprawling her back half on the small platform. Her brother's body was heavy against her. A moan came from him. She could smell his sweat and blood. The cold water chilled her body.

"Spencer? You okay, Spencer?"

"He's not." Dr. Ken stepped a few stairs down so that his head was just below the ground. He stared at her with a smile to his lips. "I'm guessing he has cracked ribs, maybe even internal bleeding."

"Did I hit him that hard?" Tara appeared beside him. Her arms wrapped around her husband.

Chrys hugged her brother. With him she was safe. It had always been that way.

"I think so. Doesn't matter though. We're not keeping him for long."

Tara threw her head back in an over-the-top laugh. Blood had trickled from the side of her mouth and down her throat. Her lips were already swelling. "I don't think she understands you."

"I'll make it simple then. Your brother is going to live long enough to watch me fuck you." Dr. Ken stared down at her with the most evil expression Chrys had ever seen on another human being.

"You come near me and I'll rip your cock off you …"

"You won't. Every time you do something wrong your brother is going to get punished," he stepped up and looked out the hole.

Chrys couldn't remember which way she had run or which way they had come from, so she didn't know what he was looking at.

He stepped back down and said, "Your brother's going to die. When depends on you. You'll be with us a long time. Tara's studied different ways to torture a person to the brink of death. And then we have the training to bring you back. I'm guessing you'll last," he looked outside again. Both of them ran up to the surface. The stairs suddenly curled upward and the door closed. Blackness overtook the room. There was the click of a lock fastening.

The cistern went quiet. Chrys listened to her brother's jagged breathing. She strained to hear what was happening above them. No sounds came through the solid walls or could penetrate the pounding in her head. Her cheek burned where she had been struck. She knew more pain was coming.

"Chrys," Spencer said and breathed in rapidly.

"Don't talk," she said. That's what they said in the movies. She adjusted her arms around him. He let out moans with each movement and she regretted it. "I'm so sorry, Spence. This is all my …"

"I need ... to ... tell you ... about ... Liam O'Donnell." All of his words were cut short by attempts to breathe.

"I don't want to hear anything about him." Tears began to flow down Chrys's cheeks. She wanted to wipe them away, only she didn't want to move and give her brother more pain. "I don't care about whatever you have with him. It doesn't matter."

"He ... knows ... about you."

"I don't care." Her brown eyes stared where she knew the door was. No light came through at all, but some sounds were starting to, muffled sounds that she couldn't make out.

"No," Spencer tried to move and pain squeezed his insides. All of his bones felt like they would shatter at the faintest touch. "He ... knows ... about ... your ... mother."

"Shut up."

A groan rolled out of his throat. There were more muffled sounds from outside. Spencer said, "I miss Dad."

Chrys sniffed. "Me too."

"I smelled ... green olives the other ... the other day. Remember Dad would," he ground his teeth together in pain, "come home ..."

"And sit in his chair eating olives from the jar and watching the sports headlines," Chrys rapidly finished for him.

The trap door opened. Light streamed down from above. Chrys closed her eyes. A voice came down. It called her name. It called her brother's name.

"Dawn?"

"Chrys, are you down there?"

It was Dawn.

"Spencer's hurt."

Chapter Twenty-Five

"Let me give you a hand, Mr. Alcrest."

"Dude, every time I've seen you, you've been flirting with my sister. Please don't call me, Mr. Alcrest." Spencer braced his hand on the arm of the wheelchair. He awkwardly tried to figure out how to place his casted hand without hurting himself.

Chrys opened the passenger door to Jessie's Beetle. They thought it would be easier for the wounded man than having to climb into the truck.

Marc, the orderly, bent over the chef and locked the big wheels of the chair. He moved to Spencer's left side and slipped his arm carefully around the patient, his shoulder underneath the other's armpit. He counted to three and the two of them stood. Spencer ground his teeth together. He didn't want to scream, but found it impossible not to make a noise. The dark man practically lifted him himself.

"You good?" Marc asked.

"Oh yeah," was all Spencer could mutter. His whole core, especially his ribs, screamed in pain. The medical tape tried it's best to hold everything in place. At least he didn't think about how much it itched. After they got him out of the cistern and strapped to a gurney he was placed in the air ambulance and flown back to the city. At the hospital x-rays said he had two cracked ribs and massive bruising across his front and back, but no internal bleeding. The doctors wanted to keep him in hospital a couple of nights for observation to make sure nothing broke off and punctured any organs. Moving hurt. Breathing hurt. Laughing was excruciating. They kept him on the happy drugs for a while to keep him still.

Spencer looked out the side window at Chrys and Marc talking. He leaned in close to her and said something that made her laugh. Her head went back. Her hand touched his arms. Spencer knocked on the window and got his sister's finger raised at him. At least it was the index finger.

"What?" She snapped as she got in the driver's seat.

"What about Dawn?"

"What about her?" Chrys stomped on the gas.

The sudden lurch of the car made all of Spencer's muscles tense and pain flow through him. "Aren't you two a couple?"

"I don't know. She said she might put in for a transfer. It'll help her career to go somewhere else." She shrugged her shoulders as she pulled the car into the street. "She wanted me to tell you it was smart of you to not hang up on her."

"I did that?" Spencer didn't remember whether he hung up or not. If he didn't it wasn't on purpose.

Chrys adjusted the radio settings. Her cheek was still red where she had been hit. "She said she was able to hear some of your conversation with Dr. Ken, so she knew where you two were going. Then they were able to put a trace on your phone and knew where we were.

Oh, Dawn found the Linques for me. They moved to Calgary. I'm going to call them and see if they want their stuff. We can ship it to them or something."

"Sure." He let out a grunt. "Any word on what they found at Dr. Ken's place?" He knew that when the RCMP arrived both Tara and Ken were there. Tara had the two-by-four still in hand. Dawn had yelled at her to drop the weapon and get on the ground. Ken got down. His wife stared at the police officers as if she didn't know she was there. She raised the board and ran forward. Spencer wasn't certain about all the details, but he knew Dawn had enjoyed herself when she pepper-sprayed the woman.

"Dawn wouldn't tell me much, something about pending court proceedings and all that. She did say that they found a room in the house basically dedicated to the women these two tortured. There were driver's licences pinned to a wall, videos of them taking turns torturing them, and some of their belongings. There was more than we knew about, Spencer." She looked away from the road. Dawn was going to tell her a lot more about what they had found, but Chrys asked her to stop. Chrys knew it could all have happened to her if many things hadn't come together. She owed much to her brother and to the police. Dr. Ken had brought Spencer out there pretending to be on his side so that he wouldn't have time to call the police. The basic plan was to kill the brother and torture the sister. As far as Dr. Ken and Tara knew they were the only two who knew anything and had any idea about what was going on. It would have worked if it wasn't for Spencer not pushing a button on his phone.

Spencer didn't say anything.

"You okay?"

He turned to his sister, reached out and moved her hair back from her ear. The lobe was torn. It was covered with a bandage, but they both knew it was never going to look the same. "How are you?"

Chrys quickly flicked her hair back to cover the ear. "I'll be okay. The doctor said I could have plastic surgery to have it look close to normal, but I'm not sure if I want to. I like my hair down anyway." Emotionally it was going to take her a while to get back to normal. She was going to be looking over her shoulder and in the back seat of vehicles for months to come.

"Maeve came to see me," Spencer said.

"Oh,"

"She wasn't taken. She was just sick of being stuck in the hospital so she went with her daughter's mother to stay at their place. It sounds like she's going to be okay." He looked out the side window for awhile and thought about the blonde singer. He knew where things stood. She had a life to try to return to. He had a life to live. "So did anyone look for a new oven?"

"It's been taken care of."

"What do you mean?" By his calculations the restaurant had been closed for four days. He didn't want to think of all the revenue he had lost. His sister just smiled. "Chrys?"

~ * ~

A shiny new range sat where the grungy old one had been the morning Liz was found in the oven. Bright blue IMPERIAL was embossed into the oven handles and there were round blue dials for the stove burners and the ovens. It had ten burners and a shelf above which was a little lower than the shelf on the old one. Pans had been place there

284

ready to be grabbed. In fact there were a couple of pans on the stove top. Customers sat at some of tables.

"What the hell?" was all that came out of Spencer's mouth.

Jessie quickly came from the hostess stand to meet him at the door. He cringed at her touch, but he was glad to feel her hand on his arm.

"What is this? I can't afford it."

Gordie looked at him from on the line, cocked his head to the side, and lifted his hands as if to say, *I don't know.*

"It just showed up." Jessie said.

"What? Oven's don't just show up."

Chrys walked past him and said, "This one did."

Jessie said, "I had everyone come to your place Friday like you said and an hour later I got a call asking if anyone would be in the restaurant on Saturday. Saturday morning a big truck showed up with the stove. They said it was all paid for and everything. Even the city energy company showed up. They dismantled the old one, cleaned the floor and walls, then installed the new one, all in the same day."

Spencer stared at Jessie. "You didn't ask who bought it?"

She shrugged her shoulders. "I just thought maybe you ordered it and didn't have time to tell anyone."

"No, I didn't even find one."

"Well this one works great." Gordie said after sliding a plate onto the pass and joining them by the door. "Can we keep it? Can we? Can we?"

"I don't know. They came on a Saturday? And the city workers?"

"Yeah, they did. You have to let us know what you're doing, Spence. We're fully booked for tonight." Jessie showed him the reservation book. There was a party booked for the evening under the name Solomon. "Gordie has an extra cook coming. We need to find a singer though. I have some calls out."

Spencer looked over the book. People didn't have private parties on Sundays. Kitchen ranges didn't just show up at your doorstep. But then serial killers didn't show up in the average person's life. His head was spinning and the pain was coming back. It was time for medication. "I'm, ah, going upstairs. I'll be back."

~ * ~

Hours later Spencer walked past the dishwashers in the back and slowly made his way out to the dining room. It was alive with noises and people. Some sat at tables, others walked around. It was more a cocktail party than a sit-down dinner. The kitchen crew was doing a lot of deep-frying and plating. Across the room Maeve sat on a stool on the stage. A week of being safe and she looked like a new person. Finding out her captors were in prison probably helped too. She had bruises and cuts on her face. All anyone noticed, however, was the music. She held her guitar, but she wasn't playing. A man behind her played the music as she sang. Spencer recognized some faces through the room. A couple were well known actors from California in town making a movie. There were some business men he knew and local politicians. There were even some reporters taking photographs and talking to people. He couldn't believe what was going on. They never had this part of society at The Alcrest.

"Spence," Jessie tapped his shoulder. She had to speak up to be heard.

"What the hell is this? Do you see who's here?"

"There's a call for you."

At the hostess stand he took the phone and pressed the flashing line button. He had to ask who it was twice before he heard. "Liam?"

"How's everything going? Did you like my gift?" The slight Irish accent could barely be heard.

"Your gift?" Spencer looked down the line. "You mean the oven? You did that? Why?"

"It was something I needed to do. My man shouldn't have terrorized you and I owed your father."

"This is too much. I really can't accept it. I don't," how was he supposed to say that he didn't want to owe the man. "I don't know when I can repay you."

"Someday then." There was silence across the line then Liam quickly asked, "How's Chrysanthemum?"

Spencer turned around. His eyes looked through all the faces in the room. His sister was by the stage clearing empty glasses and talking to a few people. "She's fine. I have to ask, Liam, what's this secret you have? Liam?" The line was dead. Perhaps it was something for a different day.

He crossed to Jessie. She turned towards him and he pressed his lips against hers.

Potato Corn Chowder

6   medium sized potatoes, peeled and rough chopped
4   medium sized potatoes, peeled and cut into cubes
1/3 C Bacon, diced
1   Onion, Carrots, Celery all finely diced (the amount of
       carrot and celery together should equal amount of
       onion.
½ C   frozen corn
       salt and pepper to taste

Method
  1.   Place first set of potatoes into a pot in enough
          cold water to cover. Turn heat to high and bring
          to boil. Boil until soft. Remove from heat and
          puree with hand blender or in a blender. Add a
          little water or stock if too thick.

  2.   I give an amount of bacon to use, but by all
          means use as much or as little as you like. Place
          into your soup pot on medium/high heat and let
          crisp up. Scoop the bacon out and drain most of
          the fat. Save it though in case you need to add
          some more or wish to use it later.

  3.   Add in the diced onion. Cook for about a minute
          or until they start to soften and then add the carrot
          and celery. When they too are softening add the
          diced potato and let cook a little while, about 2 to
          3 minutes. Next pour the pureed potato into the
          pot.. Let cook to starting to soften.

4.	Add corn and bacon to soup. Cook 10-15 minutes.

5.	Taste and season with salt and pepper.

Feel the need for seafood chowder? Back up to step 3 just before adding the pureed potato and put in an array of seafood (haddock, salmon, mussels in or out of the shell, clams, shrimp, etc.) cook them for a little while, basically until just about cooked, then add the pureed mixture.

To do it like how Gordie makes it in the book leave the skin on the first batch of potatoes. Cut them into quarters then toss in some extra-virgin olive oil, minced garlic, parsley, and grated parmesan and then roast them in an oven until soft. Puree them with water or stock and follow the rest of the recipe.

The Alcrest Gastropub Signature Honey-Lime Vinaigrette

This is the vinaigrette Spencer learned when he was in culinary school and he fell in love with it. He has kept it with him and adopted it as the signature vinaigrette for the restaurant. It's simple, easy, and tasty.

3	limes, zested and juiced
1 T	honey
1 T	Dijon mustard
	Canola oil
	Salt and pepper to taste

Method
1. Put the lime juice and zest, honey, and mustard into a large bowl. Place the bowl onto a towel so that it won't move. Using a whisk, slowly whisk in some oil. Just a little at first, maybe a tablespoon or two. As the oil and lime juice emulsifies you can add oil a little more quickly as you whisk it in. Oil should be almost 3 times the amount of lime juice

2. Season with the salt and pepper. Taste and add more honey if needed.

This is a basic vinaigrette. You can use the same recipe, but switch up the acid and the flavoring to make different tastes.

From the Author

There you have it. The end, or is it only the beginning? I know, cheesy. I'm so excited to go on more adventures with the staff of The Alcrest. I would really like to hear your thoughts on Chrys and Spencer and the story and where you'd like to see them go. I've already started work on the next Alcrest Mystery, so more are coming like it or not.

Email me at lorneoliverauthor@gmail.com

My other books, RED ISLAND and RED SERGE are part of the SGT. REID SERIES. I'm currently working on the third in that series titled RED ROVER. One thing I've learned since starting this publishing journey is that no matter what dates I state as being possible publishing dates, I'm wrong. So I'm not saying when I'm publishing anything else.

I will say, however, that a romance novel I wrote a long time ago titled JUST BY ACCIDENT (we're talking back in the late 1990's) is going through the process and should be out later 2014.

I don't know if anyone has noticed this yet or not, but I leave little connections out there in each book that either attach it to one of the other novels or the characters. For instance you might have noticed that one of Maeve's songs had the title Red Island. And Maeve is in one of the other books too. There are a few more out there. Happy hunting.

As always you can find me at
Lorneoliver.blogspot.ca
Facebook.com/oliverauthor
And @LorneOliver on Twitter

Please get in touch with me and tell me what you thought or even just say hi. Yes, I write for myself but I also write for that one reader out there who feels emotion with every tear and every fright.